More

a delicious romance

Abra Pressler

sugarbush press

CONTENTS

For Mum and Dad
Thanks for everything

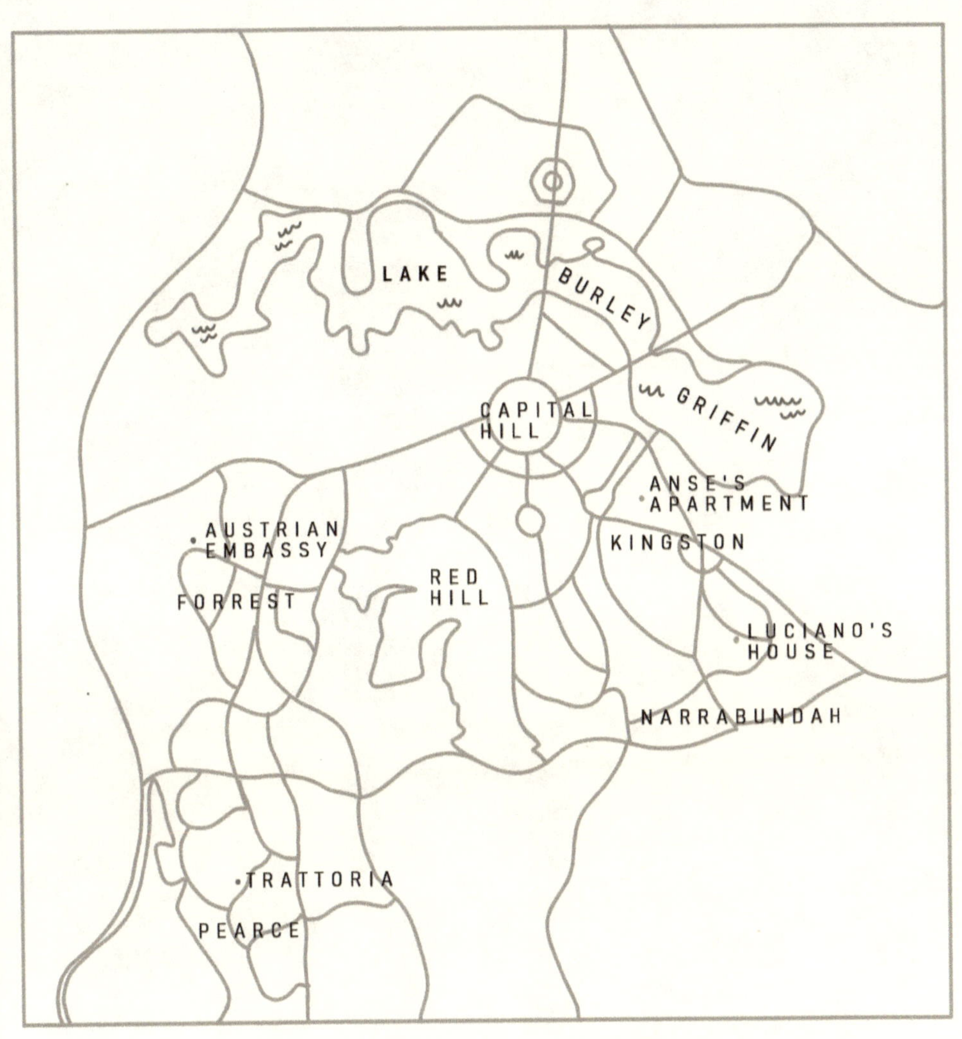

MAP OF SOUTH CANBERRA

MICHELIN STAR CHEF LORETTA JILANI PASSES AWAY

The Canberra Daily, 3 January 2019

By Evan Mason

Loretta Jilani was remembered on Wednesday as passionate, kind and loving in an emotional funeral service at St Christopher's Cathedral in Manuka. Jilani, who was fifty-three, was described by her eldest daughter, Marzia, as a woman who 'worked her way to the top and took everyone with her.'

Jilani opened *Trattoria*, an Italian restaurant, in Pearce shops of South Canberra in 1993. Previously, she worked in Milan, where her restaurant, *Ragazza*, was awarded a Michelin star in 1989.

In 1993, she emigrated with her daughter, Marzia, to Canberra. She opened Trattoria three months later and notoriously continued to work through the early stages of labour while pregnant with twins, Luciano and Corina.

During an emotional eulogy, Luciano described his mother

as, 'a woman who had a burning passion not only for cooking but for the people who visited Trattoria. She loved Canberra, and Canberra loved her. When you came to the restaurant, it never felt like you were going out to dinner; it was like coming around to our house because we lived our entire lives in that restaurant.'

While the funerary proceedings were a final goodbye between close friends and the community, the international culinary community mourned the loss of a great artist across social media. Restauranteur and international food critic, Alex Yamamoto said, 'She was a master at her craft. There was a love, a touch, a feeling she brought to her cooking so rarely seen in today's restaurants. It's an incredibly huge loss.'

Trattoria closed following Jilani's diagnosis of an aggressive form of brain cancer six months ago. There is no word as to when, or if, it will open again.

The Canberra Daily team mourn the loss of Loretta Jilani, and we extend our sympathies to the Jilani family.

CHAPTER ONE

It's one day after the funeral, three days since his mother passed, only the sixth of January, and Luciano Jilani is just trying to get a cup of coffee without anyone recognising him. Or giving him their condolences. Or asking if there is anything, he, or his sisters, need.

Yes, there is one thing he needs: a bloody strong coffee.

With the funeral arrangements, the will, and the restaurant, he's barely had time to eat, shit, or sleep. Hopefully, the coffee will help to meet two of those needs while prolonging the third.

His sisters have been steadfast and level-headed throughout the entire process and frankly, he is in awe of them. There is so much to organise, so much to decide. Corina chose the dress she was cremated in, Marzia helped pick out the rose colour—*fuchsia*—and organised catering at the wake. He'd helped where he could. At the funeral service, they'd held his trembling hands and he'd just *sat there,* barely able to process any of it until the Father had invited him to speak.

God, he needs a coffee.

Leafy oak trees line the busy street, smattering shade on the café tables across the road. A bell rings as Luciano steps out onto the road. There's barely a second to process the whiz of the bike before it zooms past him. Luciano presses his body against the side of the car but feels his sunglasses fall from his face. He hears them crush as the bicycle passes.

'Watch it, dickhead!' the cyclist barks. A *QIK-EATS* food pack bounces on the back of his bike.

'You watch it!' Luciano calls back and instantly regrets it. Both because his comebacks are always so lame and now because now all eyes are on him, and this entire situation is just a newspaper headline waiting to happen.

Luciano Jilani rages at local delivery driver days after mother's death!

It's not like he's unrecognisable: his face has been featured in at least six national newspapers and shared across social media in the days since his mother's funeral. He's tall and lanky, with olive skin and a head of chestnut hair that tends to have a distinctly Leo Sayer look if he lets it grow.

Everyone knows him in this town.

With sweaty palms, he fumbles to open the car door before cranking the air conditioner up full blast. Cold air chills his sweat-soaked skin. The car starts up with a purr.

———

'Ugh, drive-thru coffee? Really?' Marzia groans as Luciano balances three coffees and fights with the rusted fly screen door.

'The other place was closed.' It's a lie but Marzia doesn't

press him on it. She takes her coffee and disappears back into the kitchen.

Corina eyes him suspiciously. 'You okay?

Luciano shrugs and sips his coffee. It's dull and mellow. 'I almost got mowed down by a dickhead on a delivery bike.'

'Did he scratch the car?' calls Marzia.

'No, I protected it with my body, thanks for your concern, Mar. He crushed my sunnies, though.'

Corina's writing thank you cards: to the funeral home, the minister's office, the local restaurants, business people, even the local radio station who reached out to help fund treatment. It had been in vain. The chemo and radiation hadn't worked and there was no way to operate. Still, the cards are a kind gesture. One Luciano is sure he would have forgotten. She hands him a stack. 'These are ready to go to the post if you want.'

It's a mundane job but at least it'll keep him busy.

Marzia is on the phone to a client when he arrives home, hot and sweaty, and Corina suggests that they get Chinese for dinner. Marzia hears this and pauses her phone call to snap, 'Not in my car, you're not!' before unmuting the phone and continuing the conversation.

They take Corina's old Toyota Corolla to Mr Long's Chinese restaurant, their well-loved local eatery.

'Did he ask about Mum?' says Luciano as she comes back to the car.

'Yeah.'

'I can't go anywhere without someone asking about her.'

'They miss her, Luc.' She starts up the car to get the air conditioner going again. 'It'll get better. You want to go for a drive? I wanna do something real quick.'

Luciano shrugs. It's better than sitting in the car park with the car door half-cracked, sweating in the heavy heat of the day.

They drive up the narrow leafy streets of Narrabundah and Luciano presses his forehead to the glass. Corina turns towards Red Hill. The car splutters as it climbs the narrow road to the lookout.

'Why'd you bring us here?' Luciano inhales. The air is damp and heavy with the scent eucalyptus. Below them, Canberra glows red from the dying light of the sun. There are so many memories of her in this city, he's overwhelmed as they come rushing back.

'Did you see Rohan at the funeral yesterday?' Corina pulls her long, curly hair off her shoulders and into a messy bun. 'Marzia said he was sitting near the back of the church.'

'The whole thing was a bit of a blur,' Luciano admits. He barely remembers anyone at the funeral except his sisters and the Father, the muskiness of the church and the rigidity of the pews against his spine. 'Why is he back?'

'Apparently, he got kicked out of his footy club. Guess he's moved back here now.'

'Did you talk to him at the wake?'

'Didn't see him.'

'I haven't seen his dad since we closed the restaurant. Speaking of, I should go suss out the damage tomorrow.'

'You don't have to,' Corina says. 'Take it slowly.'

Luciano kicks a rock. It skids across the road and tumbles down the embankment. 'How slowly, though? Shouldn't I be trying to get things back to normal?'

'Things won't go back to normal,' replies Corina. 'But if you want to go tomorrow, I'll come with you.'

He wants to tell her he'd prefer to go by himself; to work

through things without an audience but her phone vibrates and then she's stepping away from him. The moment's gone.

'Come on.' She unlocks the car. 'Dinner's ready.'

The rich aroma of honey chicken fills the car as the takeaway containers seep warmth through Luciano's shorts. By the time they get back to the house, they've broken into the complimentary bag of prawn crackers.

Marzia is hunched over the dining table, thumbing through documents again. A half-empty mug of cold tea sits beside her.

'Food's hot.' Luciano grabs the wine glasses from the kitchen cupboard. 'C'mon, Mar, come eat.'

She waves him off. 'In a bit. I'm just working through a few things.'

Luciano spies the bank's logo on the header of a document and decides not to press it.

The cricket's on TV. It's not something Luciano would usually watch, but Corina's big on sports and he doesn't feel like bickering with her. There's a calmness to it: the monotonous voice of the commentator, the rhythmic cycle of the game.

Eventually, Marzia comes over to them. She's dressed in a pair of cotton shorts and one of Luciano's hoodies she's flogged without permission.

'Can we watch something else?' Marzia demands as she sits crossed-legged on the floor.

'No,' says Corina.

Luciano nudges Marzia's shoulder with his toes. 'Corina said you saw Rohan at the funeral?'

'Yeah,' Marzia mutters through a mouthful of Mongolian lamb. 'Omala too. He's moved back in with his parents again. Stopped playing footy.'

'Why?' Luciano asks.

'Didn't say.'

'I heard he hit the clubs a little too hard,' Corina says. 'Got involved in some stuff he shouldn't.'

That doesn't really sound like Rohan, but it has been a few years since they've seen each other.

'I don't even go for the Tigers, but I seemed to have watched a lot of their games last year,' Corina continues. 'There was one game where he literally had his shirt ripped off and—,'

'All right, I'm done.' Luciano steps over Marzia's shoulder awkwardly. 'I won't be a part of this conversation.'

'How is this not something you want to talk about?' Marzia sniggers as she takes his place on the lounge. 'The man's a beefcake.'

'No one says beefcake, Marzia,' Luciano groans. 'I'm showering.'

'Cold showering, maybe,' Corina retorts.

Luciano closes the bathroom door to the sound of Marzia's laughter. It's nice. He doesn't remember the last time he heard laughter in this house. The sounds of machines whirling had become too commonplace.

They're still talking when he cracks the bathroom door open fifteen minutes later. Grabbing the bottles from the shower, he's about to ask if Corina wants their mother's curly-haired shampoo and conditioner when he hears Marzia say, 'We have to tell him, Corina.'

'There has to be something we can do. Move a few things around?'

There's a pause. He stays in the shadows of the hallway, listening.

'I've tried. This is the only option.'

'It'll destroy him.'
Marzia releases a painful sigh. 'I know.'

I n the bleary hours of a cold January morning, Anse waits on the side of a snow-slicked road in Vienna. He shoves his cold hands deep into the pockets of his jacket and sighs, breath turning to fog in front of his face.

He checks his phone. Below the clock, which tells him his flight is departing in less than two hours, is a text from Max that simply says, 'Running late!' with a face-palm emoji.

God, he should have known better than to trust Max.

He is about to call for a cab when a black SUV barrels down the road, mounting the curb as it parks. The boot pops.

'I'm sorry I'm late,' gushes Max as Anse climbs into the front seat. He's wearing a geometric-patterned bathrobe and his hair is wild from sleep. 'Close the door, it's so fucking cold. What time is your flight again, like, specifically?'

'Seven.'

'And you have your passport? Wallet? Everything on you?'

Anse presses his hands to his pocket just to be sure. 'Yes.'

Max adjusts his GPS. 'You checked the weather in Sydney, didn't you? It's going to be forty degrees. Did you pack different clothes?

'They're in my backpack. I'll change in Dubai.' He looks at the clock on the dashboard. Now, he has one hour and fifty-three minutes until his flight and they still need to navigate the city.

'All figured out then,' Max says briskly and pulls into traffic.

Anse tries to stop his leg from bouncing nervously and instead, focuses on Vienna and its snow-lined streets. They cross a bridge. Below, people skate down the frozen canals. The trees are dormant wiry creatures that rise like fingers from the snow.

He will miss this.

He will miss the first snow, the crunch of it under his boot, the warmth of mulled wine on his palms, the cold Christmas markets. More than that, Anse will miss his local bookshop, his colleagues at the office, his friends from high school, he will miss his local bars, his gym.

'You'll have to come to visit me.'

Max shrugs. 'Yeah. Maybe.'

They get onto the highway and suddenly the airport looms. Anse's body begins to tingle. There is so little time left between his old life and his new one.

Perhaps he should say something else.

'And I *am* sorry.'

Max frowns as he parks in the five-minute drop off zone. 'For what?'

Anse falters. Yes, for what, exactly? For breaking up with him? Perhaps. But it was almost entirely mutual. Their relationship had once been a forest fire and for a long time, it had thrown off embers, never quite burning out. Until, suddenly, it did. Max had made it clear his life was in Vienna, not Canberra—a strange city on the other side of the globe he said he'd never even heard of until Anse told him he was moving there.

Max, still waiting on an answer, shakes his head. 'Best of luck, Anse.' Then, he leans across the console to press a kiss to Anse's cheek.

The car behind them beeps loudly and Max swears. Just like that, his five minutes are over. His old life is over. Anse takes his luggage from the back of the car and closes the door, waving an apology to the loitering car behind him.

It's a short walk to the airport entrance. Anse resists the urge to turn and look back on the life he's leaving behind. But perhaps Max has parked and is scrambling now to catch up with him, to tell Anse that he has changed his mind and he'll be on the next flight.

It's stupid.

But he's always been a romantic.

Max doesn't run after him.

It takes thirty hours to get to Sydney. He notes the rise and the fall of the sun through the small porthole window. Sydney in the early evening is still bright and brilliant, all blue skies and aquamarine shoreline. Immigration and customs are a blur as he boards yet another flight. As he rises above the clouds once more, he traces the line of beaches that hem the vast green land in gold. They dip back below the clouds not twenty minutes later and Anse sees flat, lush farming land rise into low hills. A city, nestled in a valley, appears in the distance. He feels his stomach churn as the plane descends.

This is it? Barely bigger than Salzburg, Canberra sprawls around the base of three mountains, one to the west boasting a particularly needle-like tower. But there is no city, no sky-rises. Surely this cannot be all there is.

The airport does little to quell the worry that he has landed in a ghost town. There are perhaps twenty other people in the vast tiled building. Airline staff and passengers included. Outside, he is directed to the first taxi in a long rank.

The cab driver takes him through darkened city streets before stopping in an apartment complex carpark and demanding an astounding amount of money. Anse hands over the cash and takes a receipt, slipping it into his pocket.

It takes him ten minutes to find his apartment in the maze of buildings and hallways. It's a lot bigger than the one he'd left in Vienna, but sparingly furnished. Decorated in a minimalist modern style, all the furniture matches. It's strangely unsettling.

He showers before collapsing into bed, not bothering to unpack. Blearily, he connects to the Wi-Fi and waits for the system to load.

Four emails filter in: one from Hannah, the receptionist from the Embassy with the subject line 'Welcome!', one from his local bookshop in Vienna, a survey prompt from the airline, and a spam email. There are eight text messages from his brother, Daniel.

Daniel: Hey, are you flying out today or tomorrow?

If today, can you get me some things from duty-free on your way through?

Alcohol mainly.

Anse? Assuming you're up in the air and not being a dick.

Get back to me.

LOL HAVE YOU SEEN THAT FUNNY VIDEO WITH THE CAT WHO CAN PLAY PIANO. Fucking died laughing. Also, get back to me.

Are you still alive?

Have you gone through duty-free yet?

Anse: Didn't get these messages until now. Got you a bottle of whiskey at duty-free. In Canberra now. Going to sleep.
Daniel: HOORAY! THANK YOU
Welcome, btw

There are no messages from Max.

CHAPTER THREE

On Monday, Corina and Marzia go back to work. Luciano hasn't brought up what he overheard. Perhaps they're working it out themselves and won't need to involve him.

Things are supposed to go back to normal on Mondays. Back to work. Back to business. Back to routine.

Luciano lies in bed and looks at the ceiling and wonders, over and over again, what is his new normal?

There is nothing for him to do.

Barely a week ago, he would rise at six—if not earlier—and sit by his mother's bedside. He'd brush her hair and teeth, pat a little blush to her cheeks with the pad of his ring finger, apply balm to her dry mouth. And she would smile, squeeze his hand gently, and if she had the strength, they would talk until the nurse came at eight.

Now, he has nothing to get up for. No mother. No work. No responsibilities.

It's midday when Corina calls him. 'What are you doing?'

'Cleaning up the house,' he lies. 'Going through Mum's things.'

'What things?' she challenges. 'Because I said to Marzia I wanted to keep-,'

He groans against her shrill voice and presses his face into the pillow. 'Chill, I'm still in bed.'

'You've been in bed all morning?'

He grunts.

'Okay. That's okay.' Her voice is calm, but he knows it's not okay. 'Let's just do one thing today, then, that's it. Are we still on for Trattoria?'

'Shit. I forgot. Sure.'

'Right, so you need to get up and eat something,' she says. 'I'm picking you up at four. Do you need me to bring anything? Do some laundry?'

'No, Cor. See you at four.'

He wishes she didn't treat him like a child. They're twins, but she's older by three minutes and she's not above reminding him if she thinks it'll help her get her way.

There is nothing to eat in the kitchen. Where are all his neighbours offering baked goods or frozen meals to get him through this troubled time? Grabbing his keys, he heads out to the nearest McDonalds to grab a breakfast wrap and a large, strong coffee.

When Corina arrives later that afternoon, Luciano is deep inside his mother's walk-in wardrobe.

'You all right in there, Luc?' Corina calls by the doorway.

Luciano throws Corina a palm-printed linen dress he remembers their mother wearing for the 2017 staff Christmas dinner. 'Do you want any of her clothes?'

'God, I never saw her out of her chef jacket.' Corina runs her hand over fabric. 'Half of these clothes have the tags on them.'

'You should look through what you want.'

'Later. We should go to the restaurant while it's still early.'

'Marzia doesn't want to come?' Luciano stumbles out of the wardrobe.

'She said she'd go later.' Luciano gives her an exasperated look. 'Don't start, Luc. It's not worth fighting with her on it.'

Trattoria is a fifteen-minute drive from the house. Warm delight stirs in him as they crest Red Hill and the meandering valleys of Woden appear below them. The Brindabellas, blue and brilliant, hug the southern edge of the city. Sometimes, in the winter, snow dusts the mountain peaks and Luciano pretends he is in the Swiss Alps, eating his way through Europe. He's never been to Europe, or outside of the country for that matter, but he thinks it must feel quite similar. In the summer evenings, the Brindabellas are bathed in the warm glow of the sun, striking against a sky rippled with pink and orange and yellow.

Surprisingly, everything is the same at Trattoria.

Not that he'd expected it to be vandalised; the restaurant is nestled in a small village of shops. Retailers look out for each other and there are numerous security cameras. Other than the restaurant, there's a hairdresser, the Ahuja family's well-loved Indian restaurant, *Pind*, the post office, and an independent supermarket chain.

Trattoria's windows are covered in newspaper pages over eight months old. The two olive trees in the large terracotta pots by the front door are dead. Maybe he should have given them away but there had been no time after the diagnosis. She'd fallen ill so quickly.

Luciano unlocks the door. The stench of rot hits him hard.

'Oh god.' Corina quickly pushes past him to open the windows and the door to the courtyard. He finds the culprit: a box of old potatoes in the walk-in pantry, festering with a diverse mix of mould.

'I knew it would be bad,' says Corina. 'But I didn't think it'd be like this. You don't want to look in the customer toilets.'

Luciano takes the rubbish out through the courtyard, avoiding the customer toilets. The courtyard is filthy. Weeds grow through the cracks in the brickwork and the wisteria grows wildly across the trellis. The tendrils catch on his hair and clothes. In a small pot, a lemon myrtle tree is blooming. It's citrus scent hangs heavy in the air. His mother had purchased it years ago against advice that it would never survive the biting winters in Canberra, but it's still here, thriving where it should not, protected from the elements by the wisteria.

To his left, a large staircase leads from the courtyard to a nondescript white door.

'I'm going up to check on the apartment!' He calls back to Corina.

The apartment reeks of stale air as he steps into the large lounge room for the first time in years. Until recently, someone had always rented the place and the apartment is well-loved with use. Off-white paint peels from the roof and walls.

'This place is smaller than I remember,' Corina says from the doorway. 'Have you seen Mum's office?'

Luciano shrugs sheepishly. 'I kinda didn't want to go in there.'

'It'll take a week alone to organise. And then there's all the furnishings, the old paintings, the kitchen equipment. Maybe we should have an auction.'

'Why would we do that?' he says. 'I'll need it all when I reopen.'

A pause. 'You want to reopen?'

'Of course.'

Corina folds her arms over her chest. 'But you'd be running the restaurant. That's a huge responsibility.'

He shrugs. 'She wouldn't want Trattoria to fall to pieces. She'd want me to get it back up and running.'

'What about what *you* want?'

'That is what I want, Corina.' He laughs at her serious expression before pushing past her and heading back down the stairs. 'You act like I haven't been working here for the past ten years to do exactly that.'

Corina is silent as she follows him to their mother's office. In the centre of the room is a desk, and from where Luciano stands there is a clear pathway made by carefully arranged documents. Filing cabinets line the back wall. He leans down and picks up a stray paper. It's an invoice from May 2014 detailing a delivery of tomatoes, strawberries and exactly eight watermelons. What she'd done with the watermelons, Luciano has no idea, but there's certainly no need to keep the invoice five years later.

'I never used to come in here,' Luciano mutters. 'She always kept the door closed. Is this what you and Marzia were talking about the other night?'

Corina places a hand on his shoulder. 'We should meet with her. It's six already.'

On the way out, Corina stops to water the olive trees in their large terracotta pots.

'They're done for, Cor, don't bother.'

She shrugs. 'You never know.'

The car ride home is silent. He listens to the radio and thinks about how much nicer the floorboards in the apartment would look with a nice polish and oil, and if maybe the same floor-boards are hidden under the restaurant's linoleum. It'd be nice to revamp the place a little before it's reopened.

The house smells like pork and spices as they walk through the front door.

'I got dumplings!' Marzia beams as she sets the table. 'How was the restaurant?'

Corina hisses through her teeth. 'There was a lot of *stuff.*'

'Mum always was a 'more is more' kind of decorator,' Marzia shrugs. 'Those big prints still there?'

'The big prints, the fake flowers, the large urns, the heavy tables no one could move,' Luciano says. 'At least they can't get stolen.'

'And Mum's office is a mess,' Corina says as they sit down to eat. 'She's probably got files from the 90s.'

'Shit,' she says. 'I'll have to tell Drew about that.'

'Who's Drew?' asks Luciano as he fishes for gyoza with his chopsticks.

'He's the financial lawyer from the firm who owed me a favour,' she says. 'He's helping us with Mum's financial position.'

Corina puts down her chopsticks. 'Wine, anyone?'

'No, thanks.' Luciano turns back to Marzia. 'What do you mean her financial position? Like our inheritance?'

'Kinda.' Marzia purses her lips. 'Mum had debts, Luc. Big ones.'

Corina takes a large gulp of wine.

Luciano frowns. 'What do you mean?'

'Exactly that. She had loans that we just don't have the

money to pay back. Everything she had was—*is*—tied up in assets. This house. The restaurant.'

'So we have to sell the house?'

Corina's head falls into her hands as Luciano's skin pricks with sweat.

Marzia's expression is neutral. There's barely a waver in her voice as she says, 'And the restaurant, Luc.'

'You're wrong,' he snaps back. 'She couldn't have been in debt that badly.'

'You can see the bank statements for yourself if you don't believe me.'

'Did you know about them?' Corina asks. 'Did she ever mention it?'

'No,' he says. 'No, of course not. Everything was fine. It *is* fine. I'm sure she has money tied up in stocks or something. There must be something else.' He gets to his feet. An idea comes to him. 'I'll take on the debt, I'll reopen the shop and pay it back.'

'That's a ridiculous idea, Luciano,' Marzia snaps. 'You have no idea about what it takes to run a restaurant.'

'*Marzia*,' Corina says gently.

'I'm telling the truth. He doesn't want her debt following him around for the rest of his life.'

'It's my life,' Luciano replies.

'Yeah, but it's *our* debt. It affects all of us, Luciano. And I vote to sell both the house and the restaurant. If we do that, we'll cover the debt and have enough to invest in something worthwhile. It's what she would have wanted.'

'You don't know if that's what she wanted!'

Marzia shoots an icy glare across the table. 'Careful, Luciano, she was my mother too.'

'She was our mother but she was my boss and my mentor. Everything I did with her was to set me up to take over that place. *That's* what she would have wanted.'

'Calm down, Luciano,' Corina says. She reaches out to him, but he pulls away.

'Please don't touch me.'

'It's a building, Luciano.' There's a smoothness in Corina's voice that makes his anger settle. He's always been quick to anger. So has Marzia. Half of their childhood and most of their teenage years had been spent at each other's throats. Corina had always been the one to broker peace. 'With the money we make on the sale, you could create something else. Something your own. I'm sorry, Luciano, but I want to sell as well.'

CHAPTER FOUR

The office is entirely unexpected. In Vienna, he'd worked in skyscrapers and modern wings of old heritage buildings in bullpen office spaces. But the Austrian Embassy in Australia looks more like a regal family home than an official building, shaded by an enormous jacaranda tree. When he steps foot in the front door a young woman with a blonde ponytail looks up from her computer.

'Anse?'

'Yes.' He clears his throat. 'Hello.'

She shakes his hand firmly. 'Hannah. I'm the one who has been relentlessly emailing you these past three months. How was your first weekend in Australia?'

'Nice. I got sunburnt.'

His accent is harsh and strong, grating even to him. Where Hannah's accent is lyrical and bright and distinctly Australian, he's sure he must sound particularly Schwarzenegger-like to her.

'Yes, I can see that.' She offers a sympathetic smile. 'Come, I'll show you around.'

He follows her down a narrow hallway lined with large golden urns brimming with native Australian florals. Hannah's heels click against the oak floorboards. The office smells of florals, and it takes Anse a moment to realise that the native bouquets in the urns aren't fake. It's a strange luxury.

They arrive at a large oak door and Hannah knocks twice.

'Franz? You in yet?'

There's a pause before the doorknob turns, and a man, no older than forty, pokes his head through.

'This is Anse Meyer,' Hannah says as Anse extends a hand. 'The new attaché.'

The door opens. Franz reveals himself as a petite man dressed in a well-fitted tweed suit. 'Pleasure to finally meet. Come in, Anse.'

Franz's office is large. Bookshelves and glass cabinets full of trinkets line the walls, and behind his desk is a large window that looks out into the shady, lush courtyard and the jacaranda tree.

'Cappuccino with soy milk, please Hannah.' Franz turns to him, encourages him to sit in the leather chair by his desk. 'Anse, do you want a coffee?'

Anse's glances to Hannah. Something in him is uncomfortable about this situation. 'I'm fine, thank you.'

Hannah leaves as Franz sinks down into his desk chair. Anse notices his desk is organised with papers in neat pile and pens perfectly aligned to his notepad.

Franz gives him a little smile. 'How is Austria?'

'Cold.'

'Ah, I miss the snow.'

'Do you get back home often?'

Franz shakes his head. 'Not as often as I'd like, I'm afraid. Work has a habit of piling up. You certainly won't be bored during your placement here.'

'I like a challenge, sir,' he says.

Franz smiles, but only the corners of his mouth upturn. Anse considers that he looks rather rat-like. 'Come, I'll show you to your office.'

There are five other people in the office, Hannah included. Franz simply introduces her as 'the receptionist' as she hands him a coffee. There is also Mary, the cultural attaché who is a painter from Salzburg, Kristoph the military attaché, and Simon and Martina in immigration. He is shown to the courtyard, which is carpeted by the lavender flowers of the jacaranda tree. Franz shakes his head.

'Pest of a tree.'

Anse thinks it's beautiful.

His office has a small window facing the street. It is strangely furnished with a deep mahogany Queen Anne desk, matching bookcase, with a tall fiddle leaf fig in one corner and a single wingback chair upholstered in emerald velvet.

'I'll let you get settled in. All briefing materials have been sent to your email. We have a meeting for an upcoming project at two in my office,' he says. 'I'll see you then.'

Franz closes the door to his office on his way out and Anse allows himself to fall back into his chair. After soaking in his new office, he hesitantly boots up the computer. What a strange, small corner of the globe he has found.

That night, Daniel rings. The first real phone call they've had for almost eight years where the line is crisp and clear and doesn't buffer.

'I can't believe you're actually here,' Daniel says. 'What was your first day like?'

'Strange,' Anse replies. He fossicks around the apartment a little more, adjusts the air conditioning; checks the shower pressure. 'But they all seem nice enough. I have my own office. It has a window.'

'Living the dream,' Daniel replies.

'How are you? How's Emmy?'

'Good.' Things between Daniel and Emmy are always just 'good', and he never likes to go into detail. 'God, I can't believe you're here. Come to Sydney this weekend, or we'll come to you.'

'Give me a bit to settle in.' The fridge is empty: he needs to go shopping, but for what, he's not sure. Milk. Toilet paper. Maybe he can live entirely on frozen meals until he scopes out the neighbourhood. 'What's Sydney like?'

'Expensive,' comes Daniel's immediate reply. 'Fucking beautiful, a wonderful city to live in, but it's expensive.'

'Watch out, the stress may turn you grey.'

'Oh ha-ha,' Daniel groans. 'I think I'm turning white. How are you not grey yet?'

'I think I got Dad's genes,' he says. 'I always remember Mum being grey.'

'Have you heard from her recently?'

He opens the fridge only to close it again. 'No, have you?'

'She sent me a message a little while ago that she got a job at a university in Oslo,' Daniel replies. 'Peter is moving there with her.'

'Good on Peter.'

'You should call her, Anse. She would love to hear from you.'

He knows he should, but he's always the one to make the effort in their relationship. He's moved across the world and he's not even sure his mother knows. Or if she does, she hasn't bothered to reach out.

'I'll think about it. How's the book coming?'

'It's not,' says Daniel bluntly. 'I keep getting stuck. There's something I'm missing, and I don't know what it is.'

'You'll find it.'

Daniel seems to ignore his encouraging words entirely. 'Did you say goodbye to Max?'

'I did. He drove me to the airport.'

'Aw. There wasn't a tinge of regret?' Daniel teases him jovially but something in Anse twists at how close the words hit.

'We've been over a long time, Dan.'

'I know but I liked him.'

'You barely knew him.'

'Yeah but he made you happy.'

'Maybe for a bit.'

A doorbell rings in the background and then Daniel says, 'Oh shit, gotta go. The groceries are here. Talk later, okay?'

'You get groceries delivered?'

'Yeah, it's great,' Daniel says. 'Emmy orders it all online. We don't even have to leave the house.'

The doorbell rings again and Daniel hastily hangs up.

Falling onto the lounge, Anse browses through the apps on his phone and downloads the highest rated food delivery service. QIK-EATS has five stars and over eighty reviews.

Less than fifteen minutes later, a man named Ahmed delivers green chicken curry and rice to his apartment.

CHAPTER FIVE

The sound of his alarm pierces the quiet morning and Luciano groans, hand emerging from the sheets to feel around for his phone. It's nine but his eyes are heavy and his head thumps with the strain of a headache. For a moment, he contemplates rolling over and going back to sleep. What is there to get up for? The fight with his sisters sweeps over his waking subconscious like a chilling wave.

They want to sell. They want to sell the house, the restaurant.

Everything he's ever known.

When he arrives at Trattoria, the olive trees are nothing more than sticks in a pot of soil, but he doesn't have the heart to throw them out.

In the kitchen, he checks the freezer and takes out the frozen meat; most of it will still be fine to eat, and it will save him money over the next few weeks. He wipes down the tables, the counter of the long bar, cleans the glass splashback behind the alcohol cabinet, and finds a half-empty bottle of vodka for his efforts.

Finally, when his arms are jelly and the restaurant smells of eucalyptus and bleach, he returns to the office.

Wading through the documents, Luciano begins the slow, mundane job of sorting them. He finds receipts for meaningless work, bank statements that detail a small but steady effort to repay a loan with a bad interest rate. A poor choice made by a mother desperate to start over again.

An hour later, he's barely made a difference. Taking a photo of his progress, he sends it to Corina.

Luciano: I know you're supposed to keep records for the taxman but this is ridiculous.

Corina: I can't believe you're really going through all that stuff.

Luciano: Someone has to.

Corina: I want to talk about last night.

He stares at his phone for a long while, typing and deleting the same message three times. What is there to talk about? He's pretty much out voted, after all. Even though he'll be the most impacted by their decisions. Even though this restaurant is the last thing he has of *her,* of *their life together.*

Luciano decides not to respond at all.

His phone vibrates with a text, but he ignores it. Instead, Luciano takes a break to make a latte at the bar. Running his hands along the counter as he passes through the kitchen, memories flood back. How many times had he sat on the corner of the island as a child watching as his mother filleted a fish? Her hand had moved with the knife, so slow and masterful, and then, twenty minutes later those same hands had changed shape entirely, no longer lean and thin and precise, but wide and warm as she kneaded the dough for a pie crust.

After coffee, Luciano turns on the oven. Soon, the kitchen is warm and alive as Luciano sings off key and flours the work-bench. He works the dough almost mindlessly, skilful without having to focus, until it's smooth and rounded.

While it rests, he gets to work on the filling: slicing crisp green apples, sautéing in butter and brown sugar and cinnamon. The syrup bubbles as the apples soften, and Luciano adds a dash of vanilla extract.

Gently, he spoons the mixture into the pie crust and slides it into the oven.

Sucking leftover syrup off his thumb, Luciano grabs at his phone. The text from Corina is still unanswered. With a huff, he types back, *Come around at six.*

———

Corina arrives just after six. Her hair, curly and voluminous, sticks to her face from the humidity. Luciano's is no better and he reminds himself to get a haircut before it gets too unruly.

'Hey,' she says simply as she walks into the kitchen. Luciano presses a kiss to her cheek. 'What are you making?'

He runs the pasta through the press again, the thin sheet draping over his forearm. 'Lasagne.'

He finishes assembling the layers of pasta, bechamel and mince before crumbling ricotta over the top and sliding it into the oven. Corina opens a bottle of wine and pours them both a glass.

'Do you want to talk about last night?' she asks.

Luciano swirls the wine around his glass. Frankly, he doesn't. 'Mum never told me about the debts.'

'She probably thought she'd get them all paid off by the time you were ready to take over,' Corina says.

'I wish she told me.' He swallows his wine. It's okay. A little too fruity for his tastes. 'I know selling it is the only choice we have right now. Maybe it's even the best choice. All the staff have new jobs and I know the restaurant needs work. I'm not even sure if I can reopen without her, I—,'

He only notices the wine glass is shaking when Corina takes it from him and hands him a tissue. Is he crying? He presses his hand to his face. Oh god, he *is* crying. Corina's brings him in close. She smells of strong floral perfume and his mother's coconut conditioner.

'I know it's hard, Luc. It's a shit choice to have to make.'

But the choices seem to hit him the hardest, he thinks. No one else is being forced to give up their dream. No one else is out of a job and possibly a home.

The alarm on the oven goes off and Corina sets the table.

'Marzia is coming back over the weekend,' she says as they eat. The lasagne is rich and cheesy. Perhaps too much cheese but Luciano's of the firm opinion you can never have *too much good cheese*. 'She's meeting with agents and getting appraisals and stuff.'

'So, clean up the house is what you're saying,' Luciano replies. A polite person would call the home 'well-lived in' while Marzia has been known to use the phrase, 'a run-down 70s government house that is worth less than the land it's on'.

'A little yes,' Corina smiles. 'Some friends and I are going out for a drink Friday night after work. You should come.'

Luciano shrugs. 'I don't know; I don't really vibe with your friends.'

'But you know Ahmed and Tatiana.'

'Sure, but we're not really *friends*.'

'I think it'd be good for you to let off a little steam,' she says. 'First-round is my shout.'

'I don't know.'

'Don't make me beg, Luciano. When was the last time you let loose a little?'

Probably eight months ago, he thinks. When he'd got drunk and slept with Evan. He wonders if Evan told Corina about their *interaction*.

'I promise Evan won't be there,' she says.

So that's a yes, then.

He gives her a half-smile. 'Fine.'

She claps. 'Great! We'll be at the Pier at six. It'll be fun, and it'll give an outlet to blow off steam before the wicked witch of Western Sydney rolls into town again.'

CHAPTER SIX

Anse's not sure what he's supposed to be doing. It's eleven in the morning and he's staring at a blank screen. He's been in briefing meetings since eight and has another scheduled for one o'clock but between now and then he has time to kill. He has already read each of his emails and now he's looking up how to care for a fiddle leaf fig.

At eleven-fifteen, he decides to venture downstairs and get coffee. Beside the coffee machine is a cupboard full of mugs. As he goes to take a dog-print mug, he hesitates. Is it a free-for-all or does everyone have their own mugs and a silent agreement not to use anyone else's? Maybe he should bring in his own mug just in case. Just to avoid an awkward run in if he accidentally uses Martina's mug. But that doesn't help the fact that he wants a coffee *now* and he has to solve this conundrum—

'Having trouble with the coffee machine?'

Anse jumps as Hannah appears beside him.

'Yes,' he lies. There's no way he's about to admit the mug problem. 'Can you help?'

'Don't bother with it,' she says dismissively as she rinses out her re-useable cup in the sink. 'Most of us just buy the coffee from the café around the corner. Want me to take you? I'm about to go.'

He follows Hannah out onto the street. It's dreadfully hot and instantly, he regrets the idea of coffee, but he can't back out now. Hannah slips on a pair of cat-eye sunglasses as they stroll down the leafy street. They make small talk about what Anse got up to on the weekend (nothing) and what he likes about Canberra (the proximity to his brother is his favourite trait, currently).

'The best thing for getting over jetlag is sunshine and exercise,' Hannah says. 'Every time I come back from a long trip, I take my shoes off in the park and ground myself. It's supposed to recharge your body and your connection to the Earth.'

'You believe that?' he asks as the barista hands him his coffee.

'Always worked for me. There's a great walk around Lake Burley Griffin. I do it every Saturday. You should join me.'

'I will try and make it,' he says and means it.

They're on the way back to the office when Hannah asks, 'When's your birthday, Anse?'

He thinks it must be for some sort of internal work birthday roster—perhaps they do a cake at the end of the month. 'August 26th.'

'Ah, so you're a Virgo. That makes so much sense,' she exclaims.

'Does it?'

'I'm a Sagittarius.' He wonders what that's supposed to

mean, but Hannah doesn't elaborate. They slip back into the office to find Franz waiting in the lobby.

'Ah, Anse, I thought you must have gone out,' he smiles. 'I've been called to a quick meeting over at the German Embassy, and I thought we could go together and introduce you to the team there?'

On the car ride to the embassy, Anse pencils in a meeting into his work calendar for nine-thirty on Saturday morning and sends it to Hannah with his phone number at the bottom. A moment later, Hannah texts him.

Hannah: Just to let you know, I only do the walk to look at the dogs. And the guys.

Anse: We'll have that in common then.

CHAPTER SEVEN

Luciano doesn't want to go out with Corina's friends, and yet he gets a haircut, irons a good shirt, and at five-forty-five, he walks from the corner of his street to the Kingston foreshore.

Lined against the edge of Lake Burley Griffin, the Kingston foreshore breathes modern scandi-inspired development, directly contrasting the old brick buildings that frame the village shops in the heart of the old suburb. That's something he's always loved about Canberra; the small cluster of shops in the centre of each suburb: a coffee shop, a small grocer, a massage parlour, and maybe a hairdresser. Just enough to get you through the day without having to trudge to the city or chain supermarket.

Still, the developments along the foreshore have reinvigorated the nightlife on the notoriously lonesome south-side. Now the area is alive with music and people and business. Corina and her friends are gathered in a busy sports bar, adequately named The Pier, though the only thing that docks at the Kingston pier are private boats, the police and the brightly coloured party boats.

Corina waves Luciano over as he walks into the bar. 'Luc, you remember Ahmed and Tatiana, right?'

Ahmed is a tall, fit man with long brown dreadlocks. Luciano's surprised to see he has one arm slung over Tatiana's shoulders, and every so often, his thumb brushes the tanned skin of her arm.

'And Luc,' Corina continues, getting his attention again. 'This is Agnes. Agnes, this is my brother, Luciano.'

Agnes has a small up-turned nose and shy smile, which immediately drops as Luciano takes the seat beside her.

'Oh, Evan was sitting there,' she protests.

Luciano stiffens and rises immediately, shooting Corina a glare. 'Sorry. I didn't know he'd be here.'

'Why don't we get a drink?' Corina pulls Luciano towards the bar. 'Please, please, *please,* don't be angry with me. I honestly didn't think he'd come. He *told me* he wasn't coming, and then suddenly he just shows up.'

Luciano rolls his eyes. 'I'm going home.'

Corina grabs Luciano by the arm and though he could shrug her off, he doesn't. 'Stay, please. He'll be on his best behaviour, I *promise.*'

Luciano hesitates.

'Please, Luc,' begs Corina. 'This is me, begging. Please stay. Just for one drink.'

'Ugh, fine,' he groans. 'One drink.'

'Thank you. You'll have a nice time, I promise.' She spins to call over the bartender. 'Two glasses of house red.'

The house red is awful. As they head back to the table, Luciano watches as Evan slides back in to sit beside Agnes. He laughs when she tells him a joke, and Luciano fights the urge to down his wine, turn and stalk out of the bar.

'Luciano!' he says too brightly. 'You've had a haircut.'

Luciano runs his hand through his curls self-consciously. 'Yeah. It was getting too long.'

'It looks good.'

Evan also looks good, though Luciano isn't about to tell him that. With dirty blonde hair, a smattering of freckles down his long, angular nose, and his normally white skin sporting a subtle tan, he's the poster boy for any Australian tourism campaign.

Mercifully, Ahmed says, 'So Luciano, how's the restaurant going?'

'Fine,' he lies. 'Things are a little up in the air with Mum dying.'

Corina pipes up. 'Ahmed was telling me he's taken up food deliveries to make some extra money. I thought that'd be perfect for you.'

All eyes are on him. Why does this suddenly feel like an intervention? Or a weird grief circle organised to get him out of the house? The skin on the back of his neck prickles with sweat.

'It could do you good, Luc,' Ahmed says. 'I just use my own car and make about forty bucks an hour on a bad shift, up to eighty on a good one.'

'More than me,' Evan injects with a laugh.

'Another one, Luc?' asked Ahmed and points to his empty wine glass. 'I'll get it.'

Luciano follows Ahmed to the bar and can't help but notice his defined calf muscles. Ahmed's always been straight, but if he wasn't, Luciano would climb him like a tree. Consensually, of course. Ahmed waves over the barman and orders a beer and a glass of wine.

'Beer, actually,' Luciano interrupts. When the bartender walks away, Luciano mutters, 'The house red is awful.'

'Noted,' laughs Ahmed. 'Anyway, sorry to bring up the whole delivery thing. It was just that Corina mentioned to me you were looking for something to do while things settle with the restaurant.' He pauses and looks back at the table. 'I didn't know that Evan would be here. Is everything okay between you two?'

Luciano shrugs.

Ahmed takes the hint. 'Anyway, I reckon the delivery app is perfect for you to make a little extra money. I only do it once or twice a week, but I know mates who do the weekday lunch run around the parliamentary triangle and make an absolute killing.'

'Really?'

A map of the local area pops up on Ahmed's phone. 'All you have to do is switch the app on, and it starts sending you orders out. It's got this whole algorithm that optimises your deliveries, so if you're taking an order from, I dunno, Kingston to Manuka, it'll look for a nearby delivery from a restaurant in Manuka before re-routing you somewhere else. You can put all kind of limits on it, too, so you're not delivering outside your area.'

Luciano downloads the app onto his phone. 'A little extra money couldn't hurt.'

'I'll send you a referral code,' Ahmed adds cheekily as he grabs the beers. 'Hey, if you ever, I dunno, want to hang out on the weekend, let me know. We could go for a hike. Physical activity is a great way of working through heavy stuff.'

It sounds like an awful idea, but Luciano isn't about to tell him that. 'Thanks for the offer. I'll let you know.'

Ahmed offers him a smile. 'Sure.'

———

The night is warm and young. Someone decides they should hit the clubs in the city and suddenly Luciano is being corralled into a taxi. There's a lightness, a joyfulness, that he hasn't felt in a long time. He knows it's the alcohol but it also feels good just to *let go*.

Corina takes his hand as she opens a nondescript door. Deep inside, Luciano can hear music thumping.

'This is how I die,' Evan mutters from behind.

Corina's friends from university are already on the dance-floor and she drops Luciano's hand to join them. Ahmed nods towards the bar.

A man with an impressive moustache serves them and Luciano orders a double gin and tonic. The alcohol floods him, warms him from the inside out, and muddles his brain to the point that he doesn't mind—or really notice—when Evan sits down next to him and leans in close.

'I was hoping we'd be able to talk,' he says over the pounding music.

'Talk about what?' Luciano half-shouts back.

'You know. Everything that happened between us?'

Everything that had happened between them? Luciano takes another sip. 'What's there to talk about? We slept together. I liked you. My Mum got diagnosed with cancer, and you didn't speak to me for *eight* months.'

Evan pulls away. 'I thought we could be mature about this.'

Luciano rolls his eyes and checks the time on his phone—it's just after twelve. Ahmed is on the dance floor with Corina, lost in a haze of bodies and smoke. Evan downs the rest of his beer and makes a show of grabbing a cigarette: a wordless invitation. With a nod, Luciano finishes the rest of his drink and follows Evan out of the club and into the cool air of the night.

The alleyway smells like piss and stale beer. Evan offers Luciano a cigarette, which he shrugs off, before lighting up.

'I'm sorry, okay?' He blows a steady plume of smoke out the corner of his mouth. 'I thought you'd need space. I didn't want to be the asshole who asked for more when you were clearly going through something with your Mum.'

'I didn't need space,' Luciano replies. 'I spent *months* trying to figure out what I'd done to fuck things up.'

'You didn't do anything.'

'I'm ordering a ride home.' He opens his phone and plugs in his address. The ride is two minutes away. Quickly, he sends Corina a message. *I'm going. Text me when you're home so I know you're safe. Thanks for the night out.*

Evan takes another drag of his cigarette and blows the smoke out his nostrils. 'I want to make things right, you know? Did you read the write-up in the paper?'

Of course. The newspaper article about the funeral. 'You wrote that?'

Evan's about to reply when a call echoes across the court-yard. 'Get the fuck out of here, you faggots!'

Stifled laughter follows. Luciano feels his stomach clench in fear. His phone vibrates in his palm; his ride is approaching. Next to him, Evan drops his cigarette to the pavement below and snuffs it out with the heel of his shoe. Luciano watches as the ember dies.

'Go back in and make sure my sister gets home safe.'

Evan doesn't protest. Without another word, he heads back into the club.

CHAPTER EIGHT

How is it possible to burn rice? Anse scrubs at the clump of blackened rice clinging to the bottom of the pot, but it doesn't come loose. With an exasperated sigh, he drops the pot back into the sink.

He'll replace it on the way home.

The weeks have melted together—quite literally as he steps out into scorching heat—and now all anyone at the office can talk about is voting for the 'Top 100' song countdown, and how they'll be spending the long weekend. Hannah is going to the coast with her boyfriend and dog. Daniel and Emmy are visiting her family in Brisbane. Asne, in contrast, has absolutely zero plans. Perhaps he'll go watch a movie. Probably run the Lake track again. Twice if he's bored.

At work, the day has an annoying habit of getting away from him. It's two-thirty when his phone rings and it's only then that Anse realises he hasn't had lunch.

'Anse! Hey!' says Daniel in German. 'How're things?'

'Warm,' he replies. 'You never mentioned how hot it gets here.'

'I'm sure I did. You probably just didn't believe me.' Daniel's German, once lyrical and rounded, has become sharp and nasally. Occasionally, he switches out words for English when he can't think of the right word in German, or if it's easier to say.

'So, Emmy has a job interview in Canberra next weekend,' Daniel says. 'Would it be cool if she stays with you? I'm sorry to ask on behalf of her, but—,'

'It's fine,' he interrupts. An email marked urgent has popped up on his screen. 'Of course, she can stay.'

'You sure?'

'Yes.' His eyes skim over the message—a meeting at the American Embassy. This afternoon. Briefing notes attached.

'She's psyched to see you.' Daniel is the only thirty-something Anse knows that still uses the word *psyched*. 'And I could really use the writing time.'

'I'd like to read it sometime.' He notes down the address for the American Embassy. There's a knock on his door. It's probably Franz. 'I have to go. Ask Emmy to text me the train times.'

There's silence on the other end, and Anse suddenly realises that he's cut Daniel off from whatever he was saying. Probably about his book. Guilt makes his stomach sink and twist. Fuck, he feels like a dick now.

'No worries,' comes Daniel's stilted reply. 'I'll talk to you later.'

Anse hangs up just as Franz opens the door.

'Did you get my email?'

———

After an entirely unproductive meeting at the American Embassy, Anse goes back to the office and orders through the QIK-EATS app. He'd planned on saving money by making his lunch, but now he's down a meal and a saucepan, so really, what's the harm? A man named Luciano is assigned to his order, and a small photograph pops up beside the estimated time of arrival. He's all tanned skin, bright smile, and curly hair.

Luciano is coming.

Arriving on a Vespa Primavera.

Hannah eyes him suspiciously as he enters the lobby, waiting for Luciano to arrive.

'Thought you were trying to make your lunch,' she teases as she fires off an email. She's a whiz at multitasking. Anse doesn't know how she does it.

His phone vibrates again.

Luciano has arrived.

Outside, the red Vespa pulls up into the driveway. A tall and lanky man pulls off his helmet and shakes out his chestnut curls. He grabs Anse's order out of the pack on the back of his bike (or is it a scooter? Anse thinks it's probably closer to a scooter) and shoulders the door open.

'Are you—,' he looks down at his phone. 'An-see?'

'Yes,' Anse says. 'But it's An-say.'

'Cool name.' Luciano smiles and Anse feels his heart rate speed up.

His traitorous fingers shake as he reaches out to grab the bag from Luciano.

'Yours is also.'

Luciano frowns. 'Huh?'

'Your name. It's also cool.'

'Oh!' Luciano laughs just as his phone chimes. 'Thanks! I gotta go. Have a nice day.'

'You too,' Anse replies.

Luciano leaves like a breeze, leaving the scent of sandalwood and cloves hanging in the air.

Hannah clears her throat and Anse realises he's still standing in the middle of the room with a hot bag of Thai fish cakes in his hand. He turns to her and is greeted with a smug grin.

'Don't say a word.'

———

Wednesday brings much of the same. Hannah is too busy for their coffee runs and Anse finds that unless distracted by a phone call or a meeting request, he can spend all day on his computer without making a dent in his workload. His emails are a constant stream of demands and invitations with the occasional meme from Hannah.

This time, the email's subject line says, *Are you coming out of your cave for lunch? I'm hungry*. When he opens the email, a picture of a waving cartoon bear is copied and pasted into the message.

I'm coming out, he types in reply. *Non-occupational email content is against the regulations.*

'Regulations *smegulations*,' Hannah says as Anse enters the foyer. 'Let's get sushi!'

They order a few hand rolls and a variety pack on the QIK-EATS app and Hannah hoots with laughter as the delivery details pop up on the screen.

'It's him!' she cries. 'What are the chances? He must live around here somewhere. Let's ask when he comes in.'

Anse groans. 'Don't make it weird. He might spit in our food.'

Luciano is coming.

Arriving on a Vespa Primavera.

'Right. Because you weren't weird at all last time he was here.'

He doesn't dignify that with a response.

When Luciano arrives, Hannah slips out into the courtyard with a gentle call of good luck.

'Hey, it's you again!' Luciano says brightly as he steps into the reception. He's dressed in a pair of black shorts and a *Sydney Swans* singlet and all Anse can think about are how smooth Luciano's shoulders are and how wildly inappropriate the outfit is for riding around on his scooter. 'Are you going to make a habit of this?'

Anse smiles. 'Probably. I can't cook.'

'Never learned?' Luciano hands him the sushi.

'Not really.' There's no time to go into family history now so he quickly adds. 'I burnt rice a few nights ago. I can't get it off the bottom of the pan.'

'Vinegar and bicarb soda.' Luciano's phone chimes. He's got another delivery. Their time is almost up.

'Pardon?'

'Vinegar and bicarbonate soda will do the trick,' Luciano elaborates. 'Leave it to soak for a bit and it should lift off pretty easily. I gotta go. See you next time.'

Anse watches as Luciano jumps back onto his Vespa and backs out of the driveway before meeting Hannah in the court-yard. She's grinning like a Cheshire cat.

That afternoon, he stops by the supermarket and picks up a small bottle of vinegar and a box of bicarbonate soda. A website tells him to '*mix equal amounts vinegar and water, bring it to the boil and then sprinkle in a tablespoon of baking powder*'. The boiling water froths. Gently, he dislodges the clumps of rice with a spatula before draining the pot and using a little soda and detergent to scrub out the marks. When he's done, the stainless steel shines.

CHAPTER NINE

Luciano gets to know his regulars quickly. There's Shae who is in the middle of exam prep; Lee and her husband Nico who have recently welcomed their first child and are struggling to find time to cook; a group of teenagers who order a ridiculous amount of pizza every Thursday lunchtime under the name Trang, and of course, there is Anse.

Towering well over Luciano's modest five-foot-nine stature, Anse cuts a figure like some Greek hero. He practically bursts out of his tailored suits. Paired with a soft, sweet smile and it's enough to melt Luciano's battered gay heart. He knows he needs to watch himself with him.

He's not sure exactly what Anse does for a job but he knows he works at the Austrian Embassy. There's a sign on the doorway welcoming him onto foreign soil. He's only ever stepped foot in the reception where a young woman sits behind a computer next to a giant urn of fresh flowers. Today, Anse is leaning on the edge of her desk. He must say something funny because her face lights up and she laughs. They look cute together, Luciano thinks.

Anse's ordered Pho from a local Vietnamese place. The fragrance of spices and coriander is delightful.

As soon as Luciano enters the foyer, Anse's eyes are on him. 'I tried the vinegar last night. It actually worked.'

Luciano scoffs. 'I can't believe you'd doubt me.'

Anse takes the order from him and their fingers brush again.

'I'm quite bad in the kitchen.' Anse gestures to the takeaway bag. 'As you can tell.'

The app chimes. He's got a new order.

Anse's lip twinges, just a little, and Luciano focuses on it. He has wonderfully full lips.

'Have a nice day, Luciano.'

Next time, he thinks, he should just turn off his phone.

———

Marzia comes back to Canberra for the Australia Day long weekend, and with her comes a storm of activity. The house and restaurant are officially put on the market, their mother's clothes are donated, and she takes Luciano to look at apartments. Even Corina thinks it's all happening too quickly, but neither of them is game enough to tell Marzia that.

Luciano meets his sisters at a local café for breakfast early on Sunday morning. Marzia looks sophisticated with a sleek bob and big cat-eye sunglasses. Corina, on the other hand, has repurposed last night's winged eyeliner into smoky eyeshadow.

'Corina told me you've started working as a delivery driver,' Marzia says as she takes a sip of her lactose-free, extra hot, dirty chai latte. She orders like Meg Ryan from *When Harry Met*

Sally: specific and authoritative. Luciano can't bring it to tell her that there's no such thing as *extra hot* milk, especially lactose-free milk. It always just curdles in the jug. Nothing ever gets above eighty degrees.

'It pays the bills while I figure things out.'

'It can't be safe delivering food on that death trap of yours.'

'The Vespa is completely safe,' Luciano grumbles as he breaks his eggs with his fork. 'And economical on fuel.'

Marzia takes a sip of her coffee and very intentionally turns to face Corina. 'How's your job going?'

Corina shrugs. 'Oh, you know, same-same. Still working in IT.'

'Have you thought about going back to school?'

'Not recently.'

'They told you that you need more qualifications to be considered for a promotion,' Marzia says. 'I don't understand why—,'

'I'll figure it out, Marzia.'

Marzia doesn't take the hint. Luciano can see it happening, the slow slide from a civil conversation into a fiery fight but he doesn't know how to stop it.

'What's there to figure out?' Marzia says. 'All you have to do is apply yourself and—,'

'I'll get around to it.'

'If you'd started it when you'd planned to last year, you'd be halfway done by now.'

'God, Marzia, can you leave us the fuck alone?' Corina snaps. The café goes silent. Luciano doesn't dare to turn around; he can already feel the eyes on the back of his head. God, Evan's going to have a field day with this headline.

Jilani siblings squabble during Sunday showdown!

Marzia scoffs. 'Jesus, calm down.'

Corina pushes her chair back with a sharp scrape.

'No,' she hisses as she gathers her handbag. 'You don't just get to come back and hassle the shit out of me and Luciano.'

'I'm not hassling Luciano,' Marzia replies. 'We all agreed that the restaurant needed to be sold to cover Mum's debts.'

'Your brother's about to be homeless all because the payout means you can afford a penthouse in Bondi.'

Even Luciano thinks that's going a bit far. The payout would get a penthouse in Manly *at best*. Across the room, the head waiter makes eye contact with him and then pointedly looks at the door. They're making a scene. Time to go.

'We all agreed this was what we'd do with Mum's money.'

'I don't fucking want Mum's money,' Corina sobs. Marzia tries to wrap an arm around Corina's shoulder only for her to push it off. 'Get off me!'

'Guys, we should go,' Luciano says. He hastily throws down a fifty dollar note as Corina stalks out of the café.

Marzia shoots Luciano an exasperated look. Across the road, Corina wrenches open the car door and, without a glance back to them, drives off.

Marzia rolls her eyes. 'What got into her?'

Without Corina, Luciano's anger at his sister sparks. 'Why'd you have to bring up the job thing?'

'What? I was just asking. You know, like what regular people talk about. How was I supposed to know she'd act like a complete psycho?'

Another spark. He tries to shake off his anger. Be cool. Keep it together. 'You knew she deferred when Mum got sick. It's been one month, Marzia. *One month*.' he fishes his keys out of his pocket. 'And don't call people psycho, it's wrong.'

'You're mad at me too, then? Sorry for trying to keep this family together. I didn't have to come this weekend, you know.'

Luciano slips on his helmet and starts the Vespa. 'I'm not sure why you did.'

———

When he pulls up at Trattoria, Luciano is relieved to see that there isn't a FOR SALE sign picketed by the side of the road. Seeing the literal sign of things to come may just break him. As he approaches the front door, he's surprised to find it unlocked. Soft acoustic music plays inside.

'If you've pilfered the wine collection, there'll be hell to pay, Corina,' he calls into the dusty air as he walks towards the kitchen.

Normally, it's Corina who defends their sister, spouting that she's 'only looking out for their best interests' because she's older and a lawyer. Marzia's always been rational to the point of exhaustion whereas Luciano prefers to go with his gut. They don't often fight. Not like that, at least.

'I shouldn't have made a scene,' Corina laments when Luciano finds her on the floor of the kitchen with a half empty bottle of red wine. 'I just *snapped.* It feels like it's just all about money and it makes me feel so,' she fumbles for the word, '*dirty.*'

Luciano doesn't say anything.

Corina takes another swig of her wine. 'I wish I could do something to save the restaurant, Luciano. But there's so much debt. There was no other way.'

'I understand,' he mutters over the lip of his glass. As much as he'll hate to see this place sold, he does understand. 'It's just hard figuring out what I want now that she's gone.'

'You put your whole life on hold for her when she got sick. I wish I could have been there for you more.'

'You did what you could,' Luciano phone vibrates in his pocket. 'It's Marzia.'

Corina scoffs into her glass. 'What does she want?'

'She's coming over,' Luciano grumbles as he gets to his feet. He plucks through a few of the white wines on the rack before finding a merlot and popping the cork.

'Evan told me you guys had a falling out,' Corina murmurs. 'I didn't even realise you liked him that much.'

'It was just a stupid fling.'

'You're not seeing anyone?'

'Maybe you haven't noticed, but I haven't really had much time to date, Corina,' he says. He means it as a harmless jab, but it comes out with a little more bite than expected. 'Twenty-five has been a real bitch.'

'We're going out for our birthday,' she says firmly. 'No arguing. We're celebrating the end of a quarter century together.'

'I'd rather observe it morosely if you don't mind. But don't let me stop you; it's as much your birthday as it is mine.'

'You could meet the love of your life!'

'At the club?' he says sceptically.

The bell above the door rings and heels hit the hardwood floor. God, she sounds like a she-devil with killer pumps as she crosses the restaurant floor and finds them in the kitchen.

'We thought we'd better dispose of the good stuff lest the sellers think it comes with the property,' Luciano replies. 'Get yourself a glass.'

Her eyes cut to Corina. 'Are we good?'

'I don't know.' She juts out her lip. 'Are you finished being a massive bitch?'

'I only want—,'

'Guys,' Luciano stresses. '*Enough.*'

Marzia's chin juts out. 'Sorry, Corina.'

'Sorry too,' Corina mutters.

It feels like they are children again, except this time Mum isn't here to break up their arguments. 'Fight in your own time. This is a holy place. Treat it with respect.'

Marzia snorts but takes the bottle. She pours herself a glass and raises it to the sky. 'Here's to you, Mum.'

Luciano does the same. 'We're selling off everything you worked for piece-by-piece.'

'If only you didn't have tremendous debts that we have to cover,' Marzia adds before joining them on the floor of the kitchen. 'Ew, when was the last time this place was cleaned?'

Luciano ignores her. Serves her right for wearing a Gucci dress as casual Sunday attire. Beside him, Corina is scrolling through her phone. Suddenly, old 90s RnB fills the room and she scrambles to her feet, glass in hand, and starts dancing to the music. 'Remember this?'

'How could I forget?' Marzia laughs. 'Rohan's eighteenth and he got so drunk he danced on Luciano.'

'I thought it was the other way around,' Corina says snidely, and Luciano is about to argue but then he's tugged up to dance beside Corina. She's an awful dancer with awkward moves and bad rhythm. Marzia jumps up to join them with a laugh, kicking off her heels. There is no fighting. No heated words. No mention of money. For the first time since their mother's death, it's just them.

How they used to be.

The real estate agent arranges the first open home of the family house on Tuesday. Streams of people tour his house, poke their head into his bedroom and wander around the kitchen. Sometimes he catches them standing in her empty room, whispering to each other. Other buyers are blatantly interested in the land, and Luciano realises with a strange mix of guilt and relief that there's a possibility the house will be demolished.

No one has mentioned Trattoria yet. It's officially on the market but there's no 'for sale' sign and no plans to host an open home. Marzia says they're looking for the right buyer. That it's a 'unique business venture'. Whatever the reasoning, it gives him time to finish cleaning it out. To say goodbye properly.

On Wednesday, Luciano arrives at Trattoria to finish sorting his mother's office. For the first two hours, he wades through receipts and statements and order forms, sorting everything into fileable records or recyclable paper. Unsurprisingly, most documents are the former.

At eleven, he stops work, rolls up his sleeves and heads into the kitchen.

Pasta is simple to make. It's eggs, flour, and the warmth and dexterity of a hand. Make a well in the middle of the flour, add an egg and begin folding until the dough is smooth to the touch. Sink a finger in the middle of the dough and if it comes out clean, the dough is the right consistency. Continue kneading until smooth and then let it rest for ten minutes before rolling. He's made it enough times that he can eyeball the ingredients and knows when the doughs done from the velvety feel of it underneath his palm.

Next, he starts on the pesto. The gas stovetop splutters to

ignite underneath the cast iron pan. He fries off onion, a clove of garlic and two handfuls of pine nuts before blending everything in a food processor. The scent of onion and garlic make him think of his mother; she is with him, working beside him, guiding his hand as he works the pasta through the flat roller.

Luciano packs the pasta into a plastic container, wraps it in a cotton bag and slips it under the seat of his Vespa.

He starts his rounds: a young man orders chicken soup from a local Chinese shop and accepts it gratefully in his pyjamas; then it's burgers to an office, Thai to a hairdressing salon, a baguette to a guy on a construction site, and finally, finally, he gets the order he's been waiting for.

This time Anse's ordered a salad from a Mexican restaurant. It's almost two o'clock. He hopes the pasta isn't soggy.

He turns off his phone. He can always turn the the app on again later, but he's not about to let another order ruin the few moments he has with Anse.

The same blonde woman is behind her computer when he arrives, but Anse's nowhere to be seen.

'Um, where is he?' he asks the receptionist.

'Anse will be here in a sec,' she answers. 'Luciano, right? I'm Hannah.'

He takes her hand and shakes it. They have met before, but Luciano's knows he's been too swallowed by everything Anse is to really introduce himself. He knows it's trite, but when Anse steps into the room, everything else seems to melt away. 'Nice to meet you.'

Anse enters through the door behind Hannah's desk and something in Luciano's brain just *breaks* because Anse's wearing suspenders. Who wears suspenders anymore—especially around the office? Luciano's fingers twitch with the urge to grab them, to tug Anse's body forward and feel it pressed against his. God, what is this man doing to him?

Anse takes the cotton bag and frowns. 'This isn't what I ordered.'

Oh right.

'It's a gift,' Luciano splutters. 'I mean, I made it for you. I have the food you actually ordered if you still want it. But I thought I'd make this for you. You know, since you don't know how to cook. And always order your food.' Luciano takes a breath. 'Let me start over.'

Anse's lip twitches into a half-smile.

'I made you lunch because you always order food and I'm a chef, and I thought, hey, match made in heaven.' Fuck, that didn't come out right. How is he so bad at this? 'Anyway, it's a gift. Have it for dinner. It'll keep.'

Anse looks back down at the cotton bag and places it on the edge of the desk. On the other side, Hannah is doing a wonderful job pretending to read an email.

'Why don't you have lunch with me?'

Luciano feels his stomach lurch. 'Really?'

'Unless you have something else to do.' He looks down at the phone in Luciano's hand. 'Other orders.'

'No!' Luciano says. 'I mean, I don't. I'd love to have lunch with you.'

'Good,' he says like that solves everything. 'I'll get bowls. Meet me in the courtyard.'

The courtyard is through two large French doors at the end of the room. Luciano takes a seat underneath the large jacaranda tree. Anse appears a moment later with two bowls and spoons out the warm pasta. The fragrant smell of basil and garlic hits him; he's ravenous but he waits, nervous, as Anse takes a mouthful.

'This is—,' Anse pauses. Swallows. 'Luciano, this is amazing.'

Pride swells inside him. 'You like it. Really? It's pretty simple.'

'It's incredible.' Anse shakes his head as he takes another bite. 'I can barely toast bread.'

'I could text you the recipe,' he offers. God, if only his mother could see him now—giving away trade secrets to the first man who smiles at him.

Anse laughs. 'That wouldn't help. I'm an awful cook. My father used to hire a chef. There was always food when we got home.' He smiles at the memory and takes another mouthful. 'How did you learn to cook so well?'

'I'm a chef but business is slow. The delivery job pays the bills.'

Anse's eyes light up. 'I have to visit your restaurant.'

Luciano laughs nervously. 'I'd like that but we're closed right now. My Mum used to be the head chef but she passed away just after Christmas. I want to re-open but I'm not sure that's going to be possible.'

'I'm sorry to hear that,' Anse says. 'My father died a few years ago. It's still painful.'

Anse's hand reaches out towards him and on reflex, Luciano flinches back. 'What are you doing?'

'You have flowers in your hair.' Anse reaches forward again to brush the few purple petals off the crown off his head.

'What bought you to Australia?'

'My job,' Anse says as he twirls the last of the pasta onto his fork. 'I'd always wanted to work overseas, and my brother and his wife live in Sydney. It's only for twelve months. At the end of the contract I'll have to go back to Vienna.'

'What do you do exactly?'

'I provide advice on policy and international issues to the office of the Ambassador. Science and environment, mostly.'

'I can't imagine you get too much drama.'

Anse smiles. 'Australia and Austria do have quite an understanding relationship, yes.'

He holds his hand out and it takes a moment for Luciano to realise that he wants to take his empty bowl.

'This was nice,' Anse says as he stands up. 'Thank you for lunch.'

No. He's not ready for this to be over yet.

'I could teach you to cook,' he blurts. 'So you don't have to order it so often.'

Confusion flickers across Anse's face. 'You want to teach me?'

'I mean, only if you want to be taught,' he says. 'We could do it at my restaurant.'

Anse considers it for a moment. 'That would be nice. I'm free on Thursday nights?'

'Thursdays are good for me too.' Friday and Saturday nights are his better nights as a delivery driver and while he'd get good money working a Thursday night, he's willing to give it up to spend time with Anse.

They exchange numbers.

'Great,' Anse smiles as he pockets his phone. 'See you Thursday.'

Thursday, Luciano repeats to himself as he remounts his Vespa. Thursday.

CHAPTER TEN

Anse meets Hannah for coffee early on Wednesday morning. Though it's early February, the afternoons are still too hot to venture outside, so he gets up at six to beat the sun. Hannah runs with her dog, Patrick, every second morning. At seven-thirty they meet in a shady alfresco café along the edge of Lake Burley Griffin. It's calm and quiet as Anse relaxes into the café chair. A swan glides along the water leaving gentle ripples in its wake. The sky is a soft cornflower blue, unmarred by clouds.

Most of the time they talk about work, books they're reading, or the occasional celebrity gossip. Today, however, their conversation circles back to a too-familiar topic—

'So, how did your lunch date with that delivery driver go?'

'It wasn't a date,' he replies. 'He brought me lunch because I've ordered so much take-away. If anything, it was an intervention. He even offered to teach me how to cook.'

'Really?' Hannah hums over the lip of her coffee. 'What did you say?'

'I said yes. I could do with the lessons,' Anse shrugs. 'It'll be nice.'

'So, it's completely platonic? No romantic feelings at all?' He doesn't know what the word platonic means. There are still a few English words he doesn't know despite studying the language for twenty years. Hannah shakes her head and leans down to caress Pat. 'What am I supposed to do with this guy, Pat? Luciano obviously likes him.'

Anse chokes on his latte. 'He does not.'

'Oh please, you should see the eyes he gives you.'

'I see the eyes. I have eyes.'

The waiter puts a slice of carrot cake on the table. It's covered in a thick layer of cream cheese icing. Anse is about to tell the waiter that they only ordered coffees when Hannah slides a spoon across the table and says, 'My treat!'

'It's barely eight in the morning.'

'Yeah and we earnt it,' Hannah grins and sinks her spoon into the moist cake. 'Ugh, it's heavenly.'

'Stop it.'

'*Kaffee und kuchen, Anse, bitte,*' Hannah teases him as she whips out her phone. 'Do you know Luciano's star sign?'

'No. Why does that even matter? And *Kaffee und Kuchen* is between three and four. It is, I repeat, eight in the morning.'

Hannah ignores him. 'It matters because I need to see if you are compatible. You know, romantically.'

'Star signs aren't real.'

'Please. I have a Virgo friend just like you and she was always dating the wrong guys. Then one day we figured it out —,' she pauses for effect. 'They were all *Geminis*.'

'What's wrong with Geminis?'

'Nothing. They're just not good for Virgos romantically.' She pulls out her phone. 'According to this website, the best star sign for you, an early Virgo, is a Capricorn, Taurus or a Pisces. You should ask Luciano what he is.'

'That would never come up naturally in conversation. He'd know.' He feels Pat nudge against his thigh and gives him a head scratch in acknowledgement.

'So? Then you could make a move.'

'No moves will be made,' he says. 'I will just be learning how to cook.'

'I don't know. The kitchen can get pretty steamy. I bet he really knows how to use a whisk.'

'That makes no sense.'

'His muscles bulging from working the dough, his skin covered in a thin sheen of sweat.'

The image is graphic. Anse's not about to tell her he's had similar fantasies about Luciano and a bowl of cabbage, how his hands worked as he massaged and squeezed the cabbage, how the brine had run down his hands as he'd sucked his fingers clean. It's awful—cabbage isn't sexy.

Hannah takes another stab at her carrot cake before pushing the plate towards Anse. Without thinking, he sinks his spoon into the cake and takes a bite. It *is* heavenly.

'I can't believe you've been here a month already. Your English has improved so much,' Hannah says. 'Don't take it the wrong way, I know you were taught proper English but sometimes you can sound a little… robotic.'

Anse stares at her, mortified.

'What?' she laughs. 'Surely you know.'

'I'll have *you* know,' he tells her in German. 'That English is a very hard language to learn and Australians are incredibly informal even in their business settings so my apologies if I'm experiencing a little culture shock.'

Hannah throws her hands up in the air, surrendering. 'Fine, fine. I'm sorry.'

Anse goes to sink his fork into the carrot cake again, but Hannah's intercepts him. They fight, using the forks as weapons, before Anse swiftly pierces a piece of cake and retreats with his prize.

'Do I really sound so robotic?' he asks after a moment.

'Completely. It's actually adorable.'

'Should I try some slang?' he says. 'G'day?'

'Oh no.'

'Hello, mate. How are ya?' His accent is awful but Hannah's laughing.

'Please stop.'

'I'm going to Maccas in the arvo, and then to the bottle-o.'

'You're so bad at this.'

Anse smiles and finishes his coffee. Hannah looks down to Pat, who is sleeping at her feet.

'We should go,' she says and nudges Pat. 'This was nice, Anse.'

'It was,' he replies. 'See you at the office.'

Hannah runs her hand over her face, wiping away her smile. 'Work mode activated,' she says in a robotic voice.

Anse scoffs in mock hurt. 'Don't impersonate me.'

———

When he arrives at the office, there are already eight emails waiting from him—the earliest time stamped at 06:31am, from none other than Franz. While he's a good boss, Franz is entirely unsociable. He rarely leaves his office and the large double doors are usually closed. For most of the day, Anse talks to Franz via phone despite the fact their offices are right down the hall from each other. There is a void between them and neither seem to want, or know, how to breach it.

His colleagues are much more friendly. He routinely runs into Martina, who processes the visas in the kitchenette. Every conversation with Martina always circles back to her four daughters in Europe of whom she is immensely proud. The youngest has just finished university in Salzburg and is working as a student nurse at the hospital.

'Are you single?' she asks him as he makes a coffee.

'I am, yes.'

'Shame, a lovely guy like you is single,' she says. 'I'd think you'd have girls hanging off you.'

He gives her a tight smile. 'No, I've never really been that kind of guy, I suppose.'

Hannah is the only one who knows he is gay and that's the way he wants it to stay. He's never been gay at work, never disclosed his sexual preferences, never mentioned a partner in small talk or brought them along to after-work drinks. There's always been a duality to his life and he's trying his hardest to maintain it.

Luciano is doing little to help the matter.

He finishes work and goes to the gym, where he runs ten kilometres on a treadmill and then spends twenty minutes on the weight machines. It gives him time to shut off; there's nothing to focus on except the burn of his muscles as he works through his sets methodically.

When he arrives home to his silent apartment, he showers

and eats another calorie-controlled frozen meal before picking something on Netflix.

Emmy isn't on social media, so he sends her a text message, which goes unanswered. He considers, for only a moment, texting Luciano.

But what to say?

Hey?

Too simple.

Looking forward to learning how to cook!

No, too needy.

In the end, he settles on—

Anse: Are we still meeting tomorrow night?

Luciano: Yep. Meet me at Trattoria at Pearce shops. 6pm.

Anse: Do I need to bring anything?

Luciano: Nope! Just willingness to learn! See you tomorrow!

Anse: Ok.

Luciano: :)

CHAPTER ELEVEN

Nope! Just willingness to learn! See you tomorrow! Luciano knows he sounded like an idiot. There are way too many exclamation points in that sentence. Who on Earth would agree to take cooking lessons from a stranger who rocks up and offers you food that they've cooked for *you*?

Honestly, Luciano's surprised he wasn't carted out by security and banned from Austria forever.

He's sure Anse has only said yes out of politeness. The week has flown by so quickly: a blur of house inspections and delivery driver shifts, but now it's Thursday and he must come up with a lesson plan.

Standing in the kitchen, he pores through his mother's old handwritten recipe books for inspiration. Too complex and Anse won't get it. Too simple and he'll think Luciano is taking the piss and won't come back. The pages are thin and delicate in his hands and crackle as they turn. His mother's beautiful handwriting is faded but legible; though there are no dates on any of the pages, the book is at least as old as he is.

Peppered throughout the recipes, he finds pictures of her old kitchen in Milan filled with people he doesn't know clipped against certain recipes. She is photographed chopping onions in her white chef's jacket. Against a cocktail recipe, he finds a picture of her with an arm around a bald man, their faces both flushed red. Against a recipe for *Lobster Fra Diavoloi*, she stands out the front of her restaurant Ragazza, her hair as wild as Corina's. Who took this photo? Perhaps his father?

He settles on a recipe towards the front of the old book. It won't blow Anse's socks off, but it's a good place to start and the ingredients are readily available from the grocer across the square. He's washing the tomatoes when his phone rings on the kitchen bench. It's Marzia.

'We got an offer on the restaurant!' she cries happily.

'What?'

'And it's way beyond what we'd ask for! It's like astounding how much they are willing to pay. Seriously, Luc, this could set us up for *life*.'

'I thought—,' Luciano clears his throat. Something is stuck there. A big, dry lump. 'I thought we were going to wait. I thought were more focused on the house.'

'Well, word gets around!' she says.

He feels cold.

'Luciano?'

'I have to go, Mar.'

'Luciano, don't hang up.'

He hangs up. Sweat pricks at his skin as he undoes the first few buttons of his shirt. It's so tight, he can't breathe. The phone vibrates again as Marzia tries to call back, but Luciano lets it ring to voicemail. Outside, he can hear distant traffic on the street, the hum of a motorbike.

That's it. Marzia will sell the restaurant, and he'll have nothing. His heart beats rapidly and something lurches in his stomach, threatening to come up.

Trattoria will belong to someone else.

Will they gut it and reopen, wearing the skin of his mother's old restaurant? Will they demolish it completely? Will he have to watch his memories, his dreams, his ambition, get levelled and built over?

His phone buzzes.

Marzia: Luciano, call me

Are you upset?

Call me?

I don't know what to tell you except that we knew we had to sell the restaurant and I'm sorry if you're not taking this very well, but we all knew this had to be done.

Luciano, call me!!

He doesn't.

This is his night, perhaps his only night, with Anse in Trattoria. He's not going to squander it.

There's a knock on the glass front door. Luciano pulls himself up from the floor and checks the time. Shit. It's five-forty-five.

'Luciano?' Anse's deep voice echoes through the empty restaurant. 'I'm early. Are you here?'

Fuck.

'Come in, the doors unlocked!'

He smooths his hair back and stumbles into his mother's

office, rifling through his overnight bag. He pulls on a black Fleetwood Mac t-shirt and spritzes cologne messily onto his wrists and neck, coughing on the spray. Perhaps he's overdone it, but it's better than smelling of petrol and sweat.

Anse stands in the middle of the restaurant wearing navy pants and a crisp white button-down; the sleeves rolled up to his elbows. Luciano suppresses a whimper at the suspenders. This is going to be a long night.

Anse is staring at a large print of the Tuscan landscape hung in a garish golden frame. He hasn't been bothered to clear out the old furniture, but if an offer has come through, he suspects he'll have to start soon.

'That was my Mum's,' Luciano says as he approaches Anse. 'It's not exactly my taste but she insisted on it.'

'It's certainly eye-catching.' Anse replies. 'Do you want me to take off my shoes?'

'No. It's pretty dirty here and I haven't seen how you handle a knife, so better keep them on. Come on through to the kitchen.'

Anse follows him, glancing around the restaurant. 'What are we making?'

'Bruschetta,' he replies with a hard 'sck'. *Bru-sketta.*

Anse chuckles. 'When I said I couldn't toast bread, I didn't expect we'd start there.'

'We start with the basics,' Luciano assures. 'Oh no. You're wearing white.'

Anse looks down at his white shirt. 'Do you want me to take it off?'

Luciano swallows. His mouth is suddenly cotton dry. 'Um.'

Without waiting for an answer, Anse slips out of his suspenders—*sweet Jesus*—and begins unbuttoning his shirt.

Luciano considers just telling him he'll cover the cost of the shirt if Anse will put it back on because now he's just in a well-fitted white tank top, the waistband of his pants snug against his hips. The business shirt really does him no favours, Luciano considers, because Anse's arms are well-defined cords of muscle.

Luciano clears his throat. 'Drink?'

'Sure.'

He pours them both a glass of merlot before grabbing the basket of washed tomatoes from the sink.

He hands Anse a utility knife. 'Dice them. Cut it down the middle, so it's got two halves, and then press the flat side to the cutting board. Try to keep it even, like little squares.'

'Little squares. Got it.'

The tomato squelches on the board as Anse presses the knife into it.

Immediately, Luciano reaches out and covers Anse's hand with his own. 'You need to slice more. Don't force the knife down. It's sharp. Let it do the work.' He moves Anse's hand, allowing the knife to glide along the flesh of the tomato. It slices effortlessly. 'See?'

'I think I'm getting it.' Luciano lets go and Anse slices the tomato again. This time, only a little bit of pulp seeps out from the pressure.

'There are a lot of different kinds of tomatoes,' says Luciano, and dear God, is he really talking about tomatoes? 'You can use any kind but I like Roma tomatoes, because they're easy to find and have more flesh and less juice than a regular tomato.' He picks up a tomato and hands it to Anse who chops it with ease.

'What next?'

'Garlic.' Luciano picks a smaller knife from his roll. 'I'll show you the easiest way to crush it.'

He peels a clove and crushes it underneath the flat of a knife with the ball of his hand. Sprinkling a little coarse salt onto the board, Luciano begins to work the clove into a paste with the side of his knife. When it's smooth, he scrapes it into the bowl with the chopped tomatoes.

'Did your mother teach you how to do that?' Anse asks.

'Yeah. She was a Michelin star chef. I've worked here since I was like fourteen. Now, though, I might have to sell the place and get a job in someone else's kitchen. Awkward because my only referee for a new job has died.'

They move onto the toast. Luciano hands Anse a loaf of crisp sourdough and a serrated knife with the instruction to cut one-centimetre thick slices.

'How different is Canberra to where you're from?' Luciano asks as he refills their glasses. Anse is carefully slicing the bread, trying to get it as even as possible, but Luciano can already tell the slices are significantly wider at the bottom. No matter. All art is flawed.

'Vienna is a lot bigger. I've lived there all my life. I had my friends, a job, an apartment in *Wieden*. It used to take me forty minutes to get to work, now it takes me five. I'm not sure what to do with all that extra time.'

'Learn to cook?' Luciano offers helpfully and manages to get a smile for his efforts.

When the bread is toasted, Anse piles the tomatoes on top of the sourdough. Luciano adds a sprinkle of basil and a little salt and pepper.

'We're done!'

'That was surprisingly easy,' Anse says as they make their way out to sit at a table in the restaurant.

'Next week we'll boil an egg.'

'Perhaps by the time I've graduated from your school, I'll be able to make a three-course meal,' he says.

'I'll write that into the final exam,' Luciano laughs.

'I'm afraid I'll need quite a bit of tutoring until I'm ready to do that,' he replies. 'Every Thursday night, then?'

'Works for me.'

CHAPTER TWELVE

E mmy looks the same as she did four years ago: long, rich dark hair and a tanned and glowing complexion from weekends spent swimming and walking bush trails. The only thing that has changed is the new lotus tattoo that runs down her left arm. She steps off the train and scans the platform. The moment she sees him—it only takes her a moment; he doesn't exactly blend in—she lets out a high pitch squeal and runs into his arms.

God, he's missed her.

'Look at you!' Emmy says as she runs a hand across his shoulders. 'You're so buff!'

'Stop it,' he shrugs her off affectionately. People are staring, so he picks up her overnight bag and shows her to the car. 'Cool tattoo.'

The lotus flower is inked into the roundness of her shoulder and the leaves fan out down her arm. 'It's the national flower of

Vietnam. It literally rises from the shit on the bottom of a lake to bloom so I can relate to that.'

'Still struggling in Sydney?'

'We're getting by,' she says. 'How are you going?'

'I'm learning how to cook.'

Emmy looks impressed. 'And hitting the gym? Seriously, the last time I saw you, we could share clothes.'

It's true. He'd been a wiry teenager; athletic and fast but with no muscle mass whatsoever. At university, he'd joined a gym on a free trial and had loved it so much he never stopped. He'd run between classes and hang out in the free weight sections on Friday nights before heading out to a club with his friends. Suddenly, he wasn't the skinny teenager he'd always been, but a six-foot-four, broad-shouldered blonde. And all eyes were on him.

'How's Daniel?' he asks and hopes the change of subject isn't too obvious.

Emmy shrugs. 'He's fine. Working on his novel, probably.'

'I had no idea he quit the job with the council,' Anse says.

'Quit? No, he got made redundant. His entire department did. Don't ask me why the environment isn't a priority anymore but they got a new mayor and his team was literally the first to go.'

'He's not looking for work?'

'A few odd jobs have got us through, but he's been set on writing this book,' she sighs. 'I mean, I support him in it because he's just so unmotivated about anything else these days. But it's shitty being the only person bringing in money.' She rolls her eyes. 'And I'm sick of living in Sydney. The house prices, the transport. I spend most of my morning getting to work and most of my afternoon getting home from work. Daniel and I maybe spend a few hours together before I go to bed to get up and do it all again. It's exhausting.'

They arrive at the apartment, and Anse shows Emmy to the sparingly furnished spare bedroom where she promptly collapses face-down onto the bed.

'This is a nice place,' she says through the pillow.

Anse shrugs. 'I think it feels like a hotel.'

After Emmy unpacks, they eat lunch. Anse makes a salad without cutting his finger off. He considers sending Luciano a picture as proof he's improving in the kitchen but then Emmy pulls out her hiking gear and all but pushes Anse out the door.

They set out to Tidbinbilla, a winding nature reserve in the south of Canberra. Through dense gum forest, Anse finds the entrance to the Square Rock carpark and they mark their names on the sign-in sheet before departing.

The bush is quiet and silver and dense. The moisture in the ground makes it uncomfortably humid and the air smells earthy, of eucalyptus and rain. As they wander into a clearing, Emmy runs towards a rusted ladder fixed to the side of a large rock, climbing it without any hesitation.

'Holy shit,' Anse hears her say from the top.

Anse climbs awkwardly, unsure if the fragile ladder will hold his weight. As he scrambles to the top, he sees Emmy standing on the edge of the rock, her ponytail blowing in the wind. As he joins her, he realises there's nothing below them but space, hundreds of metres of it, and then bushland. It's a sheer drop. No fences. No warning. Just the rounded edge of the rock, and then trees far below them. Emmy takes a seat, dangling her legs over the edge, and gazes out at the rolling hills blanketed in gumtrees.

'I've missed you,' she says after a long time.

'I've missed you too. It's nice being so close again.'

'Will you stay?' she asks. 'If you can?'

He nods. 'If I can.'

It's late by the time they get back.

'Let's order in,' Emmy suggests as she disappears into the bathroom.

Anse grabs his phone and opens the QIK-EATS app. 'What do you feel like?'

'Don't care. You pick.'

A moment later, Anse hears running water. Great.

He thumbs through the options: Greek? Vietnamese? Maybe a burger from the place down the street? He settles on Indian and orders two dishes and a side of rice and promptly reminds himself to ask Luciano how to cook rice.

The bathroom is full of steam and the floral scent of Emmy's shampoo as he jumps in the shower. He's towelling his hair dry when the doorbell rings. Quickly, he wraps the towel around his waist and steps out of the bathroom, only to run into Emmy *en route* to the front door.

She laughs as she narrowly avoids colliding with his wet chest. 'Jesus Christ, put some clothes on, Anse!'

Rolling his eyes, he continues onto his room to dress. He hears Emmy open the door.

'Hi, how's it going?'

'… Anse Meyer?' says the delivery driver.

'Yes, this is his place,' replies Emmy. Anse pulls a shirt over his head. How does the driver know his last name? It's never given out on the app. And it's not like he has a common first name. Thanks to his eclectic mother, he's never met another Anse.

'I don't have to pay you, do I?' A pause. 'Perfect, thank you so much.'

Anse meets Emmy in the lounge room where she's setting out plates on the small coffee table.

'Indian was a great choice,' Emmy says as she pours them both a glass of white wine. 'Come on, pick something to watch.'

Anse flicks through his streaming services absentmindedly. 'Who was that at the door?'

She gives him a funny look. 'The delivery guy?'

'No, I mean, what was his name?'

'I don't know. He was the delivery guy.'

'What did he look like?'

She shrugs. 'I don't know. Curly hair. Tan skin. Can you grab the beer from the fridge while you're up?'

Anse finds his phone and fumbles to unlock it.

Your food was delivered by Luciano. Provide a rating?

'Fuck,' he says.

Emmy turns. 'What?'

How is this possible? He must live close by. Shit. *Shit.*

'Seriously,' Emmy replies. 'What is the matter?'

He can't tell her he's crushing on the delivery boy. He'll look stupid and she'll only run right back and tell his brother who will tease him endlessly. So, instead, he lies. Badly.

'It's, um, my boss. Looks like I'll have a big meeting on Monday to sort out some things.'

'Shit. They email you on the weekends?'

'Yeah, just comes with the job, I guess,' he says. 'I don't mind.'

'Damn,' she says. 'Hope everything's okay at work.'

So does he.

CHAPTER THIRTEEN

Luciano tries not to let the woman bother him, but she does. It bothers him that she was in his home, which he now knows is a nice modern apartment near the Kingston foreshore. It bothers him that she knows him in a way that Luciano doesn't, but so desperately wants. It bothers him because she is beautiful with dark hair and dark eyes and is probably *exactly* his type. But what bothers him the most is that he thought the spark between them wasn't entirely one-sided. That Anse was like him. That Anse *liked* him.

Luciano groans into his pillow.

He had started his shift early, this time serving the suburbs around his home in Narrabundah instead of the offices that make up most of his clients during the week. That's how he'd arrived at Anse's apartment. The amount of food he was carrying should have given him an indication that Anse had company. Butter chicken and Rogan Josh, a large tub of rice, and two garlic naan breads.

He's jealous though he has no right to be.

Anse is not his.

Corina calls him at nine-thirty the next morning to get brunch and he woefully agrees. He hasn't been bothered to do the laundry in a long time, so he throws himself into the shower before pulling on an old grey shirt and a pair of black shorts. It's already so hot outside. His thongs stick to the road as he backs out of the driveway. It's days like this he wishes he had a car with air-conditioning.

Corina is far too bright and bubbly when he meets her at the café. She's wearing a white flowy dress and her hair is more curly than frizzy, falling around her tanned shoulders in tight ringlets.

'Are you okay?' she asks. 'You don't look very well.'

'I'm fine. I just had a bad night's sleep, that's all.'

Corina orders them both a coffee.

'Did Marzia call you?'

'About the offer on the restaurant? Yeah.' He wonders if this is all Marzia's doing. Of course she'd recruit Corina to deliver the bad news.

'What do you think?'

'You know what I think about it,' he says as his long black arrives. Luciano soaks in the scent of the coffee before taking a sip.

'Marzia wants to accept.'

'What do *you* want?'

Corina pauses, looks down at her coffee and then buys time by dumping two sugar packets very slowly into the foam.

'Corina,' he says impatiently.

'I want you to be happy, Luciano,' she replies. 'And I know

working with Mum made you happy but you have to let go. You have to let *her* go.'

She makes it sound so easy. Like as soon as he decides to let her go, he'll be free.

The problem is that he can still see her.

He can see her in his home, in his life, in every dirty corner and beautiful vista of this city. She haunts this city in the most wonderful, awful, nostalgic way.

'I don't know who I am without her, Cor.'

Her lips tighten into a thin line. 'The money could help you figure that out.'

———

It's eleven in the morning when Anse's order comes through the app. It is the first order of the day. He's elbow-deep in the toilet cisterns at Trattoria. The water, still and untouched, is almost brown and now that he's disturbed it, the entire first floor reeks of sewerage. The restaurant needs work—more work than he can afford if it's going under the hammer—but he does what he can to make it presentable.

Luciano pulls off his gloves and checks his phone. The delivery request flashes.

Anse Meyer

Confirm? Deny?

His finger hovers over 'deny'.

Confirm? Deny?

Deny. Deny, he thinks. Deny!

His finger twitches and he clicks confirm. With a groan, he gets up from the toilet floor. Why does he subject himself to this torture repeatedly? *Anse does not want you,* he tells himself even as he grabs his keys and helmet. *Anse is not interested in you.*

This time, Anse has ordered a Turkish roll from a local café. Luciano figures that the sandwich costs around seventeen dollars with his delivery fee. Surely the same sandwich couldn't cost more than five or six dollars to make. Is Anse so hopeless he can't assemble a sandwich? Or is it a convenience thing? How Luciano longs to have more money than time.

To his surprise, Anse is waiting for him in the foyer. Hannah, an ever-constant spectator to their fumbling banter, isn't at her desk. He's wearing a grey suit with a white shirt and shiny black shoes. His blonde hair is swept over and gelled. It's irritating how good looking he is. Truly.

'Luciano!' Anse gives him nervous smile. 'How are you?'

Luciano hands him the sandwich. 'I'm fine.'

Anse takes the sandwich and places it on Hannah's desk. 'Are we still on for Thursday?'

'Sure,' Luciano shrugs. He does his best to make his tone effortless. Casual. Not concerned in the least. 'Come around at six.'

'Great.'

'Good. I should go. I've got other orders.'

'Did you have a nice weekend?'

'It was fine,' he lies. *Who was that woman?* he wants to ask. *Why was she in your apartment? What is she to you?*

'Good,' Anse says. 'Mine was nice too.'

'Okay. Well, bye.'

'Bye, Luciano.'

As he heads back to his Vespa, he doesn't look back. Another order comes through the app and he presses 'confirm'.

It's better than cleaning toilets.

———

It's an hour later when another order from Anse comes through the app. Luciano looks at in disbelief because surely there are other delivery drivers in the area.

He denies it.

Anse must cancel the order because it pops up again a moment later.

'What the fuck?'

Anse's ordered two iced coffees and a muffin from a local coffee shop. The barista isn't confident they won't spill, so Luciano takes it slow as he navigates streets littered with speed humps.

'Anse says he's coming,' Hannah chirps as he enters.

'Why's he doing this?' Luciano demands. 'Surely he can go out and get a coffee. Is he really that busy?'

'I mean, his calendar says he has a meeting at two. Otherwise, I think he just likes seeing you.'

Oh. Well. He's not sure what to say to that, and doesn't have time to formulate a response because the door behind Hannah's desk opens again and there is Anse. He's lost the jacket and his sleeves are rolled up to his elbows again, which really shouldn't do half the things it does to Luciano's insides.

'Your coffee.' Luciano thrusts the package at him.

Anse fishes out the iced coffees from the paper bag and hands one to him. 'For you.'

Luciano looks at the coffee for a moment. The plastic cup is sweating, beads of water running down Anse's outstretched hand. 'You bought me a coffee? That I had to deliver?'

'I thought we could split the muffin also. You didn't seem yourself this morning.'

Really, what's Luciano supposed to do with that? He takes a sip of the iced coffee. It's almost too sweet with the melted vanilla bean ice cream for his tastes but it's strong. 'I can't believe you did this.'

'It took a few tries. My order got cancelled the first time I put it in and then it was assigned to a different driver.' Anse opens the door to the courtyard. 'You don't have other orders, do you?'

Luciano switches off his phone. 'Nah. I can take a break.'

There are eighteen emails waiting for Anse when he returns to his desk. One in particular catches his eye.

To: Anse Meyer
From: Hannah Ridley
Subject line: Dream boat
That was sooo romantic.

To: Hannah Ridley
From: Anse Meyer
Subject line: RE: Dream boat
It was a purely platonic coffee. He was obviously upset this morning.

Also, personal communication via email is a breach of the IT regulations.

. . .

From: Hannah Ridley
      To: Anse Meyer
      Subject line: RE: RE: Dream boat
      You should really stop emailing me about your love life then.

From: Anse Meyer
      To: Hannah Ridley
      Subject line: RE: RE: RE: Dream boat
      You're infuriating and I loathe working with you.
      We're just friends.
      See you at coffee tomorrow morning x
      PS. Franz can read these emails.

From: Hannah Ridley
      To: Anse Meyer
      Subject line: RE: RE: RE: RE: Dream boat
      Franz is a total romantic and would ship you two so hard if
he knew.

What is 'ship', Anse wonders. He plugs it into a search engine
but all he gets back are results for, well, actual ships.

Anse has never had a girlfriend—both in the romantic sense
and not. Attending an all-boys high school, he'd made a name for
himself playing soccer, where his lean body was naturally suited
for wing. In turn, he'd become friends with most of his team-
mates. Though he'd meet their girlfriends occasionally, they

weren't his friends. His father and brother were less helpful: his father never dated after the split from his mother and until Emmy, Daniel never kept a girl around long enough for him to get to know.

In university, he'd had female peers. It sounds clinical, but that was what they were: girls who did group projects with him, university professors, a trainer at the gym.

Girls had never been interested in him, though he wonders if perhaps he was too oblivious to notice their flirting. Or perhaps they'd known who he was. Known before he'd even known himself.

Hannah invites him to the football on Saturday morning. It's a great Australian game, apparently, and one he must watch while he's here. Even Daniel thinks it's a great idea because his team, the *Western Sydney Giants*, are playing. He even offers to send down his club merchandise via express post so Anse can 'look the part'.

In the end, it's not necessary. Hannah has a spare scarf she loops around his neck.

'Beer?' she asks as soon as they find seats in the grandstand.

'Of course.'

They've started talking in German now, because Anse is afraid he might forget and Hannah wants to try and remember.

Hannah returns with two plastic cups of watered-down beer and a bucket of chips.

'So what was going on with Luciano the other day?'

'Not sure, he didn't tell me.'

'You guys really still platonic?'

He hesitates. Hannah latches onto it.

'I *knew* it. You need to tell him how you feel.'

'It's not that simple.'

'It's always that simple, Anse.' Hannah reasons. 'Seriously, there is no bad time, except maybe after a funeral but you can always make that mortality stuff work for you. Oh! You should make a grand gesture!'

'They only do that in the movies, Hannah.'

'Not true,' she retorts. 'I made a grand gesture to Cam. He was hosting a radio show, and I called through and asked him out on another date live on air. He said yes, and here we are, four years later!'

He's never done anything like that in his life. Hell, the most romantic thing he'd ever done for Max was buy him an espresso and a box of condoms for his birthday. And he'd expected Max to drop everything and move halfway across the globe for him?

'That's not me.'

As if sensing he's done with the conversation, Hannah reclines back in her plastic seat.

The fact is he's here for a year at best. And Luciano's clearly going through his own issues.

'I'm worried I'd ruin things,' he admits eventually.

Hannah purses her lips. 'It's always a risk.'

Is the risk worth it? Honestly, he's not sure. Luciano's wonderful; perhaps his first real friend here after Hannah. He doesn't want to lose him for wanting more.

A siren sounds and the players run onto the field.

Anse takes a sip of his beer. 'So how's this game played, anyway?'

———

When Anse arrives at Trattoria for their weekly lesson, the entire place smells like eucalyptus and bleach and, if he's being honest, a little like shit. He finds Luciano deep in the bowels of the restaurant unclogging a toilet.

'Oh fuck me!' Luciano yelps and, in his surprise, drops the plunger. The toilet water gurgles and churns. Anse suppresses a gag. 'I didn't hear you come in.'

'We can do this another time if you're busy.'

Luciano shakes his head. 'No, it's fine. Sorry, I'm such a mess. I have a spare change of clothes in the office. Give me a few minutes to get cleaned up and I'll meet you in the kitchen, okay?'

Anse waits dutifully in the kitchen and replies to a few emails on his phone. When Luciano returns to the kitchen in fresh clothes, he carries the scent of cloves and sandalwood. Picking up an apron from a hook near the office, he tosses it to Anse.

'This week, we're cooking an egg. And making more toast.'

Anse's gaze follows Luciano as he disappears into the walk-in-fridge. 'More toast?'

'You have to master the basics first!'

'Are you calling me basic?' He's not sure if the joke, as bad as it was, lands but Luciano laughs as he re-emerges from the walk-in fridge. He places a handful of ingredients on the kitchen bench: two avocados, onion, garlic, a fresh loaf of sour dough and a block of feta cheese.

'Now,' he says, brandishing a sharp knife. 'Watch carefully.'

With steady hand, Luciano cuts the avocado down the middle, navigating the knife around its pit. A little pressure and the two halves come apart cleanly. The avocado is bright green and creamy in the middle.

'Your turn.'

Anse takes the knife and slices down the fruit's side, making sure not to put too much pressure on the knife.

'Now the pit,' Luciano says. 'Lodge the knife deep into the pit. Be careful. Don't chop off your hand.'

'You're being serious?'

'Of course! It's too slippery otherwise.' Luciano demonstrates by piercing the woody pit with his knife. It comes free easily.

Anse's sweaty palm grips the knife. Nervously, he looks between the avocado pit and Luciano before bringing down the knife with enough force to take a decent chunk out of his arm.

'You did it!' Luciano whoops.

Anse looks down at the avocado. The knife is lodged deep in the pit. With a small twist, it's out.

He wants to tell Luciano that it's really nothing to be proud of, but the way Luciano is smiling at him makes him feel like he's won a Nobel Prize or landed on the moon. Not successfully dissected an avocado.

'Now we cut up the onion. You're a pro at this.'

He is certainly not a professional. Still, he tries his best to mimic Luciano's perfectly diced onion. The slippery slices don't stay together and his squares aren't as square as Luciano's but they're passable. Luciano doesn't say anything as Anse tips it into the bowl with the avocado.

'So, what do you normally do on the weekend?' Anse asks as they work the avocado into a paste.

'Most of the time I'm here. Before that, I was caring for my mother so I didn't have time to do anything. Now I'm trying to figure out who I am without her.'

'How's that going?'

'Difficult.' Luciano adds salt and pepper to the smashed avocado. 'What about you?'

'My sister-in-law visited last week.' He places the phrase

gently and hopes it won't arouse suspicion, as if he's not used the last five minutes of conversation to bring it up. 'But most of the time I don't know what to do with myself.'

'Do you have a girlfriend?' Luciano asks as he cracks two eggs into a hot frying pan. They sizzle immediately.

Anse smiles over the lip of his wine glass. 'No.'

'Not back in Vienna?'

'No.'

Anse doesn't elaborate further and Luciano focuses on flipping the eggs.

'Come to the farmer's markets with me on Saturday morning,' Luciano says as he slides the eggs onto a plate.

The toast pops.

'What?'

'We can think of it as another lesson. It'll be fun.'

Well, what's he supposed to say now that he's told Luciano he has nothing better to do?

'Sure.'

'I'll text you the address.' Spreading the avocado over the toast, Luciano crumbles feta over both their plates with a flourish. 'We're done. Come on, I'm starving.'

'It's that simple?' asks Anse as he picks up his plate.

'It's that simple.'

CHAPTER FIFTEEN

Luciano meets Anse at the markets at nine-thirty on Saturday morning, keen to flee the crowds of people flooding through his house for yet another open home. Auction day is next Saturday. No serious pre-auction offers have come in for the house yet but the offer on Trattoria still looms over him. It's been a week and a half and he hasn't picked up any of Marzia's calls. Maybe she'll sell the restaurant out from under him. Maybe she'll take him to court. Or maybe, if he keeps ignoring her, the entire thing will just go away.

He spots Anse as soon as he parks the Vespa. He's wearing a black-and-white t-shirt and a pair of jean shorts with sneakers. It's the most casual Luciano has ever seen him. It feels intimate. Like something's changing between them.

'Nice shirt,' Luciano says as he approaches. 'It's weird not to see you in business attire.'

'Thanks.' The markets are busy on a Saturday. He can smell

the BBQ pork form the Vietnamese food van a few feet away. It's barely ten in the morning but there's already a line.

Anse releases a sigh, taking in the sheer madness of market day. 'Where do we start?'

'Why don't we start with a coffee?'

'Coffee sounds nice.'

There's a small coffee van just inside the marketplace pavilion that isn't too busy. Luciano orders a long black, and Anse gets a latte and a protein brownie, which he breaks in half with a napkin before handing the bigger half to Luciano.

He takes it gratefully. 'Thanks, I didn't get time for breakfast. We're having another open house, and I spent half the morning cleaning so that people wouldn't judge my life too harshly.'

Anse laughs, smiling over the lip of his coffee. 'Sounds awful.'

They browse the lines of stalls, meandering through the delicatessen stalls and into fresh produce and Luciano tells Anse about the differences between the different tomatoes on sale before buying a vine of Black Russian tomatoes. The stallholder, as thanks, offers them a sample of olives. Luciano takes one and bites into the salty flesh.

Anse refuses it. 'I don't like olives.'

The stallholder isn't offended but Luciano scoffs in mock hurt.

'I'll make you like olives before our lessons are over.'

'I'm doubtful.'

In the handicraft section, Anse buys a candle that smells like brown sugar and butter. It's the kind of scent that makes Luciano think of cosy winter afternoons spent listening to the rain and binge-watching TV. Something he can imagine happening in Anse's modern Kingston apartment.

'Why don't you stay with me when the house sells?' Anse says suddenly.

Luciano chokes on his coffee. 'What?'

'I have a spare room. You need a place to stay. It makes sense.'

Does it? Because the idea of being his roommate, of living with him and seeing what he looks like when he wakes up in the morning—all the while not being able to touch him—might drive him to madness.

'We could create a system where you didn't have to pay rent if you cooked,' he laughs. 'It'd be quite the arrangement. I'd never have to order out again.'

'Yeah, sure,' Luciano manages. 'Let me think about it.'

Throwing his coffee cup into the recycling bin, Luciano pulls out his phone to check the time. Instead, he sees three missed calls from Marzia and one from Corina.

'Fuck,' he groans. 'My sisters called. I need to take this, sorry. It's probably going to be a whole thing and I'm going to have to go.'

He doesn't want to leave. Not when they still have half of the market to browse and when, on three occasions, Anse's fingers have brushed his. It's too frequent to be an accident, Luciano had thought, and resolved to curl his fingers to catch Anse's the next time it had happened. Just to see what he'd do.

Anse's hands sink into the pockets of his jeans. 'I'll see you on Thursday night? At your restaurant?'

Luciano sighs. His phone rings again. It's Corina.

'I hope so.'

———

He takes the phone call outside, away from the crowd, plugging one ear with his finger as he answers.

'Luciano—what the fuck—why didn't you pick up?' comes Corina's hot greeting.

'Wow, hello to you too,' he says. 'I'm at the markets. What do you want?'

'We got an offer on the house.'

His stomach twists. 'And?'

'It's a lot,' Corina says. 'Like *a lot* a lot.'

'What?' His mind is buzzing as he sits on the edge of a raised garden bed. 'What does that mean?'

'Marzia says it's knocked all other offers out of the park and it's enough to pay off Mum's debts with some leftover.'

'How much leftover?' Luciano asks. He hates that his mother's life has been reduced to how much money they'll get in their pockets.

'Enough.'

'Enough?' Luciano echoes. 'What does that mean, Corina? Enough for me to buy the restaurant?'

'Marzia says if that's what you really want. Luciano, are you there?'

'I'm here.' His voice sounds strained. There's something dry in his throat and he coughs to dislodge it. *There's enough to buy the restaurant.*

'Come around and we can talk. There are still things we need to figure out.'

'Okay,' he mutters. 'I'll be there soon.'

As he hangs up. A few metres away, Anse is shouldering his way through the crowd.

'Is everything all right?'

Luciano nods. 'There was an offer on the house. The money

will cover most of Mum's debts. It'll be enough to reopen the restaurant.' Anse's hand touches his shoulder and squeezes. 'I can't believe it.'

'Congratulations. That's wonderful.'

Before he realises what's happening, Anse brings him in for a hug. Instinctively, Luciano raises his arms to loop around Anse's waist. He's warm and smells like washing powder and the musk of his deodorant.

'I'm happy for you,' Anse says into his hair.

'Thank you.' He feels Anse's hands drop away and he steps back. 'I better go see my sister.'

'Can I drive you home?'

Luciano hesitates. 'I have my Vespa.'

'I'm sure we can put the back seats down.' Anse looks around the carpark. 'Bring it around, my car's not too far away.'

He feels a little jittery, like the sudden rush of adrenaline in his system is struggling to find an outlet. Anse's hand rests on his lower back, gently guiding him to the car park. They find the Vespa near an old peppercorn tree and walk it back to Anse's small SUV and then—*holy shit*— Anse lifts it into the back of his car like it's a goddamn toy.

He closes the boot and dusts his hands like that wasn't the most ridiculous thing Luciano's ever seen.

'Well then, where does your sister live?'

CHAPTER SIXTEEN

He doesn't see Luciano until Wednesday.

It's a strangely quiet start to the week. There are no meetings and he manages to get on top of his emails. Franz is in such a good mood he shouts the team a mid-week round on Tuesday afternoon.

Today, he's just knocked off his emails and is about to get started reading a new bill from the Austrian Parliament when his office phone rings.

'Luciano's here,' Hannah says chirpily.

'I didn't order anything.' There's a pause. He hears Hannah repeat the phrase to Luciano before he hears Luciano reply, 'Tell him I know.'

'He told me to tell you that he knows,' repeats Hannah.

Anse presses his fingers to the bridge of his nose. These two. 'Thank you, Hannah, I'll be right there.'

'He says he'll be right there,' Hannah parrots back. Anse hangs up.

In the foyer, Luciano greets him with two plastic containers filled with stew. Hannah's made herself scarce.

'Figured you didn't have time to eat,' Luciano says. 'And wanted to make sure we were still on for tomorrow. And to say thanks for the other day.'

'You didn't have to.'

'I wanted to.'

The kind gesture floors him. 'I haven't eaten. Do you want to stay for a bit?' He motions towards the courtyard.

The courtyard is cool, dappled by the light that slips through the thick canopy of the jacaranda tree. Small handfuls of crocuses bloom around the base of the tree, a myriad of yellow, white and purple.

The food is still warm when he opens the container. It's a simple dish: mince and beans in a rich, chunky tomato sauce with a little rice mixed in, but it's delicious and hearty.

'This is amazing,' Anse says. 'You have to give me the recipe.'

Luciano laughs nervously. 'I'll put it on the list.'

'How did it go with your sister?'

'Fine,' Luciano replies. 'We agreed to the offer and then we talked about using my share to pay off the rest of the restaurant. Without the debt, it makes it easier. Technically they'll still own it but one day I'll try to buy them out.'

'I'm happy for you.'

'If I've learnt anything from this it's to make a will. If you ever die unexpectedly, don't leave it to chance.'

'You're right. My brother and mother would probably turn my ashes into some piece of art.'

Luciano laughs at the idea. After a moment he adds, 'there's also an apartment above the restaurant, so while I think you'd make a great roommate, I'll politely decline the offer.'

He's about to reply when, over Luciano's shoulder, the court-yard door opens. It's Hannah.

'Anse. Franz wants to see you.' Her tone is urgent. Hannah's *never* urgent.

He remembers the bill from the Austrian Parliament. It was just on carbon emissions but maybe shit's hit the fan.

He puts down his half-eaten lunch. 'I have to go. I'll see you tomorrow night as usual?'

'As usual,' Luciano smiles.

Anse slips past Hannah. 'Franz is in his office. You better hurry.'

The door is closed when he arrives. Tentatively, he knocks twice before entering. Franz is at his desk, staring at his computer. Outside, he can see Hannah and Luciano talking and suddenly he realises Franz has seen everything. If he'd opened a window to air out the musty office, he would have heard every word, too.

Anse clears his throat. 'Is there something the matter?'

Franz gives him a stern look. 'Civilians are not allowed onto embassy grounds without a guest pass.'

'You mean Luciano?'

'Unless he has an official guest pass, you have to meet your friend off grounds,' he tells Anse. 'And limit your visitations.'

'He just delivers food. Sometimes he stops in for a chat but he's harmless.'

'It's protocol, Anse. If you are meeting with your *friend*.' He says the word in a way that makes Anse's stomach turn. 'It's off grounds.'

It's a simple request. Not unreasonable. Sure, maybe he has

twisted protocol just a little, but the force of the word *friend* stabs at him. And twists. He's hurt by the accusation that he's not being professional, but he's absolutely floored by the realisation that what he is—what Franz is insinuating—isn't accepted here.

But, what can he say? This is his job. His career. His entire reason for being here.

Franz looks at him expectantly. 'Do you understand why, Anse?'

'Yes.'

'No more.'

'I understand.'

Franz sighs deeply. 'I am glad this is all sorted, then. Your draft on the immigration statement was good. I have a meeting with the German Ambassador at three and I want you to be there to meet him and take the minutes. I've sent you a request to your calendar.'

His phone vibrates in his pocket; no doubt the meeting request.

'It's a pleasure,' Anse replies before excusing himself.

'What did he want?' Hannah asks as soon as Anse steps into his office.

'No more friends in the courtyard. But the word 'friend' was used conservatively. He knows.'

'That's bullshit.'

He's about to tell her that it's not—it's just protocol and he hasn't followed the rules—but suddenly she's stalking halfway down the hallway, her heels clicking on the wooden floorboards. Before he can stop her, Hannah bangs her fist on Franz's door.

'What are you doing?' he seethes. 'You'll get us both fired!'

Hannah shrugs him off and bangs on the door again.

Franz opens the door. 'Miss Ridley, what can I help you

with?' He glances to Anse. Stern disappointment is written across his face.

'He sits out there and has lunch for thirty-minutes with him,' Hannah says. She's amped herself up for a speech of international proportions, Anse can tell. 'Mark used to stand out there and smoke a pack a day, talk on the phone loud enough for the neighbours to hear, *and* let his kids play basketball on the pavement and you never said a word to him.'

Franz looks between them. 'Those were different circumstances.'

'Hannah,' Anse says desperately. She is going to get herself fired, and she's the best thing about working here and he's *definitely* not worth being fired over.

Franz crosses his arms. 'The fact of the matter is that all guests need to have passes to access grounds of the office outside of the common lobby; a station, which I may add, you should be attending right now, Miss Ridley. And I'll remind you that while I am not your immediate supervisor, I am her closest advisor. It would be wise to watch your tone. One is seeking a career in diplomacy after all.'

Anse watches as Hannah's anger seems to turn from a simmer to an over-boil. 'You never enforced this rule before,' she fumes. 'It's lunch, Franz. This is just discriminatory.'

'And what discrimination is Anse experiencing, specifically?

Anse can hear his blood hammering in his ears. Oh no. Oh *no*.

Hannah, realising what she's said, backs off.

'If that will be all, Miss Ridley.' He turns to Anse. 'I'll see you at three.'

He closes the door.

Hannah turns to look at him, and Anse stares back. He can't believe that's just happened; can't believe she's just told him–

Because he's always had a duality to his life. It's better that way.

'I'm sorry, Anse,' she gushes. 'It just came out.'

'It's fine,' he lies. 'I think he knew.'

'It's not fine. I totally just—,' Her hand comes to her mouth. 'I'm *so* sorry.'

'I'm okay,' he says. 'Hannah, you shouldn't have done that.'

'I know. God. I know.' She sobs. 'Fuck, I need to apologise. That was so unprofessional.'

Hannah retreats back to her desk. Later, Anse receives a formal notice to all staff about the protocols of non-authorised persons on the property.

———

That night, he calls his brother.

'*Anse, vas?*' Daniel answers immediately. 'I'm busy.'

'They know I'm gay at work.'

There's a pause on the other end and then Anse hears sound of a door closing. 'What?'

He lies back on his lounge and repeats, 'They know I'm gay at work.'

'I don't understand?'

'I've never *been* gay at work.'

'Again, I don't understand,' Daniel says. 'Repeating the phrase or giving it a different emphasis is not helping.'

He rubs his temple. 'In Vienna, I never told anyone I was gay. I didn't want it to affect my career and it was easy enough to keep separate.'

'It should never—,'

'It did today,' he interrupts. 'I was having lunch with a friend. I got in trouble.' God, he sounds like a schoolboy again.

'Maybe it wasn't about that.'

'It was. It was just the way it was *said*, and then Hannah said that it hadn't been enforced in the past, and I just can't stop thinking about it.' Daniel doesn't respond immediately. 'What do I do?'

'What do you mean what do you do?'

Anse briefly thinks about throwing the phone out the window, driving up to Sydney and threatening to punch his brother in the face for being so infuriatingly unhelpful.

'Why do anything?' Daniel adds. 'Who cares if everyone knows? Isn't it better to be who you are at work?'

'You don't understand.'

'I do understand,' Daniel laughs. 'Perhaps not in the same way as you, of course, but you're not the only queer one in the family. I can't give you any advice but to be who you are, because that's all I want for you. And maybe to talk it out with like a therapist or something.'

'I don't need therapy, Dan.'

'Everyone needs therapy. Just a little bit.' His brother, never one to be serious for too long, immediately follows with, 'So, who's this new piece of ass you've been going to lunch with?'

Anse groans because he can almost hear his smile.

'His name is Luciano.'

'You banging?'

Anse rubs his hand down his face. 'No.'

'But you want to,' he laughs. 'Ah, you've always had one in every port, you dick magnet.'

'Do *not* call me that.'

And then Dan starts parading out all his ex-lovers. 'Let's go through them. Max, of course. Whatever happened to Lukas?'

'He moved back to Sweden.'

'David?'

'That was *two dates* and I regret telling you about him.'

'And Walter? Always loved that guy. Imagine a twenty-year-old named *Walter*.'

'Can we not go through my dirty laundry?' he huffs. 'Did Emmy hear about the job?'

'Yeah, she didn't get it,' Daniel replies. 'But back to who was it—Lucien?'

'Luciano.'

'Cute.'

'He's Italian. Well, Australian. His mother was Italian.'

'Extra cute.'

Anse smiles. 'I think so.'

'So why haven't you dicked him down yet?' Daniel asks far too casually. 'Or is this different? Are you waiting? Is it, dare I say, *love*?'

Anse squeezes his eyes tight. 'I don't know what it is yet.'

'But you like him?'

'Yes.'

'But you haven't asked him out?'

'No, I mean,' he struggles to find the right words. 'It's *complicated*.'

'Is it?' Daniel asks. 'You know, Anse, I've always found that you make things far more complicated than they need to be.'

'I want to,' he says. 'Luciano is complicated. He's going through some things. I'm not sure if it would be right.'

'Why don't you let him make the decision?'

Before he can answer, he hears Emmy in the background.

'I gotta go,' says Daniel. 'Emmy's just got home and I haven't defrosted the chicken for dinner, so I need to be told off for the next hour or so.'

Anse laughs. 'Good luck.'

'You too, man. Think about what I said.'

———

Hannah isn't at the front desk when he arrives at the office. There's a note on his keyboard to meet Franz in his office. Immediately.

'Fuck.'

The door to Franz's office is closed when he arrives. He knocks twice and hears Franz call, 'Come in.'

The door closes softly behind him. The few steps between the door and Franz's desk feel like a chasm between them, and steeling himself, he crosses the room.

'Sit, please,' says Franz.

Anse sits, wiping his sweaty hands down the front of his pants.

'I have to say I'm sorry for the way that things were handled yesterday—,'

But. There must be a but in there somewhere.

'It was unprofessional of me.'

But.

'And I want to offer you my sincerest apologies,' he says. 'For any distress I may have caused you in enforcing such a rule, which I will admit, had not been enforced so strictly in the past.'

When no 'but' comes, Anse clears his throat. His mouth is incredibly dry. 'Thank you for saying that. And for apologising.'

A whisper of a smile breaks Franz's mask. 'Good. I do want

to acknowledge that I had thought of your friend as just that and that there was no intention for discrimination based on gender or sexual preferences—,'

'He is just my friend,' Anse corrects and then surprises himself by saying, 'but I am gay.'

Franz is silent for a moment but then he nods. 'I'm pleased you feel you could tell me, Anse. If you'd like, I can arrange an ongoing guest pass for your friend. The courtyard is a wonderful place to have lunch in the summer, you should enjoy it while it lasts.'

'That would be nice, thank you.'

Franz writes an email quickly. His slender fingers fly across the keyboard. 'The statement on fossil fuels you wrote yesterday was excellent,' he says. 'Communications reported it was picked up by all major metros in Austria last night. The Ambassador is pleased and it's putting more pressure on Australia to adopt more carbon-neutral forms of power on the floor on the United Nations.'

Anse wonders if one hastily penned media release can really do all of that. Still, he's not about to rebuff praise from his boss.

'As you know, the Ambassador and a selected few from her team will be moving to Canada next year,' he continues. 'The transition period is always a time of great… uncertainty.'

He chooses the word carefully but Anse knows its code for layoffs.

'It's pieces like this that will secure you an extension in your current post, should you wish it. Keep up the good work, Anse.'

'Thank you, sir,' he says. He really wants to leave it at that; to accept the praise and continue with his working day, but he has to ask. 'Where is Hannah?'

'She's working at head office for a couple of days,' Franz

replies. 'With some of the international policy interns. It'll be good for her, really. She's too talented to be sitting on the receptionist desk, but until she finishes her degree, I'm afraid that it's where she'll have to stay.'

'So about yesterday?'

'Sometimes it is useful to be reminded of how one's actions may be perceived to others,' Franz comments quietly. 'Is there anything else eating you, Anse?'

'No,' he admits.

'Thank you for seeing me so early in the morning,' he says. 'I know you usually get coffee with Hannah. If you'd like, I am free from eleven for a short walking meeting. We could walk to the café on the corner you often frequent.'

He sees the offer for what it is: an olive branch. While Anse doesn't want a friendship with Franz, he can see there's something else there—a sort of strange mutual appreciation that grows between colleagues too different to meet under circumstances outside of work, but too similar to ignore.

'I'll come by at eleven,' Anse agrees.

Franz nods. 'Close the door on your way out.'

CHAPTER SEVENTEEN

'You can't ignore me if I show up at our house,' Marzia says as she waltzes through the front door early one morning. Luciano's still in his pyjamas, his hair's a mess and he's barely caffeinated.

'What are you doing here?'

'Making sure you're alive.' She pushes past him to make a coffee. Luciano would offer, but Marzia's so picky it's easier if she does it herself. 'And my colleague said everything went through on the house and the restaurant. Congratulations.'

'Thanks. For the help, I mean.'

'No worries. Ugh, you have nothing in the cupboards.' Marzia steps out of the kitchen and picks up her car keys. 'It was a shitty situation all around. Let's get breakfast. Mimosas on me.'

They have three mimosas before 11am. It's nice not to be fighting with his sisters and to finally, *finally* feel like he's starting to carve out a life he can call his own, for better or for worse.

That afternoon he goes back to Trattoria and starts cleaning up the old courtyard. The wisteria vine is lush and green and the lemon myrtle tree is heavy with unopened buds. He picks a few mature leaves and inhales the sweet scent before pocketing them for use later.

'Luciano!' a voice calls out from over the back fence.

Whirling around, Luciano sees Rohan Ahuja peek over the fence line.

'Rohan! You scared the shit out of me!'

Luciano unlatches the gate and immediately he's pulled into a hug. 'How the fuck are you?'

'Yeah, not bad.' Rohan is six foot tall and all muscle. His hair falls in lush dark waves around his face. He's as handsome as ever, Luciano considers, though the acne he'd had as a teenager has left scarring on his cheeks and forehead. 'What are you doing back?'

'Officially moved back in with my folks.' Rohan scratches the back of his head nervously and the cords of muscles in his arm flex. 'Don't know if you heard but my AFL career is kinda over.'

'I'd seen one or two news stories.' He rests the broom against the side of the wardrobe and ushers Rohan inside. 'Don't mind the mess.'

Rohan lets out a whistle escapes him as he takes in the expanse of the empty restaurant. 'This place looks so different. I saw you guys've been doing work. You're selling?'

'I just bought it.'

Rohan smiles. 'Holy shit, that's huge, Luc. Congratulations.'

'Thanks. Coffee?' Luciano slips behind the bar and pours a cup of beans into the coffee grinder. It whirls to life. 'Corina said you came to the funeral.'

'It was nice. Sad, but nice. I wanted to come up to you, but—,'

'I was a mess that day. I've *been* a mess. It's fine.'

Rohan leans against the long bar and Luciano's gaze is drawn to his sculpted arms. Briefly, he wonders if he could bench as much as Anse.

'How's your sister?'

'Corina?' They'd always been close. Luciano's surprised Rohan hasn't reached out to her first. He pours the coffee, working the milk froth to resemble swans. 'Working a lot. You should text her that you're back in town. What've you been doing during the off season, anyway?'

'Bit of work in Melbourne. Laying low. I did a carpentry course before I tried out for the team in case I didn't get in.' Rohan takes a sip of his coffee as he glances around the restaurant, taking in the old floorboards and the dusty rafters. 'Speaking of, you know it's gonna take a lot of work for you to reopen this place. The floorboards need replacing, there are cracks in the roof, and I think some of your plumbing is leaking.'

'And you haven't even seen the old customer toilets,' Luciano replies.

Rohan blanches. 'Is it even worth it?'

'You sound like Marzia.' Rohan gives him a knowing look. Both have known the force of Hurricane Marzia at one point during their lives. 'It is. It will be.'

'You'll need help.'

'Without a doubt.'.

'It'll be expensive.'

'Most likely.'

'It could take months before you're even ready to open.'

'Probably.'

'And you don't know the first thing about renovating.'

'That's also true.'

Silence passes between them.

'So, are you going to help me or do I have to beg for it?'

'I wouldn't mind you trying,' Rohan hums. Amusement dances in his deep eyes.

'Don't tease, Ahuja, what's it going to take for you to help me?'

'I'd never tease,' he grins over the lip of his coffee. 'I only want you, Luciano.'

Luciano narrows his eyes at Rohan's pseudo-flirting. Rohan is as straight as a ruler, and while they both agree Luciano does have an arse that won't quit, Rohan's never been that way inclined. No, there must be something else he wants.

'Out with it,' he demands.

Rohan shrugs sheepishly. 'I'm starting a grassroots footy club. I want you on my team.'

'I think we've fully established I'm on the other team, Rohan.'

Rohan gives him a look. 'I'm serious. I remember you could run like an absolute gun at the school athletics carnival. And you did Jiu jitsu for, what, six years?'

'Eight,' Luciano corrects. 'And it's not going to happen. I'd rather pay you. Just name a price.'

'Come on,' Rohan whines. 'I'd teach you everything you'd need to know. I've already got a couple of blokes and the season starts next month. If we don't get enough, we can't register a team.'

'Do I need to remind you what happened the last time I played footy?'

A flicker of recognition crosses his face. 'It won't be like that, Luciano. Ahmed's joined the team and—,'

'And you'll be there. That's what you said last time,' he sighs deeply. He hasn't dredged up the memory in years: eight boys on the school team who'd bullied him mercilessly. He'd been trying his hand at a new sport with encouragement of his best friend who just happened to be the team captain. 'Listen, what happened *happened* but you have to be real: footy has never really been super accepting of us gays.'

Rohan takes in a deep breath. 'I want you on the team, Luciano. If you do this for me, I'll do this,' he gestures to the restaurant with a free hand. 'For free.'

'Free?' Luciano scoffs. That's one hell of a price. 'You really want me that badly?'

'Yes,' Rohan replies. He's serious. Really serious. 'Training every Tuesday night and game day is every Saturday.'

'And you'll help me with this until it's done?'

Rohan extends his hand. Luciano takes a deep breath before shaking firmly.

'Work starts tomorrow. Don't make me regret this, Ahuja.'

———

Anse arrives late but he brings a bottle of red wine.

'I thought we could celebrate.' Anse says as they enter the kitchen. 'And I could really use a drink.'

Anse looks worn and tired. His hair, usually gelled back, falls a little over his eyes and Luciano resists the urge to tuck it behind his ear.

'You want to talk about it?' he asks as he hands Anse a glass.

'I told my boss I was gay.'

Luciano chokes on his wine. His hand flies to his chin, but the wine runs down his neck and soaks into the collar of his shirt. 'That's great, Anse.'

'I've never been 'out' at work before,' Anse clarifies. 'I'd always tried to keep that part hidden, I suppose.'

'I can understand that.'

Luciano throws Anse his apron and watches as it cinches into the curve of his narrow waist.

'Luciano?'

Glancing up, Luciano meets his eyes and knows he's been caught. Fuck. He doesn't know what's worse, the shame of being caught or Anse's amusing smirk.

'We're making a full meal this time. Chicken *cacciatore*.' Luciano unpacks the ingredients from his cotton shopping bag. 'Very simple dish: chicken, tomato passata, white wine. Herbs, onion, garlic, and olives. If this doesn't make you tolerate olives, I promise I'll officially give up.'

'Promise?'

'Promise. Now, the first step is prep. Dice the onions.'

'Bossy.'

Once again, Anse does a horrendous job dicing the onions, but Luciano doesn't complain. He takes the chopped onions and sautés them with a knob of butter and a teaspoon of crushed garlic. Pouring a generous splash of white wine into the hot pan, he stirs before reducing the heat to a simmer. As the wine begins to cook off, Luciano adds a can of crushed tomatoes.

'Simple,' Anse comments.

'Now we'll make the pasta,' he says and unwraps a roll of dough he'd prepared earlier. 'You can used store-bought pasta but please splash out and buy the good kind. Something from a delicatessen.'

'I had hoped you wouldn't expect me to make pasta from scratch every time.'

Luciano feels Anse's warm body as he leans in to watch the pasta slip through the rollers. 'Do you want me—,' he clears his throat. 'Ahem, to explain anything?'

Anse's eyes flick to him, tense and unwavering, and for a moment Luciano's transfixed.

'No, I'm following.'

'Okay.'

'Do you want another glass of wine?'

'Yes, thanks.' It's sweet relief when Anse steps away from his side. He can still smell his musky cologne, bruised and worn from the day. 'So, what made you come out at work?'

'You did,' Anse replies casually, like the words haven't just set Luciano ablaze.

Anse continues. 'It's against regulations for friends to enter the office premises without a pass.'

'I'm sorry,' he mutters. *Friends*. The word hangs between them. 'If I'd known, I never would have suggested it.'

'There was some miscommunication. Hannah accidentally insinuated something she perhaps shouldn't have, but it's no matter now.'

'That you're gay?'

'In a way,' Anse smiles over the lip of his wine. He's hanging back now, resting his elbows on the kitchen island. Luciano turns the stovetop on and adds the ribbons of fettucine to a pot of boiling water. 'She told Franz I like you.'

His heart feels like it's in his throat, but somehow, the words find their way through. 'You like me?'

Anse smiles gently. 'I do.'

'Oh.'

Anse stares at him with those too-blue eyes and Luciano can't find the words.

Because what is he supposed to say?

He's wanted this—wanted Anse—for so long.

'Luciano?'

'No, no, let me say something,' he interrupts. 'I want this but—'

'Luciano—,'

'Hold on—'

'*Luciano*,' Anse says, a little louder this time. 'The pasta is boiling over.'

He spins around. 'Shit!'

Quickly, Luciano turns down the element and takes the lid off the pot. Steam rises, curling towards the ceiling. Some of the pasta has stuck to the bottom of the pot but it's still salvageable. He leaves the lid off, letting the pasta boil gently.

Anse still beside him. 'There was a *but*.'

'Oh, right, of course.' Whatever it was, it doesn't seem to matter. Luciano licks his lips and watches as Anse's gaze drops to his mouth. Fingers touch his jawline before sweeping back to tangle in his hair. It's hard to speak. It's hard to think. All he can feel are Anse's fingers, the warmth of his body, the hammering of his heart.

Anse's gaze meets his again. 'You want this?'

He nods. God, yes.

Anse kisses him. It's gentle at first; a shy exploration as Anse pulls his body closer. Tentatively, Luciano's mouth opens and Anse takes the invitation to deepen the kiss. He's eager now, hungry for more, and Anse is kissing him frantically, hands roaming his body before settling at his hip to press Luciano against the kitchen bench. Barely a breath later, he feels Anse cup his arse and suddenly he's hoisted up. Luciano squeals.

Anse laughs, breaking away. 'You good?'

'Just surprised,' Luciano pants. 'Don't stop.'

Anse's hands and mouth and teeth are back on him in an instant, running down the length of his chest, ghosting down the column of his throat. When his hips press forward, Luciano thinks he may just pass out.

His fingers find Anse's buttons, fully intent on divulging him of that pesky white shirt when he realises: something's burning.

'Shit!' He tries to wriggle free of Anse's arms. 'Fuck, Anse.'

'Such a bad mouth on you,' Anse grins against his neck and oh god, no he can't do dirty talk right now. The tone of Anse's voice, deep and authoritative, is doing something to him. He makes a note to revisit *that* later.

Luciano pushes against him. 'No, no, fuck, stop the food is burning.'

'Oh shit.' Anse's arms loosen and Luciano pushes him away so he can get off the bench. The exhaust fan is swallowing plumes of dark smoke as Luciano turns off the stovetop and puts a lid on the chicken.'

'Fuck,' he cries. 'That pan was fucking iron too. *Shit.*'

Anse has the audacity to smile at him.

'Stop that.'

'Stop what?'

'That thing you're doing with your mouth.'

'You seemed to like what I was doing with my mouth before.'

'This is entirely your fault,' Luciano huffs as he scrapes the ruined sauce into the bin before placing the pan into the sink. 'I hope you're happy with yourself.'

'Beyond pleased,' Anse answers and then Luciano feels warm lips against the back of his neck.

'You didn't answer my question earlier,' Anse murmurs, switching sides.

'I didn't?'

Luciano lets out a shaky breath as his arms encircle his waist. Somehow, it's easier to say the thing he means, the things he *wants*, without facing Anse. He blames his eyes, blue like rock pools. 'I like you too. I mean, I like you a little less for distracting me and ruining dinner.'

'There was a but.' He squeezes Luciano's for emphasis.

'But,' Luciano echoes. 'I'm a bit of a mess.'

'I don't want to complicate your life any further,' Anse says seriously. 'If this gets too much, you can tell me.'

Luciano turns in his arms. Nods. 'Thank you.'

Anse kisses him again, sweet and slow.

'We could order in.'

Luciano huffs a laugh.

'I'm serious, I have this great app on my phone.'

Indian is the easiest and while it may be a minute walk across the square, Luciano pays for delivery. Anse's taken their wine and set up a white sheet on the floor of the restaurant like they're having a picnic.

As soon as he places the order, a message from Rohan comes through.

Rohan: You're really asking me to deliver across the square?
Luciano: Don't forget the wine. That's the most important bit
Rohan: LUCIANO WHO IS THAT MAN IN YOUR WINDOW? I can see him from across the street
Don't close the curtains!
LUCIANO

Luciano: Chill he's a friend

Rohan: He will be tonight, at least. My dad's Vindaloo isn't exactly extra-curricular appropriate

Luciano: Thanks for your concern, Rohan

Rohan: I'm just saying

Luciano: Don't forget the wine

Rohan: Get some!

Luciano: Plan on it x

Anse lies on his side on the spread tablecloth, his nose in his phone. 'Hello again.'

'Hey.' Luciano lies down on the sheet beside him.

Anse puts down the phone and takes a sip of his wine. Luciano wonders if maybe he should lean across to kiss him again but he can't muster the strength to make a move. There's an awkwardness between them now and he doesn't know how to breach it.

'I've ordered dinner,' Luciano begins. 'From an Indian place.'

'Sounds perfect,' Anse smiles, and then his hand sweeps down the length of Luciano's side and settles against his hip.

As if given permission to touch, Luciano reaches forward and runs the pad of his thumb across the curve of Anse's cupids bow, the roundness of his bottom lip. They part as Anse draws Luciano's thumb into his mouth and sucks gently.

'Holy fuck,' Luciano breathes.

The blueness of Anse's eyes darken as Luciano feels the velvety tip of his tongue against his finger. Slowly, he withdraws his thumb and replaces it with his lips. He kisses Anse slowly, passionately, a hand splayed under the curve of his jaw. He hasn't kissed anyone like this in a long time. It's always been frenzied, drunken, desperate kisses. This feels different. Anse feels different.

Just as Anse's tongue slips against his, Luciano hears a knock at the door.

'Luciano!' calls Rohan. 'Open up!'

Anse quirks an eyebrow. 'Friend of yours?'

'Unfortunately.'

Stumbling to his feet, Luciano cracks open the door just enough to see Rohan grinning like an idiot.

'When can I meet him?' he asks immediately. 'What's his name?'

He snatches the takeaway bag from Rohan. 'Never. Don't speak a word of this to Corina or Marzia or our deals off.'

Rohan scoffs. 'You're no fun. I even got you a nice 2016 vintage.'

Glancing into the paper bag, Luciano sees the 2016 vintage and *something else*.

'Why, Rohan?' he hisses as he fishes out the box of condoms.

'Just making sure you two are being safe,' he replies. 'Have fun. Remember to keep the curtains closed. Or don't. Just know that I can see you from across the square.'

'You're so weird.' He slams the door closed.

Luciano stashes the box of condoms behind the bar as he makes his way back to Anse.

Anse's lying on his back, spread out over the sheet, scrolling through his phone. For a moment, Luciano appreciates the view. He's long and lithe, taller than the sheet is long and his flamingo-socked feet stretch over the edge. He's supposed he's never noticed Anse's socks—had no reason to. Still, he wonders if they're all as flamboyantly silly.

The food is excellent: the sauce is rich and fragrant, and the meat is like butter in his mouth. The Ahuja's cooking has always been good, traditional South Indian food tapered down for the Australian palate.

'This is good.'

'It's hard to get a table on weeknights,' Luciano explains as they scrape their plates clean. 'Mum thought they might be competition when they first moved in, but that didn't last long. Rohan and I were like glue growing up.'

Anse presses a kiss to his shoulder. 'I assume that was him before?'

'He's just moved back,' Luciano explains. 'Spent a few years playing AFL. Don't worry, he's entirely straight.' He nudges Anse with his elbow. 'I'll finish this, meet you back out there in a second?'

'Sure. I'll refresh our glasses.'

Anse drops a kiss on the crown of his head, and Luciano finishes cleaning up. When he re-joins him, Anse is reading something on his phone. Whatever it is, he barely looks up when Luciano sits down next to him.

'Everything okay?' Luciano asks. 'Is it work?'

'No. Terms and conditions.'

'Oh.' That wasn't what he was expecting. Daring to slide closer, Luciano rests a hand on his shoulder. Anse doesn't react to the touch, his eyes running across the screen. 'Why are you reading terms and conditions?'

'Is it against the terms and conditions of the app to date your delivery driver?' he asks suddenly.

'What? No!' Luciano stifles a laugh. 'Anse, I don't think they would care.'

'For preferential treatment, perhaps.'

'Yeah. We're really going to exploit the system.' He places his hands on either side of Anse's face. 'Just kiss me.'

It's hard to kiss someone while they're smiling, Luciano realises. He can feel the curve of Anse's lips under his, even as Anse's mouth opens and he tugs Luciano closer. The more he tries to work it away, the bigger it gets until laughter bubbles up from Anse's throat and Luciano thinks he may just go mad with happiness.

'Stop being so happy,' Luciano mutters against Anse's jawline before sliding his mouth along the soft skin of his neck. Sucking a little, he's rewarded with a soft moan.

'Wait,' Luciano pulls back. Anse's face, kiss-drunk and tired, is adorable. 'What did you say about a date?'

CHAPTER EIGHTEEN

On Friday morning, Anse is greeted by an unsightly bruise on his neck. He examines it in the bathroom mirror before snapping a photo and sending it to Luciano.

Anse: Look what you did

Luciano: Omg I'm so sorry!

Anse: What am I going to tell work?

Luciano: That you got some?

Anse: Unhelpful

He glances back in the mirror. It's small, dark, and looks exactly like what it is. It's too warm for a scarf, and there's *no way* he's popping his collar.

Anse: While there were no complaints at the time, when we do this again, perhaps we keep markers of intimacy underneath our clothes

Luciano: Stop, Anse 😌 You're making me blush

Anse: You're incorrigible

I'll see you on Saturday

Luciano: I literally cannot wait

Also thank you for last night. It was wonderful x

His heart swells.

None of his shirts can hide the hickey, so in his hour of desperation, he calls Hannah. After nine rings, Hannah finally picks up.

'Anse? What is it?' Hannah's voice is heavy with sleep. Anse checks the time: 8.05am.

'Can you bring makeup to work?'

'What?' she slurs. 'What in the world for?'

'I'll explain when I get there. Can you hurry?' There's a grumble on the other end. 'Hannah, please.'

'Fine,' she grits out. 'Give me twenty.'

When he arrives at work, he corrals Hannah into the toilets before revealing the blue and purple bruise on his neck.

'Oh my god, Anse!' She howls with laughter. 'I haven't seen a hickey since high school.'

'Can you not tell the entire office?' he snaps. 'Help me fix it.'

She pulls out a small bottle of liquid foundation, dabs a little on her finger and reaches up to tap the liquid against the bruise.

'Sit on the loo, you oaf,' she says. 'I can barely reach.'

Supressing a wince as Hannah dabs at the bruise, Anse pulls out his phone and flicks through the morning's emails. He's got a meeting with Franz at nine-thirty, but otherwise, he should be able to spend most of his day in his office.

'This is Luciano's handiwork, right?' Hannah asks as she works on another layer.

'Hm.'

'I'm happy for you,' she says. 'And I am sorry about what happened before. I can't believe I said what I said.'

'In your defence, you were defending me.'

'*You* don't have to defend *me*, Anse,' she says. 'I know how I acted. As if… as if, fuck, as if you're like my gay best friend or some other stupid fucking stereotype. And I played into it and I just feel so *shit* about it, because you're more to me than that.'

'Hannah, it's fine.' Anse gasps a little as her fingers press against the hickey's edge. 'It's complicated. I've never been out at work; it was never something I had to worry about. It's different here.'

'Anse—,'

'There is just no 'coming out' and being done with it. Every time I meet someone new, start somewhere new, at some point, I have to 'come out' whether I like it or not. Most of the time it's easy, but sometimes it's still hard.'

Hannah presses powder to his neck. 'I can't possibly understand what that's like, but I am still really sorry.' Dusting the powder away with the brush, she stands back and reviews her work. Satisfied, Hannah clicks her tongue. 'You're done.'

'Will people notice I have makeup on?'

'Probably. But they'd notice a hickey the size of a fist more.'

'Touché.' Anse inspects her work in the bathroom mirror. The colour is a little warmer than the pale skin of his neck, but the bruise is certainly less noticeable.

'I'm proud of you and that hickey,' Hannah says as she reaches up to dust a little powder off the shoulder of his jacket. 'Come on, let's get back to work.'

They slip out of the bathroom as discreetly as possible, but he's quite sure Martina sees them. The one perk of being out at the office is at least Franz won't take the fraternisation complaint too seriously.

———

The date is a challenge to arrange at the last minute, but he manages to do it. In hindsight, he should have made it the following weekend when it's forecast to be postcard Australian weather with bright cloudless blue skies. But he's desperate to see Luciano. It's only been a day since the kiss and he's hungry for more.

Luciano tastes like toothpaste when Anse picks him up at eleven o'clock and Anse wonders if it's because he's anticipated kissing on the date, or because he's only just rolled out of bed.

Luciano presses his fingertips to Anse's hickey. 'Oh my god it looks worse, I'm so sorry.'

'Somehow, I don't think you are sorry at all.'

'Maybe just a little sorry.' Luciano's hand creeps behind his neck. 'Mostly turned on.'

For a moment, Anse considers scrapping the date and just driving them back to his apartment but he's come this far, and the look of delight when he parks near the Kingston pier is reward enough.

'So this was your master plan, huh?' Luciano takes in the flat expanse of the lake. To the west, the Telstra Tower pierces the sky. 'Take me out, murder me, feed me to the fishes.'

'Dramatic.' Anse takes Luciano's hand and leads him down to the boat house. Small motorised boats are tethered to the pier. They're greeted by a fresh-faced attendant, no older than twenty, and shown to a small motorised boat with a colourful canvas roof and a wooden table installed in the middle.

Anse stows his picnic basket towards the back of the boat as the attendant explains how to work the small motor.

'Like a motorbike,' Luciano notes as Anse tests his grip.

'The Vespa is not a motorbike,' Anse replies. Even the attendant stifles a laugh.

'Now, it's gonna be a little blowy out there,' says the attendant. Anse hears Luciano scoff and is just about to ask what's so funny when he's thrown a blanket. 'Just in case you need to rug up. Otherwise, enjoy fellas.'

Chugging away from the pier, Anse steers the boat out the narrow channel towards the lake. Luciano sits towards the front of the boat, his face tilted upwards towards the sun. The wind tousling his curls, and Anse can't help but stare. He looks gorgeous.

Glancing over his shoulder, Luciano gives him a grin. 'I can't believe you went to all this trouble. It's wonderful.'

The wind picks up a little as Anse steers the boat out of the canal. The lake looks strangely choppy as it reflects the warm February sun.

Luciano begins unpacking the picnic basket onto the table, whooping with joy when he finds the jar of olives. Anse feels the wind pick up a little as he steers towards the opening of the canal.

Then, it hits him.

'Jesus motherfucking Christ,' Luciano cries as the freezing wind whips against the boat. Luciano fumbles to save the cheese, but a few crackers fly into the water. Immediately, they're swarmed by a flock of ducks.

'Hold tight,' he tells Luciano, who is curled on the bottom of the boat. 'I'll drive underneath the bridge.'

Anse navigates the ravenous ducks and steers them under Commonwealth bridge. The large pillars shelter them from the wind but the boat rocks on the rough water.

'This did not go as planned,' Anse mutters as he settles next to Luciano's warm body at the bottom of the boat.

'Best laid plans and all that. I like this turn of events, though.'

Luciano's nose nudges his chin, a gentle request, one Anse's more than happy to oblige. The kisses are hot and gentle and everything he's wanted since Thursday night. Luciano tries to speed up the kisses, tries to demand more but Anse slows him down, revelling in the soft needy sounds he pulls from the back of Luciano's throat. When he finally pulls away, Luciano dark eyes are hazed with desire.

'You're entirely too good at that.' Luciano murmurs against his lower lip. 'To think we could have been doing this the whole time.'

'I have been thinking about it.'

'Why didn't you say anything sooner?'

'Why didn't *you*?'

'Um, hello quarter-life crisis. I wasn't exactly looking to ruin the only good thing I had going.'

That seems a good enough way to sum it up. 'Me too.'

Luciano smiles around the curve of the olive and Anse leans forward to take it from between his teeth. It's briny against his tongue as the flesh splits to reveal a soft stuffed centre.

———

'Come back to my apartment,' Anse says after they've docked. 'It's just around the corner. I have coffee.'

In truth, he has instant coffee but he doesn't tell Luciano that. It's still coffee.

'Just for a coffee,' Luciano nods.

Anse leads him through the foyer of his apartment and is surprised when Luciano hits the button for the fourth floor.

'I remember,' Luciano replies. 'I saw your name flash up and it was your home address, and I don't know.' He laughs nervously. 'Porn movies have been written on less.'

The lift opens and Anse grabs his keys. 'You wanted to?'

'I wanted you,' Luciano replies.

He can't remember the last time three words have affected him so much and Luciano is just looking at him, windswept curls and eyes darkened with desire. Opening the door, he corrals Luciano backwards until he rests on the back of the lounge.

'Take your clothes off,' Luciano demands against his mouth. Anse ignores it and kisses him.

So much for coffee.

'I'm serious!'

Anse's knees touch the ground. 'Yes?'

Luciano swallows, takes a deep breath, and nods. 'God, yes.'

Satisfied, Anse unbuttons his cotton shorts before his mouth finds him.

'Oh Anse, Jesus *fucking* Christ.'

'Such a mouth on you.' Anse murmurs. Luciano's fingers are in his hair and every so often he pulls, and the feeling sends a shiver down his spine.

A moan from above, a gasp and then, 'Anse, you should probably stop unless—,'

He doesn't want to. He doesn't stop.

'I'm serious,' Luciano pants. 'If you keep going, I'm going to—,'

Anse pulls back just enough to say, 'it's okay.'

He revels in watching Luciano come undone above him; the pull of fingers in his hair, the quiver of his stomach, the sounds that tumble from his mouth—some words and some not.

'I can't believe you just did that,' he says as Anse rises, albeit a little unsteady. Luciano rests his forehead against Anse's shoulder, breath hot against his collarbone. 'I think I'm going to pass out.'

'Please don't.'

Luciano's phone vibrates in his discarded shorts, rattling against the floorboards. Anse thinks it's only gentlemanly to retrieve it for him.

'It's my sister,' he says as he glares at the screen. 'My other sister. Marzia. I should take this. Do you mind?'

'Not at all,' Anse says. 'I'll, um, make the coffee.'

Luciano slips back into his shorts and takes the call in the lounge room as Anse boils the kettle. There's no need to be private about the phone call: Luciano speaks in Italian, his words lyrical and passionate. Occasionally, Luciano slips back to English, presumably when he can't think of the Italian word for 'settlement period' and 'renovation'.

As he makes the coffee, Anse focuses on the earthy rich smell of it and not on the way Luciano's thighs flexed under his hand, the sound of his gentle sighs, the feeling of hands in his hair.

Luciano only takes a few mouthfuls of his coffee before he says, 'I have to go, Anse. I'll, um, pay you back for the blowjob. An IOU.'

'Are there terms and conditions?'

'I'll text them to you.' He leans in to kiss him and it's wonderful. Anse thinks he could spend a long while just kissing Luciano.

When he breaks away, Luciano's gaze has darkened again.

'I really should go,' he says shakily. 'But I *really* don't want to.'

The following day, Anse receives a text.

. . .

Luciano: Terms and conditions: this coupon entitles the holder to one (1) blowjob from Luciano Jilani, to be redeemed at a mutually agreed time. Not to be used with any other discount or in conjunction with any other offers. Cannot be swapped or exchanged for other goods or services. The coupon is valid for thirty days until the date of expiry. Australian Blowjob Number: 122

Anse: Luciano, I was in a meeting

Also is that a made-up number or how many blowjobs you've given?

Luciano: I'LL NEVER TELL

CHAPTER NINETEEN

The footy may be grassroots but Luciano quickly realises this is more than a social game for Rohan. The team are an eclectic group of men from across Canberra with one thing in common—they're all enamoured with the idea of playing with a *real* football star. They fumble through Rohan's rigorous warm-up, not realising it is a warm-up until they're ordered to do a few laps of the oval.

'Come on blokes, get to it,' Rohan calls as he leads the group through the second lap. 'Two more to go.'

When they arrive back at the clubhouse, Rohan grants a five-minute water break. Two guys suddenly receive an urgent text and have to leave, while another feels too unwell to go on. Rohan lets them go with a promise to text them the details about the next training session.

'What's to bet they're blocking Rohan's number as soon as they get home?' Ahmed leans against the oval fence.

Luciano sniggers. 'How'd you get roped into this, anyway?'

'Rohan said he'd redo my shower if I'd join,' Ahmed replies. 'Thought it was a no brainer. Now I reckon I was probably better off taking out a small questionable loan. What about you?'

'Same. He offered his services and I was a fool to accept them.'

'An offer too good to refuse, eh?' Ahmed sighs. 'The devil works hard but I think Rohan Ahuja works harder.'

The next training exercise is simple back-and-forth punt kicks between pairs. Then they practice handballs, goal kicking, marking. After twenty minutes, Rohan corrals them to practice their centre bounces.

Rohan is tall and well-suited as the ruckman and selects a tall lanky man named Jeremy as his opponent. Luciano thinks Anse would be good as a ruckman if he was ever interested in trying out. Maybe if Luciano recruited Anse, Rohan would let him out of this ridiculous deal. It'd be an equivalent exchange.

'That was a bit much, don't you think?' Luciano says when they arrive back at the restaurant. 'I thought this was casual. You know, fun?'

'It is,' Rohan says. 'But some tough love will do them good. There's a premiership competition and half of those blokes haven't kicked a footy in years, if ever.'

He falls into the 'if ever' category.

Rohan sets down his equipment. Today, he's replacing the older floorboards while Luciano washes the walls and tries to decide on one of eight shades of white. They set to work, but it's not long before Rohan breaks the silence between them.

'So that bloke in the window last week…'

'Not talking about him,' Luciano cuts him off quickly.

'Ugh, you're no fun,' he huffs. 'Let me live vicariously through you!'

Luciano rings out a dirty rag into a bucket. 'Download a dating app or something. You're a footy star, surely there is a line-up.'

'*Ex*-footy star,' he corrects. 'Now I'm just a beautiful, ethnic carpenter. Like Jesus.'

Luciano doesn't validate that joke with a laugh and gets back to wiping down the wall behind the bar. ABBA's *Gimme! Gimme! Gimme!* plays on the radio. Rohan can't seem to work unless there's music playing. Noise seems to follow him: he's a loud worker, an incessant chatterer, and a bad singer.

'Luciano, tell me about him.' A floorboard snaps as Rohan rips it up. 'We have so much to catch up on.' There's a clatter as it hits the courtyard pavement, where Rohan is dumping the damaged floorboards for collection later. 'Corina said you got into a fight with Evan?'

Opening a can of white paint, Luciano begins painting a small sample square. 'Yeah, we slept together last year and he was a total dick about it. When did you see Corina?'

'I texted her as per *your* suggestion. We got coffee. Talked for a couple of hours.' Luciano gives him a look. 'Don't worry, I didn't tell her about the piece of ass you were seducing in your kitchen.'

'Good,' Luciano huffs. He puts down his paintbrush and takes a few steps back. 'Which white to do you like?'

Rohan stands beside Luciano as he considers the patchwork wall of paint in front of him. There's a slightly grey eggshell white; harbour white with a touch of blue, porcelain white which throws off a warm yellow tint. In the sunlight, the colour 'pure white' somehow looks a little dirty, marred with brown, and he's completely ruling out vintage white as an option because it is very obviously cream.

'Mate,' Rohan sighs. 'They all look the same.'

———

When Luciano slinks through the front door of Anse's office, Hannah immediately picks up the phone.

'Hey, you've got a visitor.' She simultaneously taps out an email. 'Yep, okay.' She hangs up before smiling at Luciano. 'He'll be two minutes.'

'Thanks.'

Hannah pauses typing her email and leans across the counter like she's about to tell him a secret.

'Anse brings his lunch more often since you've been teaching him,' she says.

Luciano laughs. 'He's a good student.'

The door behind the office opens and Anse slips out. He is wearing suspenders again. *Dear God.*

'Hi.' Luciano offers the tote bag. 'I brought you lunch. You haven't had it yet, have you?'

'No,' Anse says. 'Thank you.'

Hannah clears her throat. 'Anse, here's that visitor's pass for Luciano.' She slips a lanyard with a laminated pass over the countertop.

'Ah, right.' He hands it to Luciano. 'This is yours. For access to the grounds. Come on, we can talk in my office.'

Luciano slips it around his neck before following Anse down the hall to his office.

'Holy shit,' Luciano gapes as he steps into Anse's office. He takes in the wall of leather-bound books, the expansive desk, the fireplace, the crushed velvet armchairs, the towering fiddle leaf fig. 'This is *opulent*. It must be like working in a museum. Oh my god, you have a golden clock on the mantelpiece. And does that fire really work?'

'I think it is just for design. Please don't touch it though.'

Sinking into his office chair, Luciano spins around a few times. A hand falls on the top of the chair, stopping it. Luciano is about to protest when suddenly Anse's mouth is on his and *oh, they're doing this at work, then.* It's gentle and simple, more of a greeting, more of an 'I've-missed-you' kind of kiss that makes him melt rather than ignite.

'What's for lunch?' Anse asks as he perches himself on the corner of his desk.

'The dish you made me ruin last week.' He passes Anse the still-warm container from his bag.

'*I* made you ruin?' Anse grins.

'Yes, with your mouth and face.'

He kicks Luciano's sneaker with the tip of his oxfords teasingly.

'Just tell me if you like it,' Luciano demands. 'And make sure you get an olive.'

Anse rolls his eyes before taking a mouthful. Luciano waits as he chews, swallows. 'It's good,' he says eventually. He takes another mouthful. 'It would be better without the olives.'

'But they're the perfect balance against the acidity of the sauce!'

'I still don't like them. More for you.'

'More for me,' Luciano agrees.

Anse's phone vibrates on the table beside him. The screen lights up with DANIEL. Anse watches it ring but doesn't immediately reach for it.

'Do you want me to go?' Luciano asks. Maybe it's confidential international information that he can't hear.

'No, it's just my brother,' he says. '*Hallo?*'

Anse's brother talks loud enough that Luciano can hear his rapid German through the phone. He leads the conversation with a shrill, demanding tone. Anse manages to punch in a '*ja*' in where he can.

'*Warte bitte?*' he says eventually, his first real sentence. '*Ich frage ihn.*' Then, he places a hand over the base of the phone. 'My brother and sister-in-law are renting a house on the coast over Easter weekend and have invited me to stay. Would you like to come with me?'

'Erm,' says Luciano.

Easter is two weeks away—in late March this year—and is it too early to go on a mini-break with Anse? Is a long weekend *too* long?

'You can say no,' Anse adds.

'No,' Luciano replies and then immediately corrects himself. 'I mean, yes, I'll go with you.'

'Yes, you'll go?'

'Yes. Sure. Sounds wonderful.'

Anse uncovers the phone, '*Ja, er wird kommen.*'

'*Wunderbar!*' Luciano hears through the phone. The brothers exchange a quick goodbye before Anse places his phone back down on the desk.

'I hadn't realised you'd told your brother about me,' says Luciano.

'Was I not supposed to?'

'I haven't told my sisters about you. Well, I told Rohan, but that's just because he's nosy.'

I'm not even sure what this is, Luciano wants to say. It's been one date and now suddenly they're going on a mini-break to the coast, and he's meeting Anse's family, and they'll probably sleep in the same bed—

Anse's hand touches his cheek. 'I won't be offended if you don't want to go.'

'Of course, I want to go,' he replies. 'It's just the logistics…'

'I'll handle the logistics,' the hand on his cheek moves into his hair. 'You'll like Emmy. She loves to cook.'

'It'll be nice.' Anse's lips curve into a smile and Luciano, unable to resist their call, reaches up to capture them again. He does show some restraint in not running his hands though Anse's carefully styled hair because ever since the hickey incident, Luciano's been extra careful.

Suddenly, Anse's desk phone rings.

'Fuck,' he murmurs, breaking away. 'I have to get this, it's probably the New Zealand office.'

Running his hands through his hair, Luciano attempts to restyle his curls. 'I'll leave you to it.'

Anse picks up the phone and quickly says, 'I'll be two minutes; keep them on the line.'

Luciano's about to leave when a hand reaches out and pulls him back. 'Ah, what are you—'

Anse holds him tenderly and kisses him with as much sweetness as Luciano can possibly take without wanting to whimper before stepping away. 'Thank you for lunch.'

Luciano tips forward a little. 'You're welcome. You, um, shouldn't keep New Zealand waiting any longer.'

'Little bit longer,' he hushes before tilting Luciano's head up to kiss him once more. 'I'll see you later?'

Luciano nods as Anse's fingers caress his jawline. Anse's gaze is dark and fierce and possessive and Luciano doesn't want to leave, but Anse has a teleconference and the phone on his desk is flashing an angry red.

'This job is what keeps you here,' Luciano says sternly. 'Suggest you do it.'

Anse laughs a little, drops his hand and picks up his phone.

On his way out, Luciano catches the eye of a surly-looking man in an ashen tweed suit. The man glances over him once before disappearing back into his office.

CHAPTER TWENTY

'Y̶ou are so whipped.'

Anse and Hannah trudge through fallen leaves on the way to the corner coffee shop. It's early March and suddenly cool in the capital. It's as if, on the first of the month, every natural thing promptly decided that summer was over. The trees are yellowing, and the dry nature reserves are sprouting green with new life. Hannah wears a loose scarf, even though if this was Austria, Anse would consider their nineteen-degree day wonderfully warm.

'I'm not whipped.'

He's made the mistake of telling a workplace-appropriate version of his wonderfully disastrous first date with Luciano.

'You are and it's wonderful to see. When's your next big date?'

'I'm not sure.' He's never really *dated* anyone. Even when he'd been with Max, they hadn't dated. They'd never gone to the movies or took turns picking restaurants or any of those other things couples were supposed to do. It hadn't been their dynamic.

'But you're still taking your cooking lessons, right?'

'We're meeting again tonight.' He remembers the coupon, stored safely in the archives of his phone. 'I asked him to go to the coast with me over Easter.'

'A trip? Already?' she whistles. 'Have you slept together yet?'

'That's personal.'

'That's a no,' Hannah grins.

'You're insufferable.'

———

When he arrives at the restaurant, Luciano is staring intently at a blank wall with his hands on his hips. Carefully, Anse steps through the chaos: several floorboards are missing, there's a toilet in a wheelbarrow, and a large white sheet covers the long bar.

'Which colour do you like better?' Luciano says as Anse drops his satchel by the door.

Coming to stand by Luciano, he examines eight identical swatches of white paint. After a moment, he picks the top left for no other reason than to make a choice.

Luciano hums. 'Don't you think it's a bit cool-toned?'

'It's white paint, Luciano.'

'I thought that too but turns out there's an entire spectrum of white,' he replies. 'And if I choose the wrong white, it'll throw everything off. It'll be the kind of place you walk into and you'll know something is wrong, but you just don't know what. You know?'

He really doesn't know but he's not about to tell Luciano that. Instead, Anse places his hands on Luciano's shoulders and squeezes his tense muscles. 'Come on, it's six o'clock. We can debate the white paint over dinner.'

Luciano offers him a lazy grin. 'You're right. I haven't eaten all day.'

'You haven't?' Anse fails to suppress his startled tone. 'Why not?'

Luciano shrugs. 'I mean, I had breakfast. Just been working all day and lost track of time. Come on, I'm in the mood for a *calzone*.'

As Luciano heads towards the kitchen, Anse finally takes him in: the paint-stained clothes, bare feet, wild hair and clammy skin. Exhaustion leaks through his pores.

'Well, maybe I want to skip class.'

Luciano frowns. 'You'll never graduate with that attitude.'

'I think my teacher needs a night off,' he says tenderly. 'Come home with me.'

Luciano turns on the gas stovetop. Anse reaches forward and turns it back off.

'Anse.'

'*Luciano*.' He tries to sound serious. 'Come on. I'll buy you dinner on the way home.'

'But this was supposed to be a lesson!' Luciano rubs at his eyes. A streak of white paint on his hand transfers to his cheek. Anse grabs his wrist before Luciano has the chance to rub paint through his hair.

'Come home with me.'

'I really wanted to make *calzones* with you.'

'Another time,' he says. 'There's a Thai restaurant near my house, we can order in. I have a bathtub and a spare bedroom.'

Luciano groans. 'Fine.'

'Try to sound less enthused,' he laughs. 'Come. Get your things.'

On their way out, Luciano casts a glance back to the wall of white patches before locking the front door. 'I just don't want to fuck this up.'

'You won't.'

His eyes shimmer in the dull light of the street lamps. 'I might.' A hand comes up to his mouth to catch a choked sob. 'I knew it was going to be hard, you know, I was ready for hard. But it's still really fucking hard.'

Anse tugs him towards the car. 'It'll be here tomorrow.'

The most curious thing about Luciano, Anse considers as he drives them back to his apartment, is that his mind is almost constantly moving. Even sitting in the silence, Anse is convinced Luciano is ruminating, going over things in his mind, sorting out a mental to-do list as he stares out the window.

'What are you thinking about?' he dares to ask.

'Hmm?' Luciano's attention circles back to him. 'Oh, I'm just trying to figure out the floorplan. I think I'll do round tables instead of square.'

'Does your mind ever stop?'

Luciano laughs a little but doesn't reply.

At the apartment, Luciano showers while Anse orders Thai on QIK-EATS. The food arrives before Luciano re-emerges from the bathroom so Anse leaves it in the microwave rather than bothering him out of the tub. He eventually emerges wearing one of Anse's university hoodies and a pair of cotton shorts.

'Thanks,' he sighs as he collapses onto the lounge with a bowl of curry. 'I really needed that. What are we watching?'

'You choose.'

They settle in to watch *Arrested Development* as they eat because Anse has never seen an episode and that is a complete travesty as far as Luciano is concerned. As another episode auto-plays, Anse's hand caresses the delicate bones of Luciano's ankle, before wrapping around his foot and pressing his thumb into the arch. He rubs Luciano's foot in gentle circles.

'You're entirely too good at that,' Luciano sighs. 'You're too good at *everything.*'

Another episode plays and he switches feet. When the credits roll twenty minutes later, Anse turns to ask Luciano to press play on the next episode, only to find him sprawled out on the lounge, all limbs and hair, fast asleep.

Gently, he gathers him up and earns a tired protest of 'I can walk' for his efforts.

The spare bedroom is like the rest of the apartment—minimally furnished with a single bed, a bedside table with a lamp, and a dresser. As he settles Luciano on the bed, he can't help but recall Hannah's words. They rattle around his drowsy mind, unwelcome but not untrue.

He is utterly and completely whipped.

CHAPTER TWENTY-ONE

Luciano wakes to an empty apartment and a text from Anse.

Anse: You fell asleep on the lounge last night so I put you to bed

There's a coffee machine

Stay as long as you want

Sorry I didn't wake you - you needed to sleep

The timestamp marks the message at six-thirty that morning. Almost three hours ago. Quickly, he types a response.

Luciano: Thank you thank you thank you

Anse: Good, you're awake.

Luciano: How's work?

Anse: I have eighty-three emails from Austria. Two more have just come in during the time that I've been texting you

Luciano: Skip work? Come back to the apartment?

Anse: Tempting but I was reminded recently that this job is the only thing that keeps me in Canberra, and it turns out I quite like it here.

Luciano: How dare you use my words against me
Is that so? Any reason why?
Anse: Autumn is quite beautiful.

Rubbing his nose into the collar of Anse's hoodie, Luciano sinks into the scent of fresh linen and lavender as he rolls out of bed. He only manages a few steps before stopping at the doorway of Anse's bedroom.

Inside, he's made his bed, white linen stretched taut over a simple oak bed frame because of course Anse is the kind of person that makes their bed *every morning*.

Curiosity gets the better of him as he slips into his ensuite bathroom. It's tidy. Most of his toiletries stored in the cabinet behind the mirror. Opening it, Luciano finds the object of his desires: a half-used bottle of Armani cologne. He sprays a little on his wrist and takes in the scent of hyacinth and bergamot. It smells like Anse, like the nights they've spend cooking in his kitchen when he'd get a whiff of the worn scent in passing—just enough to tantalise.

Placing the cologne back on the shelf, he glances over the few other products: a can of shaving cream, a bottle of PrEP, an expensive looking shaving kit, a tub of hair pomade, and an unopened box of condoms.

Luciano immediately closes the vanity.

———

He picks porcelain white and begins painting the blank walls before he can overthink his choice. Anse texts him at one-thirty and reminds him to eat lunch, which he does, and even sends back photo evidence.

Corina finds him just after four, drinking a coffee by the bar, his black jeans covered in swipes of paint.

'Luciano! I was worried sick. Where were you?'

Dread sinks into his stomach like a heavy weight. Of course, she'd been worried when he hadn't come home last night. 'I slept over at Rohan's. I forgot to text you.'

'Why didn't he tell me?' Corina's temper doesn't abate. 'He knew I was worried sick about you. God, I'm going to *kill* him.'

Shit. Now he's gone and dragged Rohan into this mess.

'Ugh, it's not Rohan's fault,' he groans. 'I lied. I'm seeing someone. I stayed at his house, and I forgot to text you.'

Relief floods her features. 'Why did you lie?'

'It's just early days, I wasn't sure if I should tell you about him or not.' The fact that Luciano is going on a mini-break to meet Anse's family in a few days' time hangs over him. Their relationship feels serious, but he's not ready to tell Corina.

'So, who is this fine gentleman who's swept my baby brother off his feet?'

Downing the dregs of his coffee, Luciano picks up the paint-brush. 'No gossip unless you help me with the next coat.'

Corina looks down at the white paint and then to her denim dress. With a groan, she picks up a narrow brush and begins carefully painting the trim around the front door. 'So, spill.'

'There's nothing to spill. He's a diplomat from Austria.' The roller makes a sticky noise as Luciano coats it in paint again.

Corina ignores his correction. 'A *foreign* gentleman. What's his name?

'Anse,' he says. 'Be cool about this. Do *not* tell Marzia.'

'Hey, I'm no snitch.' Corina finishes one half of the doorway, pausing before dipping her brush back into the paint bucket. 'You deserve someone nice.'

'Right?' he clears his throat. It feels like the universe is finally giving him a break. 'Not that I mean to rub my happiness all in your face. Are you seeing anyone?'

'*No*,' Corina replies quickly. She finishes the other half of the doorframe before washing the paintbrush off. 'Want to get Vietnamese and have too many beers?'

'Can't,' Luciano says as he stretches to run the roller over a patchy section of wall near the rafters. 'It's our first game tomorrow. Rohan will kill me.'

'Speaking of, isn't he supposed to be helping you?' she looks around. 'Where is he?'

'Had a client,' Luciano replies as he steps back to admire his work. The first coat is patchy, but he likes the colour.

'Come on,' Corina nudges him. 'My shout.'

———

They stumble into Corina's apartment at one in the morning, laughter echoing through the halls. She's the drunker out of the two of them, so he helps her into bed before settling on his couch, sinking into the imprint of his body in the cheap cushions. Since the house sold, he's been crashing here while Rohan finishes renovations on the restaurant and apartment above it.

Pulling out his phone, he blearily checks the messages. There's a text message from Rohan reminding the team to meet an hour before the game starts for warm-up. He expects tomorrow will go as well as trying to put a bunch of crabs in a bucket: a completely awkward, uncoordinated mess, and if he doesn't watch himself, he'll probably get an eye taken out.

There's also a text from Anse.

Anse: Fuck this week. Coffee tomorrow afternoon?

Luciano: Sure. I'm playing footy tomorrow until about 2 though so if you don't hear from me, check the hospital

Anse: I didn't know you played

Luciano: I don't. That's the thing

Anse: I could show you a few things

The student becomes the teacher

Luciano: Oh, fuck, no I mean AFL, not soccer

Anse: It's football, Luciano

Luciano: It's objectively not

Anse: You're really going to argue with me on this

It's football

Luciano: Is this our first argument?

Anse: Evidently

Where are you playing?

Luciano: And let you witness my sheer embarrassment when our team gets annihilated? Ha. No. I'm not telling you

Anse: I'll find you

I have my ways

Luciano: Threats now?

Anse: What's the fun of having diplomatic immunity if you can't bend the rules a little?

Luciano: :O

Dew and sports drink coat Luciano's boots. The day is overcast and humid. Their team, the Brindabella Bilbies (because all the cool animals were already taken) are down by twenty points. Rohan kicks a goal and the crowd roars.

Luciano's surprised at the turnout. People line the oval boundary and the carpark is full to the point of spilling over. Of course, it's all for Rohan. No one is coming to see a slap-stick local team named *the Bilbies* on their maiden game. They're here to see what a professional footballer looks like in the flesh.

And Rohan puts on a show. He faces down eighteen men like it's nothing. He's weaving, climbing, doubling back and surging forward with a punt-kick to take another goal. The other team barely mark him. But one man isn't a team and the only disadvantage of having Rohan on their side is that it makes the rest of them look like bumbling idiots. Most of them are, but still.

A strangled cry of 'Fuck!' stops the play. Luciano snaps his head up to see Ahmed on the ground, clutching his leg.

Rohan is by Ahmed's side instantly. He pulls him up and against his shoulder as the first aid officer runs onto the field.

'Looks like a hammy,' he explains as Ahmed and the first aid officer hobble to the boundary. Another guy, Marcus, subs in.

Play continues.

Luciano gets a few digs on his defender as he runs along the wing. The ball bounces past him and he wills his body to surge forward and suddenly, the ball is in his hands and his defender is on his tail. He runs, surprised at his own speed, and kicks the ball before he can overthink it. It leaves his foot straight and true, flying towards the goal posts. The crowd cheers as the ball sails towards the goal. It's going to go in. Holy shit, he's just scored a fucking goal!

Smack!

'Hit the post,' the goalie cries. Luciano watches in disbelief as the large white pole shakes. The score changes by one.

In the end, they lose by thirty-eight points. The locker room is a sombre affair. The news that Ahmed will be out for a few weeks at least doesn't help lift the mood.

Luciano pulls off his sweat-soaked guernsey and throws it

into his gym bag. Beside him, Rohan is freshly showered, rubbing strong-smelling lotion into his calves.

'Good game today, Luc,' Rohan grins. 'Even I thought that was a goal.'

'Thanks.' His body is already stiff and he reeks of sweat and grass. Rohan offers him the tube of lotion and he takes it gratefully, working it into his shoulder.

'Hey!' Rohan shouts. 'No girls in the clubhouse!'

Luciano turns to see Corina standing in the doorway. She glances around the empty clubhouse —its wooden benches and open showers—before shrugging. 'Forcibly remove me then.' Her eyes flick to Luciano. 'You played well. For a while there I was worried you'd bring shame to the Jilani name in front of all those people.'

'Got a good crowd, aye,' Rohan grins as he hastily stuffs his footy boots into his sports bag.

'I think they showed up for you, not us,' Luciano corrects.

Rohan indicates back towards the doorway. 'Well, not everyone.'

Luciano turns to see Anse just beside Corina, hands in the pockets of his jeans. His hair is slicked back, as usual, but otherwise he looks wonderfully casual. Rohan gives him a gentle nudge of encouragement as he grabs his sports bag and heads out to join Corina.

'Take care, Luc,' she says before turning to Anse. 'Nice to meet you.'

'You too,' he replies before stepping into the clubhouse. Luciano's painfully aware he's shirtless as Anse's great frame towers over him.

A nervous laugh escapes him before he can stop it. 'You found me. Wait. How *exactly* did you find me?'

'I have my ways.' Anse's gaze swings downward.

'Hey, my eyes are up here.'

Anse chuckles a little. 'You weren't at Trattoria this morning, but Rohan was. He told me. You played well.'

'You're so unfamiliar with the sport that you don't realise how abysmally I played.'

'But you played,' Anse replies. 'Coffee?'

'Sure. Just give me a second to shower, will you?'

Anse nods but his heavy gaze lingers on Luciano's throat, and Luciano feels a thrill travel through him like a current. And then Anse is dipping down to press his mouth against the side of Luciano's throat and its hot and wet and *everything* Luciano wants.

Anse's continues pressing wet, open mouthed kisses down the contours of Luciano's chest. The pad of his thumb skims over a nipple and Luciano jolts.

'Anse,' Luciano gasps. Anyone could walk in and find them like this, but any thoughts of asking Anse to stop disappear as soon as his mouth drags over his clavicle. 'Do you have a thing for semi-public spaces or something?'

Anse backs away, a fond half-smile on his face. 'Forgive me. I couldn't resist. I'll wait outside while you shower.'

Never has Luciano praised the cold-water only shower fixtures in the old clubhouse more than he has this moment. He scrubs himself down and throws on a pair of ripped black jeans and a white cotton shirt. Deciding he's presentable enough, Luciano grabs his sports bag and meets Anse at the front of the clubhouse.

'Look.' Anse points towards the carpark where Rohan is surrounded by a crowd of people demanding signed autographs and pictures. 'Should we help him?'

Luciano laughs. 'No way.'

———

They go for a coffee and then a walk around the park. It's nice, but when Luciano gets a text from Rohan that he's at the restaurant, he heads back. While Rohan's holding up their end of the bargain, it doesn't feel right that he's working while Luciano's swanning around with his maybe-boyfriend.

Luciano rolls the Vespa into the courtyard, parking it beside the small lemon myrtle tree. The wisteria is dormant and bare, but the lemon myrtle thrives in the mild March sun. It's covered in bunches of tiny, white fragrant flowers look and feel like cotton candy. He picks a small tuft, rubs the flower between his fingers and inhales the citrus scent.

Lemon myrtle cake with a thick layer of cream cheese icing: simple and easy and quintessential Australian.

Duck marinated in lemon myrtle and orange, roasted over three or four hours until the meat falls off the bone.

The sound of a hammer breaks his focus, thumping like a bad headache. Following the sound upstairs, Luciano finds Rohan on his hands and knees as he lays new floorboards in the apartment.

'Almost done, Luc,' Rohan pants. 'Then to sand and polish, but you'll be right to move in the next few days.'

Finally, he'll be out of Corina's hair and in his own space. Rohan hammers the last few boards in place and then wipes the sweat off his brow.

'Let's get a beer,' Luciano says. 'That's enough work for a Saturday.'

Rohan scoffs but doesn't complain.

Downstairs, Luciano pulls two lagers from the walk-in

fridge. He's content to drink in silence, to marvel over the work they've managed to do in a handful of weeks, but then Rohan says, 'So Corina called the other night. Asked where you were. Lucky for you, I covered and said you were probably pulling an all-nighter at the restaurant.'

'Thanks, but I told her the truth,' Luciano replies. The phone in his pocket vibrates. The number that flashes up on the screen is local but unknown. 'Do you mind if I take this? Could be the contractor for the loos.'

An especially peppy voice answers the phone when Luciano picks up. 'Hey, Luciano! This is Hannah's boyfriend, Cameron. We met at the markets recently?'

He recalls Hannah's tall, lanky boyfriend. 'Yeah, of course. How's it going?'

'Yeah good, mate. Hannah got your number from Anse, hope you don't mind. Thing is, I work at the radio station, you know, CBR 102.5?'

Instantly, he recognises Cameron's voice as the same that blares through Rohan's radio every afternoon. How has he never made that connection?

'Oh shit, yeah.' He pauses. 'Am I on the air now?'

Cameron laughs. 'Nah, mate. Hannah was telling me all about your reno on the restaurant. It sounds amazing. Every few weekends, we host a live show at a local venue that needs some support. Good for us, good for the community. Think you'd be a good fit.'

'Are you serious?' He can barely process it. The publicity alone would be *amazing*.

'Yeah, of course,' Cameron says. 'We'd bring the weekend radio crew and set up a tent around eight, interview you, play some games with the crowd, and wrap up by around one in the afternoon. Most people organise a sausage sizzle for a bit of fundraising and that normally goes down a treat. Sound like something you'd be keen to do?'

'Definitely,' grins Luciano. 'Yes. *Thank you.*'

'It's honestly the least I can do. Your Mum's Strawberry Cheesecake was the stuff dreams were made of—seriously, I hope you know the recipe.' He does. 'My team'll be in touch to organise. Probably early April.'

They exchange emails and Cameron promises to call after Easter. He relays the phone call to Rohan who agrees it's a 'ripper of an idea'.

'Any plans tonight?' asks Rohan as he finishes off his beer. 'Hot date with Anse?'

'Nah, we got coffee earlier. I plan to be in bed by nine.'

'What an old man you are.' He checks his watch. 'Shit, I should go.'

'Hot date of your own?'

Rohan winks. 'Could be.'

The scent of Corina's expensive perfume hangs heavily in the air when he returns to her apartment. There's half of a cold pizza left on the counter with a hastily written note.

Gone out. Don't wait up.

Luciano reheats the pizza before settling on the couch and pulling out his phone.

Luciano: Dare I ask if your Saturday night is as fun as mine? Pizza and beer and Netflix.
   Luciano sent a photo
   Anse: Just left work and heading to the gym
   Luciano: Party animal

Anse: Do you want to come out for a beer later?
Luciano: Tempting
Anse: Come on
My shout
Luciano: Fine text me the address

The bar on the Kingston foreshore is quiet for a Saturday night. Anse is perched on a stool, his nose in his phone.

'Hey.' Anse startles but recovers to give him a warm smile. Leaning forward, Luciano intends just to give him a peck on the lips, but then Anse turns at the last moment, as if suddenly shy, and Luciano's lips graze the stubble of his chin. His skin smells of eucalyptus shower gel. 'How was the gym?'

'Good.' He waves over the bartender. 'What do you want? My treat.'

'Erm. Just a glass of house red, please.' Luciano says. Anse hands over his credit card. 'I picked a paint colour,' he says. 'The white one.'

'You'll have to be more specific.'

'Don't be mean to me.'

Anse places his hand by Luciano's, close enough that their thumbs are overlapping. Luciano focuses on it.

'Is everything okay, Anse?'

Anse takes a long sip of his beer. 'Fine.' He pauses. 'I'm not very good at being in public.'

'But semi-public is fine?' Luciano snorts but Anse doesn't laugh. 'Fuck. You're being serious. I'm sorry.'

'Sometimes I think I am doing this whole thing wrong,' Anse admits. 'I didn't *realise* I was gay until I was twenty, and when I came out to people most of them said they'd always suspected. I became fixated on the idea that they knew something about me that I didn't know myself.' Anse pauses. 'That's stupid, right?'

'Everyone is different. It doesn't make you any less.'

Anse shrugs. 'I just hate the idea of coming out for the rest of my life. Every new job, every friend.'

'So, don't,' Luciano says. 'Just be you.'

He grimaces like he's not sure it's that easy. 'When I told my brother, he said "same". Apparently, he'd played the field in university and he didn't particularly mind the team, so long as he was in the game. But he never came out. He was just who he was, and I don't know why I can't be like that. I don't know why it matters to me so much, but it does.'

Luciano dares to move his hand a little closer to Anse's, then closer still, until he's able to thread Anse's fingers between his. Luciano hopes that Anse realises that no one is looking at them and that this—whatever *this* is that's developing between them is just that. Between them.

'It's okay if you don't want to kiss in public,' Luciano assures. 'God knows I'm not one for PDA.' He looks down to their intertwined fingers. 'Is this okay?'

Anse nods before letting out a loose breath. 'That was a lot to put on you.'

'For what it's worth, I like you just as you are.'

'Do not quote Bridget Jones to me like you don't know it's one of my favourite films.'

Gleeful images swim in his head of cosy winter nights snuggled together on his brown leather sofa with Renée and Colin on the telly. 'Finish your beer. I want to show you something.'

Anse downs the rest of the beer before following Luciano out of the bar and into the cool night air.

'Oh no,' he says when Luciano passes him the spare helmet.

'Trust me.'

'I do. Just not with my life. Or the top layers of my skin.' Swinging a leg over the Vespa, he settles behind Luciano. 'This feels wrong.'

Luciano snickers. 'What are you talking about? I thought you'd be quite comfortable behind me.'

That earns him a chuckle and a light hit shoulder. Strong arms wrap around his waist, squeezing as they navigate light traffic before surging up the incline of Red Hill. The city falls away, widening to become a sea of dim amber lights as Luciano parks the Vespa on the lookout.

'I love coming here,' he says as they dismount. 'Every Canberra Day, Mum would take us up here to watch the fireworks. It's the best view of the city.'

Anse leans against the flimsy railing and looks out over the city. 'When I arrived, I thought the airline had made a mistake. It's not what I expected.'

'It still surprises me.' Luciano shoulders him gently. 'Twenty-five years on.'

CHAPTER TWENTY-TWO

On Good Friday morning, Anse arrives at Corina's apartment at 7.15 am, which is politely early for him, and far too early for Luciano, who dashes across the apartment complex with a half-buttoned shirt and wild, untamed hair.

'Good morning.' Anse hands him a latte.

'Thank you.' He takes the coffee with one hand and Anse's collar with the other, pulling him into a kiss. Unsurprisingly, he tastes like mint toothpaste.

The Eastern road leaving Canberra winds around a shallow and empty Lake George. Sporadic rain has turned the field marshy, wicks of woody wild grasses rise from the mud like fingers. In the distance, wind turbines rotate leisurely.

Luciano streams music through the car: upbeat acoustic guitars with gentle vocals, and covers of popular songs, with the odd Bruce Springsteen or Fleetwood Mac song thrown in.

'You should be warned,' says Anse as they stop for coffee near the Big Merino. And, it *is* a ram, Anse realises as he looks up. 'My brother can be a bit of a handful. Avoid conversations such as the state of the European Union, the Chelsea football team and anything to do with Oscar Wilde.'

'Why Oscar Wilde?' Luciano sucks the milk foam off a wooden stirrer in a way that makes Anse's gut clench.

'We once had a heated debate about censorship in literature. Earlier drafts of the Picture of Dorian Grey were particularly saucy for their time.'

Luciano grins. 'I love it when you talk dirty literature with me.'

They drive for another hour before Anse is directed to take an off-ramp, and they wind their way through villages along the southern border of the Blue Mountains. The landscape changes from bushland to lush rainforest as the narrow road twists through the mountain pass. Luciano is uncharacteristically quiet beside him and he's about to ask if he wants to pull over when the road reveals a quiet city. The sea sparkles in the distance. Anse follows a stretch of golden coastline until they arrive at a small white weatherboard beach house with a picket fence. The sparse garden is almost overrun by blue hydrangeas, still in flower, and clumps of velveteen flowers caress the side of the car as Anse parks in the driveway.

The front door opens.

'Holy shit!' Daniel cries as he steps down from the patio, his bare feet slapping against the floorboards. He's thinner than Anse remembers. Greyer too. 'Emmy said you'd gotten absolutely jacked. She wasn't joking!'

'Nice to see you too.' He's pulled into a warm hug. 'You're so grey.'

Daniel runs a hand through his short hair. 'I've just accepted it at this point.' Anse notices his eyes waver to across the side of the car, where Luciano is grabbing his duffel bag from the back seat.

'This is Luciano,' Anse offers as Luciano comes to stand by his side. 'Luciano, this is my brother Daniel; and Emmy is—,'

'Coming!' she calls from the door. She's wearing a long white dress over a blue bikini. Her long dark hair is still damp. Her brown eyes spark with recognition as she looks at Luciano. 'The delivery boy!'

Pink dusts Luciano's cheeks as he hugs Emmy. 'Nice to see you again.'

Daniel throws Anse a strange look.

'I'll explain later,' Anse says.

Luciano gives him a nervous smile as they are shown around the modest beach house. Anse notices Luciano admiring the glossy hardwood floors as they're led up a narrow hallway to two small rooms, each with a queen bed.

Luciano dumps his duffel bag onto one bed in what Anse can only describe as a complete power move, leaving the decision completely up to him. Daniel and Emmy are standing beside them, and Anse realises he's hesitating.

He pushes past Daniel and dumps his duffel onto the other bed.

'Okay,' Daniel says. 'Beer anyone?'

Emmy scoffs. 'At least wait until lunch.'

'Ah, you're right,' Daniel considers for a moment. 'To the BBQ!'

Emmy gives Anse a commiserating smile before pressing a kiss to his cheek. 'I'll let you guys get settled in. Join us on the back deck when you're ready.'

As soon as she's down the other end of the house, Anse slips into Luciano's room and closes the door.

'If you want to share, we can,' Anse says as soon as Luciano says, 'I don't think I want to share.'

They both pause. Luciano smiles.

'Not there yet,' Anse says.

'Not there yet,' Luciano agrees, and nibbles on his lower lip nervously.

How can he resist those lips? He wants those wonderful lips on other places than his mouth and neck so, so badly. Luciano kisses him deep and slow, and when he pulls away, Anse tips forward a little like he's not yet ready to let go. Like he wants more.

How many times have they worked themselves up only to stop? He knows they're at his brother's house, but the urge to touch him is overwhelming. Luciano suppresses a moan and Anse resolves to stop just as soon as he gets to the junction of Luciano's neck and shoulder.

———

Daniel has cracked a second beer by the time Luciano and Anse make their way onto the back deck. The backyard is small, but the deck is almost as big as the house, surrounded by wiry frangipani trees. The sweet scent of the flowers mingles with the salt spray. Across the road, waves crash against a long stretch of golden sand.

Daniel looks like a natural with BBQ tongs in his hand and thongs on his feet. His skin, which had always been so pale and blemish-less, is slightly deeper and covered in freckles. Behind him, Anse hears Luciano offer Emmy a bottle of red wine as a thank you. Something flutters in him at the gesture.

Daniel nudges him. 'How long you been going with this one, then?'

'Just over a month. How could you tell?'

Daniel cackles. Actually cackles. Anse has forgotten his brother's bizarre laugh. 'Remember to keep the curtains shut. I saw you two making out in the bedroom when I was warming up the BBQ.'

'Noted.'

He taps Anse's beer with his before taking a long drink. 'We have a lot of catching up to do.'

They eat lunch, and at some point (Anse doesn't know when because he's had a lot of beer and Daniel keeps giving him more) Luciano and Emmy leave them at the outdoor table to walk along the beach.

It gets dark quickly. Daniel almost sets a frangipani tree on fire trying to light a citronella candle to stave off the mosquitos.

'All I'm saying,' Daniel slurs as he leans across the table. 'Is that… we shouldn't continue… to publish the edited Grey. It's the twentieth—twenty-first? Fuck I don't know—century.'

'I know what you're saying—,'

'Don't play the diplomat with me, Anse Meyer!'

'I'm not, I'm not,' Anse stifles a laugh. 'All I'm saying is that there is *also* merit in showing censorship as an accurate portrayal of a time in history.'

Daniel flops back into his chair. 'Why do you never let me win arguments? I just think there's a purity in showing it how it was written.'

'Daniel.' Emmy appears at the door. 'It's late.'

'We have a lot of catching up to do! Five years!'

'Seven,' Anse corrects.

'Seven? *Fuck*.' He turns back to Emmy. 'Seven years to catch up on.'

She sighs and disappears back into the house. A moment later she reappears with two beers. 'Last call. Then bed.'

Daniel takes the beer eagerly. 'Okay, I promise.'

'Good.'

Daniel catches her hand and gives it a slight tug. 'Hey, I love you.'

'I love you too,' she hums. 'Drink water before you go to bed. Both of you. Luciano wants to go to the beach tomorrow and you're both coming.'

'Fine, fine,' Daniel grumbles.

'And no more arguing,' she says as she closes the sliding door.

'We weren't arguing. We were *debating*.'

Anse opens a final beer and they clink the glasses together.

'To family reunions,' Daniel crows and takes a long drink. 'You spoke to Mum recently?'

'Fuck. No, I should call her.'

'You really should.'

The sliding door opens again a moment later and Anse turns, expecting to be berated by Emmy again, only to be pleasantly surprised.

'Do you mind if I join?' Luciano appears with three beers in hand. 'I grabbed these from the fridge, I hope that's okay.'

'Of course, sit, Luciano, sit,' Daniel declares with drunken grace. 'What an interesting name that is. What does it mean?'

Luciano pulls out a seat beside Anse and places the beers on the table. Daniel grabs his, grinning like a cat who got cream. The night is quiet and balmy, and all Anse can hear is the beating of his own heart and the crash of the waves against the sand a hundred metres away. Luciano looks so beautiful, his olive skin bathed in the warm glow of the backyard lights.

'My sister and I were a surprise pregnancy. My mum thought twins were the devil's work, so to appease him, she named me after him.'

Daniel stares across the table, his beer paused in mid-air. Then, his face cracks as he cackles. 'Are you serious? That's fucking hilarious.'

'No,' Luciano grins. 'I don't know. Maybe. She had a weird sense of humour.'

Sticking true to last call, they stumble into bed at last, despite Daniel's insistence that Emmy's old man keeps the good port 'around here somewhere'.

With some effort, Anse manages to get up the hallway before falling onto one of the beds—he's not sure whose—in a tangled mess of limbs. Luciano collapses next to him, laughing into his shoulder. He knows he'll feel awful in the morning, but right now he just feels warm and light and *happy*. Luciano props himself up on one arm to look down on him, curls falling around his face.

Words slip out of his mouth before Anse can stop them: how much he likes his curly hair, his brown eyes, and how much, how very much, he likes Luciano and how happy—*happy*, there it is again—that he's come along with him this weekend.

'I'm happy too,' Luciano says, and then says something else, but Anse doesn't quite catch it. Sleep hits him hard.

CHAPTER TWENTY-THREE

Luciano wakes before the others. Walking to the corner of the street, he finds a hamlet of shops: a butchery, café, hairdresser, and an independent grocer. It's already twenty-seven degrees outside and humid as fuck, but he'd drink coffee in Hell if they served it.

By the time he gets back to the house, Emmy is cooking breakfast and the smell of bacon hangs in the air. They'd spent the night talking and drinking wine, and when the wine had run out, Emmy had uncovered her dad's good port. Occasionally, their chats paused and they'd listened in on Anse and Daniel's conversation. Luciano had revelled in the sound of Anse's drunken and carefree laughter.

'It'll be a slow morning, I think,' Emmy says as the bacon spits in the pan. 'Bets on if they get up before midday?'

'Anse never sleeps in.' He doesn't really know this for certain but Anse's always texting him at ridiculously early hours. 'Ten bucks he gets up before midday.'

'No external interference. Doors must be open. Players must step out of their bedrooms and into the hallway.'

Daniel appears in the kitchen at 11.34 am. Luciano holds out his hand. Emmy scoffs before shoving a crumpled ten-dollar note into his palm.

'You guys drank an entire case last night.'

'I was *forced*,' Daniel replies. 'He kept opening more beers, and what, I'm not going to drink them? That's a waste.'

'Yeah, Anse really twisted your arm.'

'I'm telling you he is a bad influence on me.' Daniel pads over to Luciano, coffee in hand. He looks like a mess: unshaven, hair up in all angles, bags under his eyes. 'What're you reading?'

Luciano shows him the cover of the book, procured from Emmy's father's sizable holiday reading collection.

'Oh no,' Daniel groans before turning back into the kitchen. 'I can't handle another Oscar Wilde know-it-all.'

Anse appears at 12.05 pm and while he's showered and dressed, there's no hiding his obvious hangover. Luciano calls it split and gives Emmy back $5. Anse mutters good morning to his family before leaning down to press his lips to the crown of Luciano's head.

Casting a quick look to make sure Emmy and Daniel are in the kitchen, Luciano shimmies down the sofa and says, 'Spi-derman kiss.'

Anse laughs but leans forward a little more until his mouth finds Luciano's and wow, this is a weird kiss. It feels almost too low, like Anse is kissing his chin. He laughs halfway through it when Anse tips forward with a wince.

'Headache?'

'Only a small one,' Anse assures him.

After breakfast they head down to the beach with vibrant

towels slung over shoulders. Pitching an umbrella in the soft, warm sand, Anse and Daniel do a good job of pressing through their hangovers but are quick to spread their beach towels underneath the umbrella and lay down.

'You're not coming in?' Luciano asks.

Anse slips his sunglasses on. 'No, I don't like the ocean.'

'He can't swim,' Daniel corrects.

'I can swim.'

'Anse's afraid of sharks,' Emmy supplies helpfully.

When Anse doesn't deny it, Luciano snorts. 'There are no sharks.'

'Statistically, there are.'

'Don't try and argue with him, Luciano,' Daniel says. 'As we discovered last night, it is a complete waste of time.'

'The chances that a shark will come into shallow waters *and* attack you is so statistically low, it's almost impossible.' Anse opens his mouth to retort, but Luciano continues. 'Especially factoring the number of times you've set foot in the ocean, those number decreases even more. You can't argue with facts.'

'He'll try.'

Anse picks up his e-reader. 'I'm fine here.'

Luciano strips off and spreads sunscreen across his shoulders, arms and face before following Emmy into the waves. The water is refreshingly warm. Beside him, Emmy swims underneath a large crashing waves and pushes towards the breakpoint, where the water turns calm. He follows her, deftly navigating the swell of the waves. One breaks against him, slaps him in the stomach and the sting of saltwater makes him hiss.

'Anse told me you're teaching him to cook,' Emmy says as he reaches her. The sea swells, lifting them from the sandy floor as a large wave forms, breaks and hurtles towards the shoreline. 'That's not a small task.'

'Our first lesson was how to toast bread.'

Emmy's long dark hair floats around her shoulders. 'Since their dad died, I've been worried Anse wasn't coping. He's always been independent, but we used to go weeks without hearing from him. I know it's been hard on Dan.'

Luciano looks back to Anse sleeping on the beach. 'He mentioned he died a few years ago.'

'He's not that close with his mother, either,' Emmy says. 'Don't tell him I told you, of course.'

'Sure.'

'I like having him this close,' she says. 'If I could be selfish, I'd keep him here.'

A wave washes over them.

'So would I,' Luciano replies.

———

When they finally decide to head back into the shore, Anse is standing knee deep in the shallows. With a shirt off, he's as pale and sculpted as a marble statue.

'Luciano!' Anse calls, and then again, his tone rising with panic. 'Luciano!'

He feels the water drain away from his body, sucking into the swell of the wave. In a split second, Luciano weighs his options: stay still and be thrown forward like a ragdoll to the shoreline; or do his best to ride the wave and hope he doesn't get dumped in the process. Neither are good options.

He dives just as the wave hits his back and feels himself fall. Shells graze his stomach and shoulders as he's swept along the seafloor by the undertow. The wave takes him into the shallows and when he finally breaks the surface, Anse is a few feet away. Luciano pushes his hair from his face and tries to recover, even as he gasps for breath stumbles forward, disorientated from the tumbling.

Anse catches him around the shoulders. 'Easy.'

'I'm fine.' Luciano brushes him. 'How's your head?'

'No complaints yet.'

He dodges Luciano's elbow jab.

'Are you going to come out deeper?

Surprisingly, Anse nods. The water grazes his navel as Luciano leads him out deeper, towards the breakpoint.

'How do you find this enjoyable?' Anse grumbles. A wave rolls past them and it lifts Luciano from the seafloor. Seeing the opportunity, he uses Anse's shoulders as a lever and plunges him underwater. Anse thrashes violently as Luciano escapes from his grip with a manic giggle.

'Luciano!' Anse splutters.

Anse surges forward and tries to grab him, but Luciano is quick and darts out the way.

'Get back here!' he cries.

Luciano feels a hand wrap around his ankle a moment before he's dragged backwards through the water. Spluttering, he tries to fight off his captor but it's useless. Anse traps Luciano in his arms, pulling him flush against his body.

'Caught me,' he coughs.

Luciano feels Anse cup the curve of his ass and feels a mixture of delight and embarrassment.

'You really—,'

He doesn't finish the sentence before Anse throws him out of the water. His body spasms, legs kick out, and he hits the water with a smack.

'I can't believe you just did that,' he splutters as Anse swims towards him. For once, Luciano hates the grin on his face.

'You started it.'

'You're such a child.'

'Come here.'

Tugged back into Anse's arms, Luciano kisses him until they're both breathless.

———

In the evening, they drink delicious wine and Daniel cooks another BBQ and they play Cluedo.

'I am *always* Professor Plum,' huffs Daniel and swipes the token. 'You're the Colonel.'

Emmy is Mrs. Peacock. 'The Dame Judy Dench of the Cluedo cast.'

Anse turns to Luciano. 'Who are you?'

'Miss Scarlett,' he replies. 'Naturally.'

Daniel wins by declaring himself the murderer, with the candlestick, in the kitchen, and the group break off. Emmy goes to bed while Daniel catches the end of the cricket, playing silently on the television in the lounge room. Anse pulls both Luciano and his latest novel into his lap, settling in to finish the last few chapters.

'Hey,' Luciano presses his foot to Anse's thigh. 'Want to go on a date?'

He puts down his book. 'Now?'

'Yeah.'

'Luciano, it's nine-thirty at night.'

'I didn't realise I was dating such an old man—,'

'I'm three years older than you.'

'Come on,' Luciano pesters. 'Date me. Date me. Date me.'

'Yes, begging is a great way to convince someone to date you, Luciano.'

'I'm getting the car keys. You're either coming on my date or not.' Luciano finds Anse's car keys before sliding on a pair of thongs. 'What?' he says when Anse shakes his head. 'It's strictly casual attire.'

'Fine,' he groans. 'But we're home before midnight.'

Luciano directs him to the supermarket but orders him to stay in the car. It takes him fifteen minutes to return but when he does, he's carrying a bag full of groceries and a bottle of wine.

'Now to the beach,' Luciano demands.

'Bossy.'

They park back at the holiday house and walk the dimly lit track towards the beach, their thongs slapping against the cement. The moon glitters over the ocean and the wet sand. Luciano spreads a towel down and begins preparing a rather complicated cheeseboard.

'You're kidding me,' Anse says as Luciano lights a tealight and sticks it in the sand between them. 'Luciano—,'

'I know, I know, it's too much.'

Anse takes his hand, stilling his efforts. 'This is the most romantic thing anyone has ever done for me.'

The dim light from the candle hides Luciano's deep blush. Cutting a piece of gouda, he hands it to Anse. 'Try this one, it's my favourite. It's made in the Netherlands.'

Anse takes the slice of cheese, settling against the soft sand. 'So how much has Emmy told you about my tortured past, then? You two seem to be getting along.'

'We rarely speak of you, Anse.'

He laughs. 'I see.'

'She's going to show me her mum's phở recipe.'

'Ah, she wouldn't just do that with just anyone.' Anse picks off a grape and presses it against Luciano's mouth. He parts his lips and bites down, grazing the pads of Anse's fingers. A thrill runs through him as Anse's eyes darken, but he pulls his fingers away. Instead, he stretches out on the rug, his body long and lithe. Luciano watches him for a moment; watches the flicker of the candle highlight his profile; the way his chest rises and falls with each breath and tries to ignore the tightness in his own chest.

'What will you do when your time her runs out?'

Anse's ocean eyes flick to his. 'I'm not *dying*.'

'You know what I mean.'

Anse's gaze turns to the night sky. 'Suppose I'll have to go back. At least for a bit.'

He knows, deep down, it's too early to be talking about this. About what their fledging relationship means; if they care about each other enough to make such decisions.

Anse turns to him, head pillowed on his elbow. 'Do you want to be my boyfriend, Luciano?'

The way he says it makes the question sound like a trap. 'Do you want me to be your boyfriend, Anse?'

'Yes, very much.' There's no hesitation in his voice, just calm and clear and assured, and the strength of the resolution floors him just a bit.

'I want you, too.'

'Well, that settles it. Now I have something to come back to.'

Luciano's fingers pick at the thread of the beach towel. 'Ten months from now—,'

'Nine,' Anse corrects.

'*Nine* months from now, what would we do?'

'I'd just have to apply for a visa.'

It all sounds so simple. Anse rises to his elbows and leans in to capture Luciano's lips in a soft kiss. The air is cold but Anse's body is a furnace as he shifts over the blanket to press against Luciano's body, and oh *yes*.

When Luciano is thoroughly ravished and left with a mark on his neck that will be a hickey by tomorrow morning (Anse had muttered, 'revenge is sweet' into his ear before biting down on his earlobe), they gather the remnants of the cheeseboard and walk back to the house.

Anse pins him against the kitchen bench and kisses him deeply. 'Stay with me tonight.' Luciano gives him a questionable look. 'Or we could go to a hotel.'

'That's even more suspicious,' he hisses even as he lets Anse drag him up the hallway and into his bedroom.

Luciano slides off his jeans before slipping between the sheets.

'I should let you know you're technically on my side,' Anse says as he pulls off his shirt.

There's no restraint or shame in how eagerly Luciano reaches for Anse as slips into bed. Anse is just as eager, hands gripping Luciano's hips, tugging him closer.

'My brother's just down the hall,' Anse says as Luciano's hand moves lower. '*Luciano.*'

'Just…' Luciano kisses down the length of his chest and pushes Anse onto his back. 'I'll stop if you want me to stop.'

'I don't really *want* you to stop.'

Luciano smiles and edges down the bed. 'Don't be too loud, okay?'

Anse groans when Luciano presses his mouth just above the hem of his boxers.

'Yes, okay,' he gasps. 'But just to be clear, this isn't, a, oh my god, redemption, *fuck*, of the voucher.'

Luciano looks up. 'Anse, what did I say about being quiet?'

'To be.'

'Good.'

And then his mouth gets back to work.

CHAPTER TWENTY-FOUR

Anse finds it concerning to wake up and not find Luciano curled in the sheets beside him. He rubs his eyes, adjusts his boxers and remembers, for a brief second, the feeling of Luciano's mouth on him, the way his hair had felt so soft tangled between his fingers as he'd whispered praise in the dead of the night.

Unsurprisingly, he finds Luciano in the kitchen reading a recipe off his phone. For a while, Anse lingers by the doorway and watches. How does he manage to make cooking look so effortless? He stirs a pot, checks the recipe, takes a sip of his coffee all within a flurry of a few seconds.

'Morning,' Anse says from the doorway.

Luciano jumps, a hand flying to his chest. 'Fuck, you scared me.'

'You're up early.' Anse leans over to boil the kettle for coffee.

'Couldn't sleep.' Luciano picks the wooden spoon back up

and continues stirring the viscous dark chocolate sauce. 'Watched you sleep for a bit, though. That was nice.'

'Creepy.' He watches as Luciano takes the pie crust out of the oven. 'What are you making?'

'A chocolate tart. It's Easter Sunday.'

'Is that customary here?'

'Not really. Every Easter, Mum would make an amazing chocolate tart, and we *only* had it on Easter Sunday. She never made it any other day. She'd wake up before us and plant the Easter eggs in the garden and around the house, and then she'd make the tart.' Anse dips a finger in to taste the filling that clings to the side of the bowl and his eyes almost roll into the back of his head.

'She wanted it to be a tradition—,' he pauses, clears his throat. 'Anyway, I thought I would try and make it for you.'

'I wish I could have met her.'

Luciano's face twists into a smile and grimace. How it can possibly be both, Anse is unsure, but the crinkle of his nose tells him they are wonderful, painful memories to recall. 'She would have liked you.'

'What was she like?'

'She was beautiful, courageous and fiery,' he said. 'She grew up in Northern Italy and moved to Rome to start a restaurant, won a Michelin Star, divorced her husband—my father—and immigrated to Australia. He was violent to her, drank and gambled away most of her money. I've never met him, and he's never been in touch. She came here with Marzia and found out she was pregnant, opened another restaurant and forged another life. She could speak three languages. I was in awe of her, always trying to stand toe-to-toe with her.'

He tips the chocolate filling into the pie before tapping the tin on the bench top. Bubbles rise to the top of the filling, but Luciano quickly smooths them away with the swipe of a butter knife.

'She had huge debts that she never told anyone about, and I think sometimes she knew she was sick long before she actually went to the doctor.' Suddenly, his body lurches forward and Luciano gasps, shakes, and begins to sob. 'This is just really fucking hard, sorry.'

Anse catches his shoulders and steers him towards the small dining table. "Let me make you breakfast. I recently learnt how to make toast.'

Luciano laughs wetly. 'Thanks.'

He slides the tart into the fridge before starting on the toast. 'Have you been to Italy?'

'No.'

'You'd like it there. People actually ride Vespas unironically.'

'You wound me.'

He places the toast and coffee in front of Luciano before sitting beside him at the dining table.

'Sometimes I don't know why she didn't trust me enough to tell me about the debt. Other times I understand she wasn't ready to go. That she thought she'd get things straightened out before we inherited everything.' He lets out a shaky breath. 'It's my own fault but I'm in a lot of debt, Anse. If the restaurant doesn't work, if I can't make it as a chef, I don't know what else I'd do. There's nothing else I'm good at.'

'You're an excellent chef, Luciano.'

'I was when I was with her.'

'You'll find your feet.' Luciano makes a face like he doesn't really believe him and Anse realises nothing he can say will bring Luciano out of his mood. 'Give it time.'

'I'm sorry I'm such a mess.'

'Your mother died. You don't have to be sorry.'

'I feel I'm lumping all this emotional crap on you,' he says.

'I don't mind,' Anse replies honestly. 'I'm sure I'll occasionally give you 'emotional crap' to deal with.'

Daniel and Emmy wake up closer to nine and find Luciano and Anse relaxing on the patio.

'Beach?' says Emmy, already in her swimmers.

Emmy, Daniel and Luciano swim while Anse runs a two-kilometre sprint along the curve of the beach, and then back. It takes him just under half-an-hour. Luciano calls him into the surf as he makes his way back to their umbrella.

'Just watching you made me tired,' Luciano complains as swims out past the break point. He ducks under the water to wash the sweat off his face. When he resurfaces, Luciano swims closer and pushes his hair back. 'You look like Draco Malfoy.'

Anse makes a grab for him, but Luciano slips out of his reach just in time.

'Come on, I'm hungry.'

As they swim into shore, Anse sees the lifeguard hammering a sign into the soft sand.

'Oh look, the lifeguard is putting up a sign,' Luciano echoes his thoughts. 'Oh…'

'Luciano, is that a sign for jellyfish?' Anse groans.

Luciano laughs and tugs his hand a little harder. 'Ah, good thing we're getting out then!'

After lunch, Luciano serves his chocolate tart, which is quite simply the most amazing thing Anse has ever tasted, bar anything.

'Holy shit,' says Daniel as he takes a bite. 'Luciano. Stay, forever, please.'

Emmy not so subtly mouths *marry him.*

————

The next morning, Luciano hugs Emmy and Daniel goodbye and Anse promises they'll—yes, they'll, they're a *they* now—make the trip up to Sydney soon. They pack the car, get a coffee and finally the long weekend falls away behind them as they rise into the steep hills that cup the coastal city.

'That was nice,' says Luciano 'I like your family, Anse.'

'Most of the time I like them too.' They're edging in on Canberra and, Anse realises, the end of the weekend. 'Do you want to stay the night?'

'What?'

'You already have your things and I could drop you home when I get up for work in the morning.'

Luciano is silent for a moment. 'You're not sick of me?'

'Of course not,' Anse says. 'Unless you're sick of me.'

'Definitely not.'

'So, you'll stay?'

'Sure. I love that giant tub of yours.'

Luciano lounges in the bathtub for longer than Anse can believe is necessary or possible. When he eventually emerges, his skin flushed and wrinkled. Collapsing besides Anse on the lounge, he lets out a satisfied sigh. 'So, do you want to Netflix and chill, or just kind of, you know, *chill*?'

Anse turns to him and raises a brow. 'In my room?'

'Preferably, yes.'

He switches the television off, kisses Luciano passionately and says, 'Give me two minutes.'

He gets up and heads into the ensuite, fishing out the box of condoms in his vanity. Pocketing one, he briefly considers perhaps taking two. He's never used *just* one. But then he doesn't want to presume, to insinuate that *has* to happen, because it doesn't, and he certainly doesn't want to pressure Luciano into anything.

'We should really—,' he's about to say *have the 'talk'* but then he steps back out into his bedroom and Luciano is only his boxes, and Anse whatever as he catches sight of Luciano's chest hair and the way it tapers downwards.

'I thought you'd be naked,' Luciano blurts.

'Oh, I can be if you want.'

Anse places the condom onto the bedside table and notices how Luciano eyes it. Grabbing the hem of his shirt, he lifts it off and tosses it into the washing basket, which makes Luciano laugh.

'You don't throw things on the floor, do you?'

'Why would I? The washing basket is right there.'

Luciano shakes his head and climbs across the bedspread, rising to his knees to find Anse's lips. His hands eagerly smooth over Anse's chest, warm and soft, and goose bumps prick the back of his neck. Luciano smells like clean linen and lavender soap, and his mouth is soft and wanting as it opens to his.

Anse gasps, jerks suddenly, as Luciano grasps him through his briefs.

Luciano pulls back. 'Fuck, was that not okay?'

'No,' he protests. 'I mean yes. It's fine. It just surprised me.'

Luciano visibly swallows and nods before lying back on the stark white bedspread, all tan skin and dark curls and red, kiss-swollen lips. Anse leans forward, brackets his body with his own, and kisses him. Fingers skim up his spine, feather light, before tangling in his hair as Luciano pulls him down. Anse shivers in delight as Luciano's thighs lazily fall open, encouraging him to press forward and—

Luciano hooks his leg over Anse's hip, heel against the small of his back. Before he has time to process it, he's flipped and pressed against the mattress, held down by a solid weight. Above, Luciano grins smugly.

'I did Brazilian jiu-jitsu for a few years,' Luciano shrugs. 'Comes in handy.'

Anse smooths his hands up Luciano's thighs.

'I don't think I can tonight,' Luciano says as Anse's hands settle on his hips. 'I'm sorry.'

'There's no need to be sorry,' Anse replies. There's a nervousness to his lover that Anse knows they won't overcome tonight. 'I only want what you're willing to give.'

His hand rises to smooth down Anse's side, settling at his hip, and he catches Anse's eye as if to say *is this still okay*? Anse arches up into his hand, a silent invitation. Hands slip into his boxers and then warmth blooms in the pit of his belly, familiar and welcome.

Luciano slides off him in favour of curling against his side, encouraging Anse to roll-over until they're face-to-face, cheeks pressed against the pillows. He likes it better this way; transfixed by Luciano's darkened gaze.

'Can you touch me too?'

It doesn't take long. Luciano comes undone with a shudder and a groan, and Anse marvels at the pucker of his brow, the way he says his name tumbles as the tension in his body builds and then all at once, falls away.

————

The alarm blares. Luciano groans against the pillow as Anse blinks awake.

'What's the time?' Luciano mutters.

Anse grabs at his phone, switching off the alarm. 'Six-thirty.'

'Why the fuck is your alarm set for six-thirty?'

'I normally go for a run,' Anse murmurs into the warm skin of Luciano's shoulder. 'But I think it's raining.'

He can hear the pattering of rain against his window.

'Shower?'

'Coffee.'

Anse peels himself off Luciano's body and instantly misses the warmth. 'I'll shower and then make you a coffee.'

'Best boyfriend ever,' he hums into the pillow.

When Luciano finally makes his way into the kitchen, dressed in a pair of light wash skinny jeans and a white graphic tee, Anse hands him two pieces of toast and a large mug of coffee.

'Really leaning into this toast making thing, aren't you?'

'Maybe if the chef who runs the class wasn't so preoccupied with his new boyfriend, I'd learn a little more.'

'We have skipped a couple lessons, haven't we?'

Anse steals a bite from Luciano's second piece of toast. 'I'm showering. Then I'll drop you home.'

Luciano insists on picking a tie for Anse to wear. Unsurprisingly, he chooses a pastel blue paisley tie Anse bought for a wedding a few years ago. It's not at all his style. But out of all of his ties (who needs twenty ties, Anse?), of course Luciano picks it.

'I'll be made fun of,' Anse protests.

'It's a *tie*.' Luciano throws him the tie and continues to rifle through his wardrobe. 'You like solid colours a lot, don't you?'

'I think I have one or two prints in there.'

'I don't think I'd classify stripes as prints,' Luciano scoffs. 'How many white shirts can one man have?'

'They're all different.' Anse laces up his oxfords.

'Are they?'

'Rich coming from the man who couldn't pick a shade of white.'

'Funny,' Luciano deadpans. He continues snooping through his wardrobe. 'I don't even own one suit and you have a full-on tuxedo in here. 'Do you have a top hat to go with it?'

Anse ignores him as he packs his satchel and finds his keys. 'Shall we go, dear?'

———

They arrive at Trattoria twenty minutes later, and Luciano immediately notices something's wrong. Newly installed downlights light up the restaurant spectacularly. The walls are now a crisp white and gorgeous round pendant lights hang from the ceiling. The floorboards are glossy with varnish, and the heavy scent fills the restaurant.

'Did Rohan do all this?' he mutters as he continues through to the kitchen. Anse follows silently. The new white subway tiles replace the old brown tiled splash-back. The bench tops and cooking stations are impossibly clean. Further along, Anse can see fresh shelving has been installed along the side of the hallway leading towards Luciano's office.

'Did you know about this?' Luciano demands. His voice is strained as his chin quivers. 'Tell me the truth—,'

Dread twists around him. Maybe this arrangement had been a

bad idea. The restaurant is the most important thing to Luciano, and now he's gone and fucked with it.

'Luciano, I—,'

He doesn't get a chance to finish his sentence as Rohan and Corina leap from the office and shout, 'Surprise!'

'Aw, fuck.' The smile on Corina's face drops immediately. 'You hate it, don't you?'

Anse places a hand on Luciano's shoulder. 'Are you okay?'

Luciano nods and relief washes over Anse. He doesn't hate it, then.

'How could you guys do this in one weekend?'

'It wasn't easy.' Marzia strolls in, dressed in figure-hugging athletic wear and carrying two large tins of empty paint. 'Hey, you must be Anse. Marzia.'

'I am. Nice to meet you.' Her almond-shaped eyes are strikingly green, and she looks at Anse with such an intensity, it's almost a relief when her gaze turns back to Luciano.

'Do you like it?'

'I love it,' he replies. 'I can't believe you *did* this.'

Corina leads Luciano on an enthusiastic tour. Rohan hangs back, pats him on the shoulder and says, 'Thanks for letting us know. Did you guys have a nice weekend?'

Anse nods. 'And you?'

Rohan laughs just as Luciano calls, 'Rohan! Is that my keg hooked up to the bar?'

'What? It was thirsty work!'

'Continuing on,' declares Corina as they make their way to the customer bathrooms. 'Okay, now this one is a bit out there.'

Luciano bursts out laughing as Corina opens the door to the bathroom. The stalls are black, and glossy chequered tiles run halfway up the wall. The rest of the wall is painted a vibrant yellow.

'Your bathroom upstairs is much tamer,' Marzia assures him. 'Corina picked the colour.'

'You like it, right?' Corina badgers.

'Sure.' Even to Anse, the answer isn't convincing. It's certainly a statement bathroom. 'Wait, you did upstairs, too?'

Rohan pipes up. 'Well, when we heard you were entertaining so frequently these days...'

All eyes turn to Anse.

Luciano shoots Rohan a dirty look but the man simply shrugs. 'They got me drunk. You know how easy I am when I'm drunk. Plus, they wanted to know more about the bloke that got you to get away from all *this*,' he waves his hand around, 'for four entire days.'

Marzia says, 'We've got one more thing to show you and then we'll go upstairs.'

Corina leads them through the kitchen to the back office. Once an overflowing, disorganised migraine of a room that made Anse feel itchy just thinking about it, the office is now organised and fresh with simple beige carpet and stark white walls. Filing cabinets line the back wall. The most striking feature, however, is the huge, ornately framed painting of the Tuscan countryside.

'No,' Luciano groans. 'The painting lives!'

'This way, Mum will always be looking down on you,' Marzia nudges Luciano with a grin. 'Judging your decisions.'

'I can't believe you guys did this. In *one* weekend.'

'I know,' says Corina. 'Rohan and I reckon we should go on one of those home renovation shows.'

'We couldn't have done it without Anse, who did absolutely

nothing but go on holiday with you,' Rohan adds. 'Really, it's the definition of sacrifice.'

Luciano turns to look at him, tears welling in his eyes, and Anse's heart flies into his throat. Someone—probably Corina—says that they'll meet Luciano upstairs and suddenly they're alone.

'You lied to me,' Luciano finally says with a wet laugh. He wipes his face on the back of his hand.

'Not really. I just didn't tell you the entire truth.'

He scoffs as Anse pushes a curl behind his ear. 'Your brother did tell me not to argue with you.'

'That advice will bode well for our relationship.' He hesitates. 'Do you like this?'

'I love it, and I love you.' There's no hesitation in his voice as he says it. He simply lays it out, confidently, for Anse to do with as he wishes.

His hands settle on Luciano's hips. 'You do, do you?'

Luciano laughs wetly and nods. 'I did expect you just to say *I know*.'

Anse frowns. 'Why would I say that?'

Luciano opens his mouth, looks as if he's about to say something, and then closes it again. 'Don't worry, it's silly.'

There's something Luciano isn't telling him, something that he's not quite getting. Still, he persists. 'I love you too.'

Is it too early to say such a thing? He's not sure. All he knows is he *feels* far too much, so much that it's overwhelming, and it's a relief to give some of it to Luciano. To know the feelings are accepted by him. Reciprocated.

'Luciano!' Marzia calls from above. Someone stomps on the floor above, causing dust to rain down on the.

'Hey, watch the floorboards!' Rohan protests.

'I should get back to them, and you need to go to work.' He kisses him briefly. 'See you Thursday night?'

After four days with Luciano, it seems like an awfully long time.

'Thursday,' he nods.

CHAPTER TWENTY-FIVE

It's a welcome surprise to see Ahmed at footy training, stretching out his hamstring. He looks up as Luciano tosses his water bottle onto the grass beside him.

'Rohan hasn't broken you yet, then.'

'He's given it a good go.' Luciano sits down on the slick grass and begins to stretch. Across the field, Rohan is setting up exercises using brightly coloured cones and ladders.

'Right, gents!' calls Rohan. 'Look alive. Three laps around the oval. Try to keep up.'

Luciano suspects that Ahmed doesn't have a problem keeping up with Rohan, but he falls into step with him purposefully.

'How's Tatiana?' Luciano pants. 'You guys still doing long distance?'

'Yeah, it's killing me though.' Ahmed puffs. 'We got in a huge fight the other week over whose turn it was to see the other. It was stupid. I think it's really taking its toll on us. We gotta make a decision but I've got my gym here and she's got a job in Sydney. Who gives up what?'

Luciano hums in agreement. He wants to continue talking but his chest feels tight and his legs are burning. Ahead, Rohan turns so he's running backwards. Luciano almost wants to punch the grin off his stupid face.

'Two laps to go! Keep it up. Anyone who doesn't beat me back to the clubhouse has to do fifty additional sit-ups.'

Ahmed glances at Luciano.

'He's serious,' Luciano says.

They both pick up the pace.

————

Anse appears on his doorstep on Thursday night, his gaze heavy with desire. 'Are we alone?'

Luciano barely has time to nod before he'd scooped up into Anse's arms. He laughs as he's walked across the floor and into the kitchen. There, he's kissed within an inch of his life before Anse presses him against the island bench.

'Holy fuck,' Luciano breathes as Anse sinks to his knees.

Afterwards, he feels muddled but very satisfied, and to Anse's obvious amusement, fumbles his way through the cooking lesson.

Pulling out a tray of beef steaks from the walk-in fridge, Luciano sets out separate plates for yoghurt, flour and finally, panko crumb.

'*Schnitzel*?' Anse asks in disbelief. 'Why? You can just buy them.'

Luciano gives him a flat, unamused look and hands him a small metal hammer. 'After dinner, I dare you to tell me *to my face* that these are not any better than what you buy at the shop. Get tenderising.'

There's a euphemism in there that Luciano simply won't entertain as he watches Anse use the meat tenderiser on the steaks.

'The flour seals in the moisture,' Luciano explains as he coats the meat. 'Then the yoghurt to help the panko crumb coat. Most of the time you use egg, but yoghurt can create a thicker crust.'

It's not the yoghurt Anse turns his nose up at. 'Panko crumb?'

'It'll be good, I promise.'

If the look on Anse's face is anything to go by, it must cause him great pain to stay silent as Luciano dips the steak into the panko crumb.

'My dad used to take us out for dinner every Tuesday night,' Anse says as the schnitzel sizzles in the pan. 'It was back when you could still smoke in restaurants. We went to the same place every week. He bought our first beers there.'

'How did your father die?' asks Luciano.

'He had a heart attack.'

'Fuck, I'm sorry, Anse.'

'It's fine. It was a few years ago now.'

The oil in the pan hisses as Luciano turns the schnitzel over to reveal a crisp golden coating. 'This is almost done; can you get the plates?'

They eat on the desk in the study. The beef is so tender it almost melts away at it hits Luciano's tongue. It's delicious, and he loses himself in the meal, suddenly ravenous. When Anse puts down his fork, the clatter makes Luciano look up.

'Luciano, that was…' he clears his throat. 'Incredible.'

'Better than the frozen ones?'

'There's no comparison,' Anse replies. 'I don't...' he shrugs, laughs a little. His voice is wet with emotion. 'It was like being back there.'

'So, things between you and Anse are—,' Marzia trails off, waiting for Luciano to answer. They're sitting in her hotel room drinking coffee and drafting budgets, job advertisements, policies and procedures. Earlier, Luciano had sarcastically commented about how *fun* it was to write contracts, only for Marzia to nod back enthusiastically. He's not made another snide remark since. If Marzia's willing to help him with this, he's not about to look a gift horse in the mouth.

'Fine,' he answers.

'No, I meant, are you getting serious?' she clarifies as she taps away at her keyboard.

'Yeah, we're serious.'

'What's his visa like?'

'Twelve months. From January.'

Marzia's lips pull. 'Shit.'

'I know.' It's not lost on him that almost as quickly as they got together, they'll have to say goodbye again. 'We have a plan. Well, half of a plan.'

'You could get married,' Marzia suggests.

Luciano almost chokes on his coffee. '*Marzia*, you are not suggesting what I think you're suggesting, are you? That's fraud.'

'It's not fraud if you're actually in love,' she says. 'I'm sending you the job advertisement for your Sous Chef. You'll need a Kitchen Hand as well. Have you finished your menu yet?'

'Um,' says Luciano. Marzia's eyes narrow.

'Have you *started* it?' Luciano shrugs again, and Marzia groans. 'You need to write your menu, Luciano. Identify stockists for inventory, test the recipes, train your staff. If you want to open in two months' time, you need to get it together.'

'I know,' he replies. 'But with finishing up the renos and organising this community day on Saturday, I just haven't had the time. I promise I will, though.'

'It's just food, Luciano,' Marzia says. 'How hard can it be?'

Luciano decides not to dignify the question with a response, and Marzia starts talking about food hygiene and handling certifications and liquor licences. At four, he leaves and starts his shift delivering food: it's a Friday night, and he needs the money. At seven, he texts Anse, who says he's eating sushi at home after a particular long gym session. Luciano wants to snuggle on his couch so badly, but another order comes in, so he stashes his phone into the storage compartment underneath the Vespa's seat.

He collapses into bed at eleven, undressed but not showered, and at the last minute, remembers to put on an alarm for six to help the radio station crew set up for the community open day.

CHAPTER TWENTY-SIX

Luciano: Anse, can you come to the restaurant? We NEED you. PLEASE. I'm so out of my depth, there are so many people here

Anse: I'll be there soon.

You can do this

Luciano: I'M DROWNING.

Anse: You're not.

I was last weekend

Luciano: OH PLS!! JUST HURRY UP AND GET HERE

Anse arrives at Trattoria at eight-thirty. Immediately, he's greeted by a crowd of people and loud, pumping music. Across the square, he can see Corina at the coffee stand calling out orders to a crowd of waiting customers. A large garish bouncing castle is pinned down on the small patch of grass in the middle of the square, but he can barely hear the children's squeals over the pounding beat of a popular RnB song. Inside Trattoria, Anse can see Luciano posing for photographs by his long bar, his elbows resting awkwardly against the counter.

'Anse!' Corina calls from the coffee stand. 'Anse, over here!'

She throws him an apron as soon as he is close enough. 'What's this for?'

'I need you to start on the sausages.'

The woman behind the bar looks him up and down. She has dreadlocks down to the small of her back, intertwined with rings and bells. 'You want a coffee?'

'Yes, thanks.' He extends a hand. 'Anse.'

She takes it, shaking firmly. 'Omala. Rohan's sister.'

'No chit-chat,' Corina interrupts as she refills the grinder with a packet of coffee beans. 'Anse, can you start up the barbecue.'

Anse approaches the barbecue like it's a wild beast. He picks up the tongs, but they feel strange in his hand. How had Daniel made this look so effortless at the beach house?

'It's easy, I promise.' Corina slips in beside him to turn on the gas. The barbecue lights up with a *whoosh*.

'Luciano told you I can't cook, didn't he?'

'It may have come up.' Corina lays out the sausages on the sizzling flat top. 'It's easy: cook them for ten minutes until they're brown then put them in the tray. People will grab a slice of bread; you just have to put the sausage between it. And ignore how sexual that sounds.' Someone calls her name across the square. 'I have to go. You've got this.'

It's not long until the smell of cooking sausages beckons Anse's first customers, and then the lines don't stop. He goes through eight loaves of bread in less than thirty minutes—and he only knows it's been thirty-minutes because the radio crew do a 'secret sound' competition at exactly nine-fifteen, which is the gritty audio of Omala's grinder. Corina pats him on the shoulder and hands him a coffee at ten. He's already halfway through a dozen trays of sausages when a man arrives with more.

'Heard you needed more meat.' He hands the packs to Corina.

'You're a literal life-saver,' she beams. 'Evan, this is Anse, Luciano's boyfriend. Anse, this is my friend, Evan.'

Anse puts the tongs down and extends a hand. 'Thanks for bringing more sausages.'

'No worries,' Evan says. 'Omala, can I trouble you for a long black?'

'You and eight others,' calls Omala over the sound of the coffee machine whirling. 'It'll be a wait.'

'Yeah, no worries.' Evan stands silently, awkwardly, as Anse packs the sausages away.

'Where are you from?' he asks. 'Your accent, I mean.'

'Austria,' Anse replies. 'I work for the embassy.'

'Right. Cool.' Evan clears his throat. 'I, um, work for the paper.'

'Interesting.'

Anse turns the sausages again, but they're barely brown on the other side. He sighs and flips them back. Evan stands in front of him, waiting for his coffee with his hands in his pockets. The silence stretches out, uncomfortable and heavy between them, and Anse puts on another handful of cut onions just to *do* something. He hates the intimate hell of small talk. Aspiring diplomat he may be, but international leaders don't have time to chit-chat. He'd rather debate policy for hours than talk about the weather.

'How'd you and Luciano meet?' Evan says, the first one to break.

'Through work,' Anse replies. He's about to ask Omala where that damn coffee is when she slides it across the table.

'Thanks again Evan,' Corina smiles. 'I can't believe how many journos picked up the story. We even have a TV crew here. Luciano's over the moon.'

Evan smiles as he glances at the crowd. 'Where is he?'

'He's inside,' Corina says. 'You should say hello.'

Evan's glances from Corina and Anse. 'Yeah I might. Nice to meet you, Anse.'

'You too,' Anse replies as Evan walks away. He can't shake the feeling that there's something he doesn't know, but he can't linger on it as the line for the sausages —*oh shit* they're burning —moves forward.

———

He turns off the barbecue at one in the afternoon. The last four sausages are sold to three hungry children and an overwhelmed father. The radio crew have left and the square is quiet again. A few people linger to chat with Luciano and to get a photo with Rohan, who has been helping Luciano with the interviews and the tours of the restaurant.

Rohan flexes his bicep as he poses for a photo with a group of young girls. Corina scoffs.

'He's ridiculous,' she mutters. Omala laughs.

Luciano finally finds them late in the afternoon. His hair has been curled and styled, held with pomade and hairspray. The white button down, tucked into tight black pants, is creaseless and he's even wearing a pair of black polished oxfords. He looks positively dashing as he sips on a long black coffee.

'Nice shoes.'

'They're Rohan's. And they're a size too big for me, so I'm wearing two pairs of socks.' The shoes wiggle loosely on his feet. 'I can't believe you cooked sausages.'

'I didn't get much of a choice.'

Luciano rises to his tiptoes, chin jutting out in silent question and Anse answers the request, kissing him gently.

'Ack, get a room, you two,' Corina snaps and Anse thinks that sounds like a perfectly fine idea. 'Anse, use your muscles to help me move the BBQ into the back of Rohan's van, would you?'

Anse pulls away, but Luciano takes his hand.

'I'll come over this afternoon,' he says. 'Let me shower first and then I'll be around. Say, five-ish?'

'Okay,' he says. 'I'll cook dinner.'

Luciano grins. 'Yeah, sounds good.'

Corina groans. Luciano shoots her a look, but she doesn't back down. 'Anse. Heavy BBQ. Need a big strong man to help me.'

'Go,' says Luciano. 'I'll see you later.'

———

By five, the chicken is in the oven and the vegetables are floating in cold water on the stovetop. It's nothing fancy—he's not the professional chef in this relationship—but he's marinated the chicken, made the stuffing, bought the vegetables from the markets, and stood in the kitchen for a good hour. If the way to a man's heart is truly through his stomach, then this is his grand gesture. This is his running-through-the-snow-in-his-underwear, trying-to-beat-the-clock-to-midnight-on-New-Year's, climbing-the-fire-escape, kissing-in-the-rain kind of grand gesture.

His doorbell rings at five-fifteen. Anse throws the tea-towel over his shoulder and buzzes Luciano through, only to open the door to find him in a pair of black tracksuit pants and a shirt. The earlier glow of his skin has been washed away, and even his hair falls a little limply around his face. He looks exhausted.

Luciano drops an overnight bag by the door and Anse feels his stomach flutter.

'Was I supposed to dress up?' Luciano asks as he takes in Anse's outfit: a pair of grey trousers and a t-shirt. 'Or is this your usual Saturday afternoon attire?'

Before he has a chance to respond, Luciano slips into the apartment. 'I'm teasing of course. Dinner smells amazing. I'm starved.'

Following Luciano back into the kitchen, he pours two glasses of pinot noir . 'I've become quite an excellent student recently if only my tutor would notice.'

'Perhaps you could apply for extra credit with your barbecue skills today,' Luciano suggests as he curls up on the lounge. 'Don't mind me. Please continue.'

Soft acoustic music plays from Anse's speaker system as he seasons the potatoes and slips into the oven. The chicken is browning nicely. According to his phone, it has another hour in the oven and then he should pull it out and cover it, otherwise, it could go dry. He didn't even think chicken *could* go dry.

'We made six thousand dollars today,' Luciano swirls the wine around his glass. 'I can't really believe it. And I'm going to be on TV. It's kinda unbelievable, don't you think?'

'No, I don't. You're incredible, Luciano. You need to give yourself more credit.'

Luciano shies away at the praise as Anse sits beside him.

Placing his hand on his thigh, he gives it a gentle squeeze. 'You know we have to have this talk now.'

'What talk?' Luciano cottons on. 'Oh. *That* talk.'

He knows it's a talk they probably should have had before now. 'My last test was in December. Just before Christmas. It was clean.'

Luciano picks at his nails awkwardly. 'Mine was in February. I'm all good, too.'

'And we're exclusive.'

'Right.' Luciano nudges him. 'And… how do you normally? I mean, I'm all prepared to, um, bottom, if that's fine with you. I've never really done anything else.'

'Sure. I like it both ways, if you're ever amendable to—,

'I'd love to,' Luciano says perhaps a little too quickly.

Anse laughs a little and reaches across to squeeze Luciano's knee. 'All agreed, then? Any other burning questions?'

'My safe word is raspberry, just so you know.'

'Shit, mine is a weird German word. I'll adopt raspberry if that's fine with you.'

'Nice doing sexual business with you, Mr Meyer,' Luciano shakes his hand.

Anse laughs as the awkwardness slips away. 'You too, Luciano. I think you'll find yourself a very satisfied customer.'

Luciano snorts. 'I certainly hope so.'

Anse feels Luciano settle against his side, a comforting weight against his body. 'This is my first relationship, you know. Like, real relationship.'

Anse looks down. 'Really?'

'I was kinda nervous to have sex because I didn't want you to think I just wanted something casual, but then the more we serious things got, I just kept thinking it was *weird* that we hadn't had sex yet.' He looks up. 'That's stupid, right?'

'Not stupid.' Anse pulls him in a little tighter. 'I was in an on-again off-again relationship for a few years with a person who started out as a friend with benefits. We'd never built an emotional connection, never really had very good chemistry. That's what I value the most in our relationship—the way you make time to be with me, when you fall asleep on the lounge next to me, when you take a weekend off just to hang out with my family—that is far more important to me.'

He's not sure if now is a great time to air his dirty laundry, but if it helps Luciano overcome this nervousness, then he's more than happy to share.

'I could tell you were nervous the other night.' He smooths a hand down Luciano's shoulder. 'I want you all the time, Luciano, but I don't need to get physical to feel connected or valued, or loved, by you.'

Luciano burrows into his side. 'I'm not really sure what to say to that.'

The alarm on his mobile phone rings. He kisses the top of Luciano's head. 'Dinner's ready. Come on.'

Anse pulls the chicken from the oven and the smell of coriander, chilli and lemongrass fills the kitchen.

'I'm so impressed you've cooked an entire meal,' Luciano says as he sets the table.

'And three hundred sausages.'

'Oh yeah, those damn sausages,' he mutters. 'Ugh, I smelt them cooking and wanted one so badly but Marzia said I'd get tomato sauce on my white shirt. She's right, but still.'

Dinner is, surprisingly, delicious. The chicken is moist and well-seasoned, and while the vegetables are perhaps a little bland, the roasted potatoes are soft and buttery. Luciano clears his plate and then helps Anse wash up, curling his arms around his middle.

'I'm really proud of you,' he says as Anse turns in his arms. Luciano's full lips are stained red form the wine and Anse can't seem to look anywhere else. 'I really want to go to bed.'

Anse wonders briefly if he means he wants to sleep, but then Luciano's hand is on him and Anse sucks in a sharp breath. His touch is searing, and there's no misinterpreting what he wants. Anse knows he wants it too, more than anything. His hands rise from Luciano's hips, slip under the soft cotton of his shirt to smooth over the hot skin of his back.

Luciano rises to kiss him, all soft and warm and wet, his body thrumming with desire. Their bodies fit together so well that Anse thinks this is where Luciano belongs; that his body must be bespoke in the perfect way it moulds and melts against him.

He takes it all. Greedy with handfuls of clothes and skin as he pulls Luciano closer, positions him just right.

'Stop that,' Luciano complains against his lips. 'Not here. Bed'

Scooping Luciano into his arms, he's rewarded with a squeal as Luciano does a wonderful impression of a koala, clinging to his neck and shoulders. His hot mouth drags down Anse's throat and nips at his collarbone, making it very difficult to open the bedroom door.

When he gets to the edge of the bed, Anse removes his hands from Luciano's rear and drops him.

'Anse!' Luciano squeals as he falls onto the mattress and whatever he was about to say promptly dies in his lips as Anse takes his shirt off. And now, he's not a vain man, but there's a certain *pride*, a certain *smugness* that blooms inside him at the way Luciano looks at him, at the way hands travel down his chest like a form of worship.

'I, erm, um.' For once, Luciano's romantic words fail him. 'You look, I mean, you are. *Fuck.*'

Anse flicks open the first button of his trousers. Drags down his fly.

'Take off your clothes, Luciano.'

'You do it.' Luciano kisses him fiercely. Anse tangles his fingers through his curls before breaking the kiss to push Luciano back against the pillows.

Throwing Luciano's shirt away, Anse trails open-mouthed kisses down his chest, revelling in the way he squirms with desire and pure, unbridled joy. It's heady to be trusted like this, to be trusted by him, and all Anse wants to do is bring him pleasure *repeatedly*.

He feels Luciano's thighs tremble as he places a kiss to the soft skin. 'Is this okay?'

'Of course.'

'You'll tell me if you don't like it?'

Luciano nods, curls dark against the white pillow, loosening a nervous sigh as Anse settles between his legs, plants a kiss on the crease of his hipbone and thigh.

It's is a familiar game they know, are both comfortable with, and while Anse has always liked giving blowjobs, they're positively wonderful with Luciano. He revels in the way his lover falls apart, often gasping his name, only to come back to him slowly, leisurely, and entirely unravelled.

Tonight, it doesn't take long. He arches against the sheets, and Anse's name tumbles from his mouth, hugged by a string of curse words and half-hearted prayers. Placing a kiss to the soft skin of his inner thigh, Anse slowly trails his mouth back up his lover's body.

There's a warm flush on Luciano's cheeks, and a dark, hungry desire in his eyes that makes Anse's stomach flutter. And it's all for him. He is so greedy. He'll take all, if he's allowed.

Luciano rises to his elbows to push Anse onto his back and then spends a torturous amount of time tracing the defines of Anse's stomach with his mouth.

Leaning across, Anse grabs the pack of condoms and a small bottle of lube. Luciano squeezes a generous amount of lube on his fingers.

'Go slowly,' he murmurs into Luciano's curls. He cradles the other man to him, letting him set the pace. Luciano's hands find Anse's shoulders and there's a twisted kind of pleasure in the bite of his fingernails as Luciano begins to move slowly.

Anse thinks he's seen the expression on his lover's face somewhere before, in some museum in some European city, carved into marble and heralded as a piece of classical art. Anse's hands leave the divots of Luciano's hips and smooth up the long planes of his back, and then back down again, to the curve of his rear. A playful slap and Luciano laughs. Oh, it's been a while since it has been so wonderful.

Luciano says something, a string of words Anse can't understand because Luciano's faltering, his thighs quivering. Anse's hands find his hips. A cry. Hands scrunch the sheets beside Anse's head.

Later, Anse traces patterns on the small of Luciano's back, watching in mild amusement as his eyelids flutter, desperately fighting off sleep. Sweaty curls splay out over the pillow, and Luciano, bathed in the yellow light from the bedside lamp, glows pink. Words, sweet like honey, fall from his mouth easily, lost between the mess of sheets and pillows and skin. Luciano presses against him and not for the first time, his body feels like home.

Outside, he can hear the rain hitting the windowsill, and then comes Luciano's breathing, shallow and warm against his shoulder.

CHAPTER TWENTY-SEVEN

In the warm haze of the morning, Luciano wakes to the heavy weight of Anse pressed against his back, warm breath caressing the nape of his neck and the comforting smell of clean linen and rain.

Wiggling a hand free, Luciano finds his phone. 7:19am.

Behind him, Anse grumbles sleepily and tugs him closer. There's no rush to get up on a rainy Sunday morning, so Luciano settles into the cocoon of blankets and warm limbs and, for the first time in a long time, lets his worries go.

They'll be there tomorrow: the restaurant and the menu and the sobering realisation that he's not as good a chef as his mother, and what if he stuffs this all up—

He pauses.

All those worries will be there tomorrow.

But this moment won't exist tomorrow. Perhaps there will be moment like this, but it won't be exactly the same. If he's lucky, perhaps there will be thousands of moments like this.

Behind him, he hears Anse take in a deep breath. Feels him shift a little as he wakes up.

'Do you want to get up?' Anse voice is heavy with sleep.

'Not really,' Luciano replies.

'Good.'

It would be so easy to stay in this bed all morning, Luciano thinks. Everything with Anse is easy.

Luciano knows he can be wild and erratic, he flies from one task to the other, but Anse is grounded, steering him back to his focus, encouraging him to complete one thing before moving to the next.

And he knows that Anse is a work-a-holic with a heavily scheduled routine. That he's a detail-orientated perfectionist who sometimes has trouble communicating with the two languages in his mind and the language of his heart.

And, Luciano's not delusional in realising they haven't really worked through anything *hard* yet.

That this part of the relationship doesn't compare to the difficulties they may face down the road.

Yet, he'll take the hard gladly because the easy is just so incredibly wonderful. Anse snuffles behind him as he drifts back to sleep.

Later, Luciano browses through Anse's small bookshelf: he's got a small collection of what look to be German crime novels and a pile of books he's borrowed from the library. He takes one out, thumbs through the yellowing pages and inhales the vinegar scented pages. Replacing it, his eyes spot a thick bounded A4 document.

The Vanishing Detective
By Daniel Meyer

'It's about a detective who can travel through time. It's quite good.' Anse says explains from where he's serving up breakfast in the kitchen. 'Now, do you want ham and tomato or salmon and cream cheese?'

'Ham and tomato, please.'

'Perfect, because I wasn't going to let you have the salmon,' Anse grins.

'Will you read me some?' Luciano says as he flicks through the book. Anse has scrawled comments in red pen along the borders, noted spelling errors and punctuation mishaps. 'Just from where you're up to. You can fill me in on the plot.'

Anse gives him an apprehensive look. 'You want me to read it out loud?'

'Yeah, your voice is so deep, you'd be a great narrator.'

'Not with this accent,' Anse mutters and Luciano's about to correct him because he *loves* his accent, but then Anse opens to his bookmark. 'The main character's name is Seamus Viktor.'

'*Seamus Viktor*?'

'I know. My brother is awful with names. I'm quite sure he and my mother pulled names out of a hat when I was born and then combined the two. Dad just wanted to call me Peter.'

'Peter definitely doesn't suit you,' Luciano laughs.

Anse clears his throat. 'Anyway, Viktor has just woken up in hospital after a brutal shoot-out in an old warehouse. The only problem is he's woken up thirty years in the past. The reader knows this, but Viktor doesn't. There's a little date mark at the top of the chapter.'

'Smart.'

'Daniel is quite a good writer as it turns out.'

'Is that pride I hear in your voice?' Luciano nudges him teasingly.

'Don't tell him, please. It'll just go to his head.'

The story is surprisingly complex and Luciano's quickly enamoured wirh the plot. Nestled between Anse's body and the back of the lounge, he can feel the vibrations of his body as he reads, adding inflections and changing his voice to suit the characters. The warmth of his body is comfortable, cosy even, and Luciano doesn't realise he's closed his eyes until Anse stops talking.

'What are you doing?' he mutters.

'I'm going to tell Daniel his book put you to sleep.'

Luciano elbows him.

———

In the afternoon, Anse makes—*makes,* like Luciano wouldn't willingly follow Anse to the edge of the world—Luciano join him on a walk around Lake Burley Griffin. The rain has cleared, but dark clouds hang threateningly by the edge of the horizon. The air is muddy and fresh as they wander up the southern edge of the lake, pass the National Library of Australia, and around the loop of the lake. Luciano stops five times to pat the dogs that come up to them.

Along King Edward Terrace, the looming maple trees have turned brown, and Anse takes Luciano's hand as they walk through the parklands. To their right, the Old Parliament House, the Aboriginal Tent Embassy, and the large spire of New Parliament House dominating the sky, it's flag as big as a double-decker bus.

They walk through the clearing between the National Portrait Gallery and Questacon and Luciano tells Anse about the time Marzia had been too scared to go down the Questacon free-fall ledge, and how every year they visited the War Memorial on the day before ANZAC Day with their mother, and the one time a sky-whale dominated the skies over Canberra. The picture Luciano brings up on his phone is horrifying. Luciano calls it art. Anse is not so sure.

They get coffee from at the National Library and sit on the edge of the lake, watching the sun set over the War Memorial, the sky like a field of colourful poppies.

———

Trattoria is empty and quiet when Anse drops him home.

Home.

'You could stay another night?' Anse suggests as they trudge up into the apartment. Luciano closes the window he'd opened to let out the stench of wet paint. The apartment is cold and barely furnished. He'd invite Anse to stay, but why would he want to stay *here*? With his mother's old mis-matched second-hand furniture and a mattress on the floor when he has a beautiful modern apartment?

He kisses him goodbye. 'I'll be fine, I have work to do.'

Later, Luciano crawls into bed and opens his laptop. There are three applications for the head waiter position waiting in his inbox. He flicks their applications to Marzia for vetting, not bothering to check their resumes.

It's nice to be on the same page with her for once. Often, he's wondered how she's managed to become as successful as she is; the answer has come in the form of one-thirty am emails, of three pm follow-ups, of notes on his business plan and a list of questions to ask his new accountant. She's got connections as a lawyer and a bank of favours to cash in, and Luciano's grateful for the help.

Still, the menu taunts him.

He opens a word document and types: MENU.

M E N U

Menu

MENU

'Fuck.' He deletes word again and again. Marzia's advice floats back to him. Focus on the food. How hard can that be?

———

It's seven in the morning when Rohan finds him in the kitchen chopping tomatoes.

He lingers by the kitchen doorway, thick arms crossed over his chest. 'You okay in here, Luc?'

'I'm good.' He drops the knife to take a sip of coffee. 'Great even. I *finally* figured out why I couldn't write the menu!'

'Yeah? Why's that?'

'Because I haven't eaten everything off the menu! What kind of chef would serve something they haven't tasted before, let alone cooked!'

Rohan doesn't look convinced.

'Are you going to stand there, or are you going to help me eat?'

They spend most of the morning eating, which is both entirely bizarre and completely wonderful, because though Luciano's careful to only cook as little as he can to just get a taste, by lunchtime, there are a dozen dishes scattered between them. Rohan enjoys the *tagliatelle al pesto Genovese* (because it's fresh and tangy, made from fresh basil in the courtyard) and the *Cacciatore* (there's no way Luciano is taking the *Cacciatore* off the menu, though he hopes to burn it less). They both agree to ditch the dark chocolate and beetroot cake from the menu.

At midday they break for coffee, and Luciano continues working through the desserts.

'Honestly, Luciano, this is a waste of both our time.' Rohan sinks his fork into a slice of decadent chocolate cheesecake. 'We both know this is going to be delicious.' He takes a bite. 'Ah, I'm right again.'

Luciano takes a bite. The chocolate is smooth and creamy where it melts on his tongue though the crust is perhaps a little dry. 'That's the last of it then. The last item on my menu.'

'And with the furniture delivery next weekend, you'll be ready to officially reopen.' He claps Luciano on the back. 'Proud of you. You did it.'

Luciano scoffs. He hasn't done it. Not yet.

He won't feel like he's 'done it' until the doors close that first night. Until the jitters he feels when he thinks about opening go away.

'Hey, are you okay?' Rohan sounds frantic but far away. 'Luciano?'

Spots swim through the air between them but he can't blink them away. A wildness takes over his body. His heart beats rabbit-quick. The realisation that he's no longer in control attaches to him, strangles him until it's hard to breathe. Something warm presses against his hand, but he can't curl his fingers around it. Whatever it is, it somehow stays in his grip. Looking down, Luciano realises it's Rohan's hand.

'There you are.' Rohan squeezes his hand. 'Just breathe. Focus on your breathing.'

To Luciano's surprise, he keeps talking. 'Do you remember

the old nature reserve down the block? Remember how it was just bush before all the houses were built, and me and you and our sisters used to go down there and play for hours until our family called out for us to come home?'

Of course, he remembers. That patch of bush had been a million things to them—a natural playground, a pirate ship, the wide and unruly gardens of an abandoned mansion—until one day it was fenced off to be developed into apartments. The land might have been a million things to them, but the fence had quickly reminded them it wasn't theirs.

'You remember the cubby we made there and me and Omala stole Mum's old sheets to make the canopy and she got so mad at us because they were old heirlooms from my *Dādī*?' Rohan lets go of Luciano's hand and replaces it with a glass of water. 'Have you had a panic attack before, Luc?'

Luciano shrugs. He feels better now. 'Yeah, sometimes. It's no big deal, honestly. I've just been super stressed about the restaurant.'

'Luc—,'

'They're scary but they always pass.' It's a lie, but this is the last solid ground of their friendship. If Rohan presses forward, it'll be into unknown territory, into things never spoken about, into things Luciano is still scared to talk about. 'Finish off the cheesecake, I'm going to start on the dishes.'

'When I did my ACL, I was pretty much told that was my career done,' he says as Luciano packs the dishwasher. 'You know, I'd worked almost all my life to play footy and they suddenly said that even with the surgery they weren't sure if I'd be able to take the field again. After I recovered from the surgery, I cleared every medical exam, attended every training session. I was absolutely determined to get back out on the field. Like, wild horses couldn't have stopped me, you know? But when they finally cleared me for play, I couldn't do it. I just stood on the boundary line and I couldn't move.'

'Why?' Luciano asks at last.

Rohan shrugs and picks at his nails. 'I dunno. It was a lot of things. I didn't think I'd be as good. I wanted people to remember how good I was before, not how shit I was after.'

Luciano tries to remember back to Rohan's return to the field; there'd been speculation for weeks and when he was finally named on the team, it was all anyone could talk about at the restaurant, all he read about online or heard on the news. But he doesn't remember anyone doubting his ability. They were all just pleased he'd be back on the field.

'But you went back out there,' Luciano says. 'How'd you do it?'

'I got a therapist and we tried to work through a few things. She really helped me. But I couldn't play footy. Not at that level.' Rohan purses his lips. 'They were right that my career was over after the injury. One way or another.'

'I always thought you were let go after the injury. I didn't realise—,'

Rohan loosens a heavy sigh and wipes his hand over his face again. 'It was easier for people to make assumptions but maybe I should have said something at the time. I don't know, Luciano, it's fucked. But I guess it's kinda my way of saying I know what it feels like to try to live up to something. Even if that other thing is your mother. Or who you used to be.'

Luciano crosses his arms over his chest and leans against the edge of the sink. It's easier not to look at Rohan when he talks, so he finds a spot of the floor and focuses on it.

'I don't sleep through most nights,' he says slowly. Evenly. 'I wake up stressing about things that aren't a big deal. I've always worried. With Mum gone, it's like everything is amplified. Now I need to worry about *everything,* but even when I know things are okay, I still worry. I can't stop.'

'Have you told someone about this?'

Luciano shrugs. 'Not really. I think Anse knows, but he hasn't said anything about it.'

'Your sisters?'

He shakes his head.

'I could go with you if you want. If you wanted to talk to someone, you know, professionally.'

'I don't know.' Luciano knows Rohan can read his hesitation for what it is: fear. Fear of acknowledging the problem. Fear of admitting that he needs help. Fear of the way Rohan, or Anse, or his sisters, or anyone else will react when they hear he needs help, because there's still something in him that is convinced that he's still in control, that this is something he can overcome. 'Would you go with me?'

'Of course, Luciano,' Rohan replies and the lack of hesitation, barely a breath between question and answer, warms something deep inside. Unsure what to do with the surge of feelings, he throws a dirty tea towel at Rohan's head.

———

Anse answers the door half-naked. He's still in his gym shorts, his broad chest glistening with sweat.

Luciano looks him up and down. 'Do you always answer the door like this?'

'I knew it was you. I was about to get in the bath,' he replies. 'Care to join me?'

Luciano throws his overnight bag in Anse's room before following him into the steamy bathroom.

Anse cooks dinner again and while he *doesn't salt the pasta*, he does an admirable job of making pesto. As Anse pours their second glass of crisp chardonnay, Luciano digs into his satchel and presents Anse with a piece of paper.

'Congratulations. You've officially graduated from the Luciano Jilani Culinary School!' He whoops and then pulls the string of a party popper. Streamers fall between them. 'I didn't know if you had a middle name or not, so I just left it off.'

Anse reads over the paper and then glances up at Luciano, visibly confused.

'You don't like it,' Luciano summarises.

'It's not that,' Anse answers quickly. Perhaps too quickly. 'Of course, it was always my dream to graduate from such a *prestigious* institution.'

'You've come so far, I wanted to celebrate that.'

Anse looks back down at the certificate. 'I just don't want to stop with the cooking lessons. I enjoy them. Even before we got together.'

Luciano scoffs. 'And here I was thinking they were just a way to get in my pants.'

'In German, we say *zwei Fliegen mit einer Klappe schlagen.* It means to hit two flies with one swat.'

'Holy shit you're hot when you speak German.'

Anse raises a brow. 'Noted for later, *leibling.* I'm being serious, though. You will continue to teach me?'

'As long as you're willing to learn.'

He's not sure when he dozes off—probably between the third and fourth episode *of RuPaul's Drag Race*—but he wakes to the sound of the shower running in the ensuite. Feeling for his phone, it tells him it's just after six in the morning. Despite the early hour, there's a text message on his phone from Rohan. The therapist office has a last-minute cancellation, and would Luciano like to come earlier?

If you are okay to go by yourself, call and confirm it. Otherwise, we can go together but I couldn't get you in until next month. Sorry, these things are sometimes hard to book into. Whatever works best for you.

'I have an early meeting so I can't stay for breakfast,' Anse says as he shoulders on his suit jacket and kisses Luciano on the cheek. 'You fell asleep on the lounge last night.'

'Before or after Katya's lip-sync?' Luciano wraps himself in Anse's bathrobe, which is black and soft and entirely too big for him and follows Anse into the kitchen.

'After. Can't believe she went home.' He puts the kettle on for coffee. 'Still, it was barely nine.'

'Yeah, I had a bad night's sleep the night before.'

'You're working yourself too hard. You need an assistant. Someone to help you.' Anse grabs his satchel. 'I'll talk to you tonight. Stay as long as you want today. Don't watch ahead on *RuPaul's Drag Race*. I'll know.'

'I can't believe you've never watched it. I mean, it's practically pre-requisite knowledge as a gay man.'

Anse rolls his eyes. 'Goodbye, dear.'

CHAPTER TWENTY-EIGHT

The early morning meeting is entirely unnecessary. What could have been a single email is blown out of proportion and has Franz and the Ambassador's assistant arguing over pedantics for at least twenty minutes. To think he's given up breakfast with Luciano for this. Anse leaves the meeting with a splitting headache and is about to retreat to his office to down some painkillers when Franz calls him into his office.

Franz isn't one for small talk and launches into the conversation immediately. 'I'm taking annual leave for two weeks from Friday. I need you to take on more responsibility.'

It's not meant to sound like Anse's not pulling his weight, and yet it still rubs him the wrong way. 'What do you need me to do?'

'I've sent a schedule of meetings to your email along with detailed handover notes,' he says. 'You will need to report to the Ambassador weekly, if not more frequently, if requested. You'll need to chair the weekly team meetings and the policy meetings.

Hannah will look after communications, but she'll need your help with media. I won't to lie; it will be a busy two weeks.'

This isn't helping Anse's headache. 'I'm sure we'll manage. You won't have to worry.'

Franz let's out a relieved sigh. 'I know it's in good hands with you, Anse. I'm aware you're almost half-way through your contract with us, and it's obvious you've become an integral part of the team.'

He can read between the lines. Prove yourself here and you might get to stay. 'Thank you.'

He doesn't ask why Franz is going away; they don't have that kind of relationship, and while Anse knows it's none of his business, he can't help but wonder. Is he going on holidays with friends? If so, what are Franz's friends like? He pictures them as stiff academics, writers of literary novels, the kind that win awards the papers write about, and the odd politician.

'I understand I'm not giving you much time to prepare and I apologise,' Franz says. 'Something… unexpected has happened and I won't be contactable for much of my leave.'

Anse feels a tinge of guilt at his own thoughts. Perhaps someone is ill or worse.

'I'm sorry your leave won't be an enjoyable time.'

Franz purses his lips. 'I am also. Thank you, Anse.'

Anse retreats from Franz's office and makes a coffee in the kitchen. Luciano has sent him a message asking if he wants to invite Emmy and Daniel to the opening night of Trattoria, and he makes a note to call them after work.

'Hey, you,' says Hannah as she walks into the kitchen. She's dressed in a pair of wide-legged black pants, black shirt and a pair of outrageously bright fuchsia block heels. 'Saw you at Trattoria's community day cooking up a storm.'

'You didn't come to say hello?'

'I didn't want to distract you. You were obviously trying very hard not to burn the sausages.'

'I was,' Anse admits as he sips the coffee. It's bad, but he doesn't have time to walk down the corner shop. His unchecked email inbox has just passed one hundred according the app on his mobile. There's email both flagged 'urgent' and marked URGENT in the subject line. 'Franz just told me he's going away.'

'Yeah, he told me it'll be the Anse party for two weeks,' Hannah grins as she reaches past him to open the cupboard and grab a coffee mug. Only then does he see it.

'You have a ring on your finger.'

'Finally, you notice!' It's a statement solitaire diamond with a gold band. Simple, yet gorgeous. 'He proposed over dinner. At home. Completely unexpected. He cooked us a meal on Saturday night and was insistent on eating at the table, even though we were four episodes deep in a *Will and Grace* marathon.'

'It's lovely. Congratulations.'

'Thank you.' Hannah presses the buttons on the coffee machine and Anse thinks he really *should* go and attend to those emails, but then Hannah says, 'How's Luciano?'

'Good,' then he corrects, 'Stressed. He's preparing to reopen the restaurant.'

'It's opening soon?'

'It is. I put you on the list to come to the opening night. Cameron is invited, too.' Hannah's about to say something when Anse's phone rings in his pocket. It's the embassy. What international crisis has he missed now? 'Shit, I need to take this.'

He takes the call in his office and then tackles his inbox. A few hours later, there's a knock at his door, perhaps a reminder for lunch, or that Luciano is here, but it's Hannah, coat slung over her arm.

'Are you going home soon?'

Anse glances at the clock. It's six. Shit.

'Fuck.' He still has twenty-three unanswered emails, each flagged as urgent. 'I didn't realise it's so late. I have to finish this.'

Hannah gives him a sympathetic smile. 'Don't stay too late, Anse.'

He doesn't leave the office before seven for the rest of the week. On Friday, he gets back to his apartment only to find Luciano's let himself in. There's clean laundry in the dryer and dinner in the oven.

He apologises through frantic kisses until Luciano wriggles in his arms and says, 'Anse, dinner will go cold.'

Let it, he almost wants to reply, but doesn't because Luciano's gone to all this effort, and despite the fact he really wants to take him to bed and work out all the tension of what has been one hell of a week, he sits down and takes a sip of wine and says, 'How was your day, dear?'

Later, Anse presses his lover into the mattress and takes him apart slowly.

Anse rolls onto his back, breathless and flushed and *satisfied* when suddenly Luciano throws a leg over his waist.

'I don't think I'm done with you yet,' Luciano grins devilishly as Anse runs his hands up his muscular thighs. God, he is wild for this man.

———

When they get to the oval, Rohan gives them a such a hard look that Anse is taken aback.

'Clubhouse in five, Luc,' he barks.

Anse glances towards Luciano. 'What was that about?'

'Rohan looks down on sex the night before game day,' Luciano explains as he ties his shoes. Anse doesn't have the guts to ask how he could possibly know. 'See you after the game.'

'Good luck.'

He watches Luciano run toward the clubhouse, shivering at the idea of running around on a freezing mid-May morning in shorts and a sleeveless guernsey.

The Bilbies win, but not by much.

Luciano comes back to the car smelling of freshly mowed grass and sweat. Mud stains his red guernsey, though he quickly shucks it for a pair of trackpants and a hoodie.

'Want to go on a date?' Anse suggests spontaneously.

'I'm covered in sweat and grass,' Luciano complains. The clubhouse only runs cold water and he's refused to shower after the games.

'It doesn't matter.'

They drive south towards the Brindabella mountains, blue-green giants in the warm morning light. He parks at the base of the hiking trail and Luciano immediately balks.

'Anse, it's an eight hundred metre elevation.' He looks up at the trail that meanders through the trees. 'If I collapse, you're carrying me back here.'

'Deal,' Anse says and they set off on the walking track.

Luciano trudges behind, uncharacteristically quiet and Anse's about to suggest they turn around when Luciano sees an echidna waddling across the trail a few metres up ahead. They hang back and let it cross, watching from afar. The path widens to a rocky slope and Anse climbs the boulders first before reaching down to help Luciano climb. He tugs hard as Luciano navigates the last stone. He stumbles, surges forward and hits Anse's chest.

Luciano shoves him off with a laugh. 'I can't believe you just pulled that on me. Bloody oldest play in the book.'

It takes almost an hour to reach the summit, and Luciano complains for the last twenty minutes, but finally they reach the lookout and Anse spreads their picnic blanket along the edge of the rock. The wind tousles Luciano's hair gently.

'Okay,' Luciano admits with a sigh. 'This is pretty great.'

Anse opens the wine. 'Told you.'

He doesn't remind Luciano that they still need to walk back to the car.

On Sunday, they eat croissants in bed, and Anse doesn't mind because he's going to change the sheets anyway. Luciano, sore from the football, soaks in Anse's bathtub until he's prune-like and smells strongly of peppermint and lavender. Sheets flap as they dry on the balcony.

'Are Emmy and Daniel coming to the opening night?' Luciano asks from the table, and Anse realises he's drifting off while reading Keats.

'I think so.' He dog-ears the page he's on.

'Can they sit next to my sisters? Or is that just asking for trouble?'

'They'll be fine. Coffee?'

'No, thanks,' Luciano mutters. 'Apparently, the Minister of Culture's secretary can't sit next to Marzia—Marzia's complaint, not hers—so now I have to rearrange *everything*.'

'It's not a wedding.' Anse kisses Luciano's head. 'It's a *Trat-toria*. Shove them all together.'

'What do you mean?'

'Push all your tables together.'

Luciano turns, horror in his eyes. He opens his mouth to speak but pauses, looks back at his computer, and laughs a little. 'That's actually not a bad idea.'

CHAPTER TWENTY-NINE

I t's Saturday.

The Saturday.

When Luciano steps into his kitchen for the first time, there are six hours before his first dinner service. He makes the sauces, then marinates the meat. It's been a while since he cooked for a hundred people but he's thankful his muscle memory remains; his hands are quick and nimble as he works against the clock. When Rachel, his new sous chef, arrives, she begins making dough for pasta and Madison, his head waiter, works through her safety checklist.

Ned, the barman, rocks up early and makes Luciano a celebratory espresso martini, which he drinks in the bathroom of his apartment as he dons his chef whites for the first time.

'You look great.'

Luciano jumps, almost spilling his martini all over his white jacket. Anse looks entirely too smug.

'Fuck me, I forgot you had a key.'

'I'm only annoyed I didn't get here ten minutes earlier.'

'That would have been more *Psycho* and less sexy. Speaking of sexy,' Luciano steps back to admire his lover who is dressed head-to-toe in black. He runs his fingers down the satin collar of Anse's suit jacket. 'You look good.'

'Special occasion. Thought I better dress up,' he says. 'Daniel and Emmy are downstairs with your sisters.'

'Fuck, people are here already?'

'Don't worry, they're being well-looked after by the barman. We still have time.'

Luciano turns to check himself in the mirror. His buttons are straight, his whites crisp and unstained, his hair is tamed back and out of his face. Heavy hands settle on his shoulders.

'You look great.'

Luciano leans back into the touch. 'What if tonight's a hot mess?'

'It won't be. You can do this.'

'I'm just risking so much.'

'You can do this, Luciano.'

A knock at the door makes them both turn. 'Mister Jilani,' calls Madison. 'The first guests have started to arrive.'

Anse raises his eyebrows. '*Mister* Jilani.'

'I'm trying to just get them to call me Luciano, or chef,' he huffs as he grabs his toque blanche. The hat is mostly for show, but it's was his mother's and it's supposed to be symbolic.

The restaurant is full of people. Madison navigates trays of poured beers, wine and champagne. Earlier in the day, he'd pushed the tables together and let Corina decorate the space; she's covered the tables with crisp white cloths and clusters of delicate native flowers are strewn around the room. There's a photobooth at the entry of the restaurant with a branded flower wall. The flash of a camera lights up the room.

'You did it.' Corina hands him a bouquet full of the same flowers that scatter the room. 'Congratulations, Luc.'

No one else has noticed him yet, and in he reaches out to grab Corina's hand. 'I'm terrified of screwing up, Cor.'

Anse squeezes his shoulder.

'You learnt from the best,' she says.

The words hit him hard. She's prepared him for this.

'To Luciano.' Marzia raises her glass to toast.

'To Mama,' Luciano adds.

A crease forms in Marzia's chin as her jaw clenches. 'To Mama.'

The small crowd claps as Luciano steps into the kitchen for the first time. It's clean and organised as Rachel works through the prep for the entrées. The small menu serves him well: there are only three choices for entrée, and they're ordered in mostly almost equal amounts. It's getting the food out which is the issue. The kitchen makes the dishes faster than the waiters can manage, and Ned can't peel himself away from the busy bar. Madison is fast, but not fast enough. He's about to go out and start delivering the dishes himself when he hears someone call, 'Thanks chef,' through the serving window. He whirls around only to see Anse walking back to the table, a plate in each hand and an apron wrapped around his waist.

The second course service passes without an incident. Ned manages to leave the bar to get the last of the meals out, and then there's a respite, a brief water break for the kitchen staff before dessert orders begin.

Chocolate tart with Madagascar vanilla bean ice cream.

Loretta's Tiramisu.

Lemon myrtle cake with whipped cream and pistachios.

'We've got this, chef,' says Rachel as the orders come through. 'You should go and enjoy yourself.'

Out on the floor, he can hear the joyous chattering of his friends and family, the clink of wine glasses, and Daniel's distinct cackle. Rachel gives him a hard stare.

'There'll be enough nights when you can't leave the kitchen. Go while you can.'

Throwing his apron on the hook, Luciano steps out of the kitchen and is immediately handed a glass of merlot by Ned. For a breath, he just hangs by the bar and soaks in the scene before him: sixty people sit in his mother's old restaurant, the space alive once again. The ghost of a memory of how it used to be bites at him, a lukewarm mix of melancholy and nostalgia.

He finds Anse like a boat to a lighthouse, a calming beacon across a sea of people. He's sitting between Daniel and Corina, a grin on his face as he listens to Marzia tell an outrageous story, her hands moving rapidly.

Anse smiles as Luciano slides in next to him. There are still a few bites of his lemon myrtle cake left on his plate, so Luciano scoops them up with his dessert fork. He turns to Anse and kisses him, tasting the sugar icing that lingers on his lips.

CHAPTER THIRTY

In the week following the reopening of Trattoria, they find time for themselves in the quiet hours of the morning.

Anse wakes in Luciano's bed more often than his own now, and as the nights grow colder, he relishes the warmth of his lover's body against his. Sometimes Luciano is also awake and they make slow, gentle love as the sun rises. But mostly, Anse he studies the way Luciano's eyes twitch as he sleeps, and commits to memory the splay of his eyelashes against his cheek, the murmured noises he makes just for him. Where Luciano would call the ritual 'creepy and uncomfortable,' Anse calls it 'quality time with a busy boyfriend'.

The write-up in the paper about Trattoria's opening night success has booked Luciano out for the next four weekends. Great for business. Not so great for their relationship. Still, he has no grounds to complain.

Luciano's eyes flutter open as Anse kisses his brow. 'I have to go to work.'

'What's the time?'

'Seven.'

'Ugh!' Luciano rolls his face back into the pillow.

Anse presses his mouth against Luciano's bare shoulder. 'I love you. See you tonight.'

'Call in sick. Stay in bed with me.'

'Very tempting.' Anse swings his legs over the bed and slips into Luciano's shower. Luciano's apartment reminds him of his own back in Vienna. It's old, with cracking walls and cornices, polished wooden floorboards and a kitchen as large as the lounge room, which is perfect for someone like Luciano. It's holistically furnished; where his apartment looks like it's straight out of a hotel furnishings catalogue, Luciano's apartment is full of eclectically mismatched furniture of various colours and styles, like he might have gotten it entirely from a second-hand shop.

'Don't laugh but I kinda did.' They eat breakfast on a wobbly three-legged dining table. Anse sits in his suit while Luciano's dressing gown gapes to reveal a tantalising amount of chest hair. 'Hey, my eyes are up here.'

'We should go on a holiday together.'

Luciano chokes on his coffee.

'You're joking? When would we have the time?'

'I have leave. You could ask Rachel to fill in for you. We don't have to go right now, just in a few months. Something to look forward to.'

He's pulled twelve-hour shifts every day for the past week-and-a-half just to get ahead of the next day, only for his effort to be for naught by the time he arrives the next morning because the government, or the press, has moved onto the next big issue. It would be nice to have something to look forward to, Anse considers as he kisses Luciano goodbye. Even if it's just for a few nights.

Still, Hannah has been steadfast through all the extra work: reminding him to eat, to drink coffee, and, most importantly to go home. She's not above calling security on him.

She's done it twice.

Most nights, he arrives at Trattoria just in time for dinner service. Sometimes he covers the bar, as Ned has started driving deliveries on Luciano's Vespa, and other times he waits tables, chatting with patrons—though if he is asked 'whereabouts in Germany are you from?' one more time, he may explode.

'You're the most overqualified waiter I've ever had; I couldn't possibly afford to pay you.' Luciano hands him a glass of wine before collapsing on the lounge.

Anse's feet ache from pacing back and forth across the floor, so he kicks off his oxfords and places his feet on Luciano's lap.

'I'm sure you could think of a few ways.'

Hannah catches him on the way into work. It's late May, and she's dressed in a pair of dark stockings, a floral dress and a fuzzy-black jumper.

'Franz is back.'

'Right on time.' It's a relief. While he hopes he's done a good job, he won't miss the long nights, or the sound of his phone going off during the night, *or* the sound of Luciano complaining when his phone goes off during the night.

Hannah lingers by the doorway. 'Michael from the Canadian Embassy told me that they've filled the last place on the Canadian team.'

His heart quickens. 'Do you know who got the job?'

'No idea. If it was someone from the office, they're keeping it quiet.'

He's not guaranteed a job when the next Ambassador starts their assignment next January, but if someone from the office is moving on, then there will likely be positions to fill here.

'Anse!' Franz calls from his office doorway. 'A moment?'

'You're being summoned,' says Hannah gravely.

Anse brushes past Hannah, adjusts his tie and steps into Franz's office. It smells musty from being locked up for so long, but there's something reassuring about seeing Franz behind his desk again. His face is cleanly-shaven, but Anse can see he's nicked himself with the razor near the curve of his chin.

'How was the leave?' Anse says as he takes a seat. There's an extra-large coffee on Franz's desk.

'Productive,' Franz replies as he types out an email. He sends it off before turning his narrow grey eyes to Anse. 'How are you?'

Should he answer honestly? If so: wrecked, exhausted, and a little bit horny.

'Fine,' Anse replies. 'It's good to have you back.'

Franz gives him a tight smile. Perhaps the first smile he's ever seen grace Franz's face because immediately Anse thinks how strange it looks. 'You did a good job while I was away. People noticed. *I* noticed.'

'Thank you.'

Franz takes another sip of his coffee. 'I'm going to Brisbane at the end of July. It's a three-day meeting and then a two-day summit. The Ambassador will be there, as well as the in-coming Ambassador. It would be advantageous to have you come with me.'

'Of course,' Anse says. 'Thank you for thinking of me.'

Satisfied, Franz turns back to his computer. 'Now go home.'

'Pardon?'

'I can see the hours you've put in over the last few weeks. Your well over your flexible leave balance. Enjoy your Monday, Anse.'

'But there's the Greyson negotiations—,'

'Work can wait.' Franz pauses and turns back to Anse. 'I'll admit, adjusting to the Australian culture was more difficult than I anticipated. You would think it would be easy knowing the language and what not, but it was the mindset that was the most difficult for me. The work ethic is also notably different.' He pauses. 'It's not a bad thing to have a 'sickie' once in a while.'

He's *not* about to tell him Luciano suggested the very same just that morning.

'But life is too short not take a Monday off occasionally, Anse. You're welcome to stay, of course, I cannot force you to take leave. But I do hope you will go.'

So, he leaves. He doesn't turn on his computer or check his emails. He doesn't even write an out-of-office. Instead, Anse says goodbye to Hannah, drives back home to Luciano's apartment and slips between the covers.

'I knew you went back to bed after I left for work,' he says into Luciano's tousled hair. Luciano rolls over, delight dancing in his eyes.

CHAPTER THIRTY-ONE

Snow comes early in June, well before the Queen's Birthday weekend, and Luciano curls against Anse's body in the crisp early mornings, lamenting as he slips out of the covers to go to work, or to the gym, or whatever he busies himself doing in the early hours of the morning. Now that Luciano works late, Anse doesn't hassle him out of bed as much, but he still scoffs at the way Luciano stretches out across the mattress as he gets up.

'You could come for a run with me.'

'I *run* a restaurant.' Luciano replies into the pillow. He feels a kiss against his cheek and then the door to the bedroom closes and he drifts back to sleep.

Most mornings, he'll get up around ten-thirty, make a coffee and go downstairs to start on the prep. Today, he makes pasta, a few cakes and a fresh batch of pesto, using the rest of the basil plant before it's destroyed by frost. In the afternoon, he samples three new local bottles of red wine. The merlot is lovely, and he orders two cases, but he passes on the pinot noir and shiraz.

The rest of the afternoon is a blur of bookwork and stocktake. Briefly, he checks his social channels. Corina runs his Instagram and Facebook account and he sends her a few shots of the recipes, an artsy shot of a wine glass and a picture of Anse wrapped up in a blanket watching last night's episode of *Ru Paul's Drag Race*. The third photo isn't for sharing on the internet, but just as a teasing brag.

Corina sends back a photo of Rohan cooking her dinner.

Corina: You've inspired him. He made pasta.

Luciano: OMG. Was it good?

Corina: God no

Luciano: Also, why wasn't I invited to the dinner party?

Corina doesn't reply to his last message.

———

'Let's go to the snow.' Anse's talented fingers work out a knot in Luciano's shoulder. 'Luciano?'

'What?' his voice is heavy with sleep.

'I miss the snow.' Anse presses his thumbs between Luciano's shoulder blades.

'I hate the snow.'

'I hate the ocean.'

'Touché.' He's too blissed out to have a serious conversation. That, he realises, is probably Anse's plan. Wicked man.

'It could be that break away we talked about.'

'I thought the break was in a few months. Ow, fuck!' Anse's fingers dig into a sore spot against his spine. He'd overextended at footy this afternoon; gone for a mark when he knew he shouldn't have, and now he's paying for it.

'Sorry.' His warm hands disappear for a moment only to

return with more lavender oil. 'We could go up to the mountains. Have a break away.'

Between the restaurant opening and Anse's job, they've barely had time to themselves. Something like guilt crawls through his gut at the thought that he's been neglecting some aspect of their relationship.

'That'd be nice.' Luciano tucks his chin against his shoulder, looking back at Anse as his long fingers rub work on his lower back. 'Have you heard anything else about your job? You know, what happens after December?'

Anse keeps focused on the task. 'Only that the Ambassador is moving on to Canada. Hannah says the Canadian team has been filled. There might be some restructuring here.'

'What if you don't get it?'

Luciano hears the squitter of the oil bottle and is about to tell Anse he's had enough when strong hands begin working the muscles of his left thigh.

'We'll figure it out,' Anse says. 'We have time.'

Six months. They have six months to figure it out.

'If you were offered a position, would you stay?' Luciano's leg goes to Anse's shoulder as he works the front of his thigh.

'Of course I would.' He kisses the inside of his ankle.

'I'm being serious.' He wants to turn over, but he can't. It feels ridiculous to be talking into his pillow. 'It would mean you wouldn't go back to Austria for a while.'

'I have nothing there anyway.' Luciano knows that's a lie. There's his family's apartment and the friends that he mentions occasionally. Plus, he couldn't imagine just *leaving* his hometown permanently feels as dismissive as Anse is making it out to be.

Anse drops Luciano's leg back onto the bed and, to his surprise, falls down onto the pillow beside him.

Luciano sits up on his forearms and scoots closer. 'I'm not ready to lose you.'

'You haven't lost me, Luciano.'

'I might.'

'We'll figure it out when we get there.'

'But we know it's coming, we should plan —,'

Anse kisses him. Luciano knows it's just to shut him up, but his traitorous body melts anyway.

'So,' Anse murmurs against his lips. 'Where did we land on the snow?'

———

Luciano takes the first Sunday off in June and Anse rents a cottage in the Blue Mountains. While it won't be skiing conditions, they can still go on hikes and sample cheeses from the local dairy farms. Luciano makes it clear he's in it for the cheeses.

They detour through Sydney to meet up with Daniel and Emmy. Their home is a beautiful Victorian townhouse with white painted bricks and navy-blue iron lattice. Emmy welcomes them into the house which is longer than it is wide, and frightfully cold.

It's a warm winter morning, so they sit on the deck and have an early lunch. Later, as Daniel and Anse work through the notes on his manuscript, Emmy gives Luciano a tour of her compact backyard garden.

'Sometimes I just dream of living on a property, you know,

being able to have a real garden,' she says as she picks a handful of spinach.

'No luck on the job front, then?'

'I put in for a transfer but it's always a luck of the draw.' The pristine white head of a cauliflower pokes through a spiral of thick leaves. 'How are things going at the restaurant?'

'We got a few good reviews. One in *Food Weekly* which really helped put it on the map. We're ramping up our delivery service too. No one goes out in Canberra in winter, so we'll have to go to them.'

'That Tuscan pork belly you made recently looked amazing. Anse is a lucky man.'

'I'm aware.'

Luciano looks up to see Anse standing on the edge of the garden bed.

'Ah, we were saying only nice things,' Emmy says as she gives Anse a handful of small dirty beetroots. 'Here. Last of the season.'

That night, when Anse and Luciano are alone in the small cabin on the edge of the Blue Mountains, he mixes the beetroot with cocoa and makes a deep, rich cake that causes Anse's eyes roll back into his head—a feat which he's only ever been able to achieve a handful of times, and never with food. He barely lets Anse finish the slice before he slips onto his lap, chasing the flavour on his lips.

The morning is briskly cold. Light floods into the large panoramic window and Luciano wakes to snow dusting the mountain peaks. Beside him, Anse is deep asleep. It's almost seven in the morning, but he's not about to protest the surprising lie-in and rolls to join his lover in slumber.

A moment later, Luciano jumps to the harsh call of his name.

'We overslept!'

Luciano blinks and checks his phone. It's almost ten in the morning. Damn. They really did.

'So?' he scoffs. 'It's a holiday.'

Anse stands in the doorway to the ensuite, brushing his teeth. The towel around his waist is secured by a very flimsy knot. A small bead of water trickles down his chest and Luciano follows it through the contours of his abs, into the thin trail of hair that leads—

'Come back to bed.'

Anse looks down at his towel and Luciano's heart quickens. Hooking his finger into the top of the towel, he begins loosening the knot. It unravels from around his body, hanging from where Anse holds the towel by his navel.

'Well that was quite the show,' Luciano grins only to get a mouthful of damp towel as Anse hurls it across the room.

'Get up,' Anse says as he shuts the door to the ensuite. 'It's a three-hour hike.'

'I promise I could go for three hours if that makes any difference.' His call is ignored. Defeated, Luciano falls back into the pillows.

'Up,' Anse orders again as he emerges from the ensuite wearing latex leggings and a hoodie. 'Or no cheese.'

With a heaving sigh, Luciano gets out of bed and trudges into the shower. 'Just a fair warning. I'm going to complain most of the way.'

———

His legs are on fire.

He's never felt so betrayed by his body before.

That's not entirely true: there was that one night he threw up after only four beers, and another night when a one-night-stand had told him it's completely *normal* and not his fault *at all*.

Ahead, Anse struggles for breath as they climb higher. The mountains are misty and snow-capped. It looks cool as fuck, but Luciano still would have preferred making Anse puff in a wildly different way.

Anse waits for him at a lookout, and they catch their breath while gazing out over the ravine. The sky is overcast and every now and then Luciano feels light rain hit his cheeks.

'I think there's a cable car a little higher,' Anse says as he takes a sip of water. 'It'll take us to the summit.'

The girl at the tourist information centre had said there'd been reports of snow up on the summit this morning; it was a steeper hike, but Anse had a sort of child-like fixation on seeing snow. They hadn't come all this way to *not* see snow.

'You're giving me a massage when we get back,' Luciano groans as they continue upwards. 'Even Rohan doesn't work me this hard.'

The cable car cuts through the cloud cover, revealing eucalyptus gums dusted in snow. Luciano breath fogs up the glass to look below. The treetops drip with powdered snow like thick icing. Despite the clear sky, the summit is still covered in a blanket of snow. It's a little slushy around the cable car, but by the lookout it's wonderfully loose and fluffy and Luciano quickly forms a snowball, pegging it at his lover's head.

'Fuck off.' Anse cries as the snowball hits him between the shoulders.

'There. We came. We saw the snow. We got cold. Can we please go back to the cabin now and lie in front of the fire and take off all our clothes?'

Anse makes a show about considering the request, bobbing his head back and forth, before letting out a laborious breath. 'Fine.'

'Ah, thank you for compromising. You're so wonderful. Truly, the best boyfriend.'

'Wait.' Anse stops him with a gentle hand and pulls out his phone. 'I want a photo.'

'Then take one.'

He gives Luciano a look. 'Of us. Together. I want to send it to my Mum. I realised we don't have any photos of us together.'

Luciano is about to crack a joke, but then he realises Anse isn't joking. And he's right. They don't have any nice photos together; no other photographs other than the ones he takes when Anse's not looking.

'Fine.' He trudges through the sludge back to the misty lookout. It really is a gorgeous view. He slips under Anse's arm as he takes the picture, and then, at the last minute, grabs his head and kisses him passionately.

Luciano Jilani is with Anse Meyer at Evan's Lookout, Blue Mountains, NSW

(Eighteen likes including Max Gruber and others)

Comments

Rohan Ahuja: Good to see you keeping up that off-week fitness, Luc! 😉

Corina Jilani: Omg you guys are soooo cute

Marzia Jilani: You're near Sydney and you didn't tell me?

CHAPTER THIRTY-TWO

The end of June is a blur. Anse goes on an unexpected trip to Sydney when Franz gets sick. He spends four days stuck to the Ambassador's side, drinking coffee, going over documents and speaking almost entirely in German.

The Ambassador, Her Excellency Amelia Wiess, comes from Graz and has a husband and twin girls at home. On their first day, she asks Anse to call her Millie when it's just them. Not Amelia, or Mrs Weiss, and certainly not Her Excellency.

It's all quite smooth sailing after that.

'How do they feel about moving to Ottawa?' Anse asks as they get a drink in the airport lounge. It's a forward question, but Millie considers with a shrug.

'Not well,' she says. 'The children started school here. They have their friends. My husband has his work, his friends. We've been here for five years. It will be hard to uproot our lives and say goodbye.'

'I find myself in the same situation,' Anse admits.

The flight back to Canberra takes only forty-five minutes and Anse can't help but think back to the last time he'd seen the city from above: so low and spread-out and completely unremarkable. Now, he knows the mountains, the curve of the roads, the vein-like streets that will take him from the airport to his home, to his bed, to his boyfriend.

Though he needn't have worried about getting home to Luciano, because as Anse comes down the escalator to collect his baggage, he sees Luciano waiting for him in the middle of the empty airport, wrapped in a large coat and scarf.

'Finally,' Luciano groans as he launches himself into Anse's arms. Anse catches him on reflex, and Millie laughs as she passes them and continues on to the baggage carousel.

'Luciano,' he chides. 'You're making a scene.'

Luciano, never one to be discouraged, shrugs him off. 'You are worth making a scene over. Is this a new suit?'

'It is.' He drops Luciano and instead takes his hand before joining Millie by the baggage carousel. It's such a humbling experience: even the Ambassador to Australia doesn't get her baggage quicker than anyone else.

'Your Excellency, this is my boyfriend, Luciano,' he says. 'Luciano, this is Her Excellency, Amelia Weiss, Ambassador to Australia.'

'Nice to meet you, Your Excellency. You should come around my place for dinner one night. Free of charge of course.'

At the Ambassador's perplexed look, Anse quickly adds, 'Luciano runs a restaurant. Trattoria, in Pearce.'

She turns back to Luciano. 'You're Loretta Jilani's son.'

Luciano's eyes light up. 'You knew her?'

'Of course.' She steps forward to pick her bag off the carousel. 'That woman taught me how to trick the twins into eating vegetables with her bolognese. I'd love to take you up on the offer.' She turns back to Anse and shakes his hand firmly. 'Have a nice weekend, both of you.'

'I like her,' Luciano says as he takes Anse's suitcase back to Rohan's van.

'Why don't you just get a car?' Anse sighs as he climbs in the front seat. It's full of tools and equipment and three takeaway coffee cups.

'The Vespa is me. It's *iconic.*'

'It's not practical.'

Anse does his best to ignore his lover's abhorrent driving skills, but neither can ignore the awful park job Luciano does as he pulls up out the front of Trattoria.

'Manuals,' he shrugs.

———

Franz is sick for longer than expected. Hannah makes everyone in the office get flu shots but then a new environmental policy from Germany drops and it looks like Austria's going to back it and it could make international relations *tight,* to say the least. He spends all afternoon and much of the evening poring over policy until his eyes are heavy and security hassles him out of the office.

'You're going to get sick,' Luciano tells him on Saturday morning as he stretches for footy. It's early July and freezing. Anse has three layers on *and* gloves.

'You're running around in a singlet and shorts for an hour-and-a-half. Remind me again how this is a winter sport?'

'Won't be for much longer,' Luciano huffs. 'If we don't win this game, we probably won't make finals.'

They don't win the game. Ahmed nails a few last-minute goals but it's not enough.

Monday creeps up on him like a headache.

Luciano, barely awake, rolls over to check on him. 'Anse? You're still here?'

Blearily, he checks the time on his phone. It's nine-thirty. Fuck.

'I'm late,' he groans and heaves his aching body out of bed. God, he feels awful.

'You're sick,' Luciano's voice is thick with sleep. 'You were coughing all night.'

'I'll just work from home, then.'

Luciano presses an icy hand to his forehead, then to his cheek. 'You need to rest, Anse. You're all hot.' He clambers out of bed and disappears into the kitchen, reappearing sometime later with a glass of water and two small pills. 'Do *not* check emails on your phone.'

'Bossy,' Anse complains as he puts his phone down, both because Luciano asked him to and because he can't seem to focus on the screen.

Luciano makes a pot of chicken soup before he goes to work but either Anse's tastebuds have gone on strike or it's the blandest soup Luciano's ever made. Eventually, he tires of *RuPaul's Drag Race* and goes to bed.

'Anse, you're hot all over.' Someone has climbed in next to him and is unbuttoning his shirt. A cold hand rubs salve on his bare chest.

'Did you like the soup?' A pause. 'Anse?'

The cold lasts four days.

Then Luciano gets it.

CHAPTER THIRTY-THREE

In retrospect, Luciano knows he should have cast out Anse to recover in his own apartment, delivering him enough soup to sustain him during his enforced quarantine. He would have only had to suffer his whining. That would have been preferable over the hell he's been dragged through for the past few weeks.

The cold makes its way through his team. First, the head waiter Madison gets it. His accountant who works off-site gets it. Even Rohan has the sniffles one afternoon.

'Luc, bad news,' Rachel emerges from the office with a solemn look on her face.

'Don't tell me.'

'Ned's just emailed that he's got the flu. Doctor's orders to stay off food service for a week.'

'Fuck,' Luciano groans as he begins peeling onions. 'Shit. Okay, you focus on food service with the team, I'll take any deliveries that come through.'

Service begins without a hitch: they've got six bookings,

totalling forty-two people. It's a cold July night so walk-throughs will be minimal. It's the takeaway that will make them the money. It's one of Marzia's genius ideas: taking the prestige of dining in the restaurant, a curated menu of pasta, slow-cooked meat and hearty vegetable dishes, and serve it in eco-friendly sugarcane fibre containers.

He's confident in his plan. Service is where Rachel really shines. During prep, she's quiet, driven and focused, but as soon as service starts, the kitchen comes alive. He's never known someone to have as much fun when they cook as Rachel. Even his own mother became a different person during service, shaped by years in the rigours of European culinary schools and restaurants.

Luciano gets it. It's a business after all, but Rachel brings so much *excitement* to the kitchen. She has a crop of electric blue hair and routinely wears bright red lipstick to work. Her hands are fast, and her apron is never messy, and she has a directness to her that's firm but not rude. It's a pleasure to watch her work.

Running his hand across the Vespa's cherry red paint, he greets the scooter like an old friend before loading up the deliveries.

The curly inner suburb roads are poorly lit by dim electric lamplights in frosted glass casings, but in their light, Luciano sees his breath turn to mist.

Looping through the suburbs and liaising with the team back at the restaurant, Luciano gets through twenty orders before he makes a fuel stop near Anse's office.

Anse greets him at the embassy doorway and takes the warm container of food gratefully. 'It's fucking freezing out here. Where's Ned?'

'Sick,' Luciano breathes as he hands Anse his dish. A notification comes through on his phone. 'Shit, I gotta go.'

'Kiss me, at least,' Anse complains and Luciano runs back to him, hastily grabs the collar of his jacket, tugs him forward and kisses him passionately.

'Now I *really* have to go.'

'I need to talk to you after work.'

That makes Luciano stop in his tracks. 'Like… *talk* talk?'

'Franz's going to Canada. He was the vacancy from our office.'

Luciano's phone rings again. He really needs to get going. 'Shit, what does that mean for you?'

'More late nights, probably.'

'I feel like we barely see each other.'

'That's because we barely see each other.' Anse presses a kiss to his forehead. 'I'll see you when I get home. We can talk about it more.'

He mounts the Vespa as fog settles in the valley. The streets are quiet and dark. The last order of the night is to a man in a townhouse in the next suburb over. Back at the restaurant, they've met their KPI. It's been a good night.

Kicking up the stand on the Vespa, Luciano pulls out onto the street and lets the scooter coast down the hill. Ahead, a Jeep approaches the intersection at the base of the hill. Luciano watches as the car slows briefly, but then the tyres begin to move again and the car lurches forward.

Luciano slows down, but the car keeps coming.

Luciano's heart stutters. The engine is far too loud and too close. He tries to turn the Vespa, but he feels his control slipping away. He looks up.

All he sees is bright white light.

CHAPTER THIRTY-FOUR

'It's unlocked!' Anse calls out as Luciano knocks on the door to the apartment incessantly. 'Did you forget your key again?'

The door opens slightly. 'It's not Luciano. It's me. Rachel.'

Fuck, he thinks and scrambles to find his discarded boxers. 'Shit, give me a second!'

'It's cool,' she says through the crack. 'Um, is Luc here? I'm just ready to lock up.'

'He's not with you?'

'No. I thought he was up here with you.'

Anse towels his hair dry and meets Rachel by the front door. 'I haven't seen him since he dropped dinner in my office a few hours ago.'

Fear flashes in Rachel's eyes and it makes Anse's stomach clench. 'He didn't come back from his delivery round. I've called and called his phone, but I think it's dead.'

Anse finds his phone and calls Luciano's mobile. It goes straight to voicemail. 'Fuck. I'll call his sister.'

Corina picks up after three rings. 'Hey, what's up?'

'Is Luciano with you?' he asks, straight to the point.

'No?' Corina says. 'Is he not with you?'

'No. And he hasn't been back to the restaurant since earlier this evening.' Rachel is now pacing the floor, her heavy-duty shoes squeaking on the floorboards. 'Maybe he's with Rohan.'

There's a pause before Corina says, 'Rohan's with me right now.'

'Fuck.' He pushes his wet hair from his face. What does he do now? He can hear Rohan talking in the background, but he's not exactly sure what he's saying—the phone isn't close enough and his accent is too strong. 'What's he saying?'

'Hold on, I'll give him the phone.'

'Anse, mate,' Rohan says, his tone clear and confident. 'We're going to meet you at the police station in Woden, do you know where that is?'

'I can look up directions,' he says and then hangs up. Rachel is waiting by the door as Anse grabs his coat. 'We're heading to the police station.'

'I've got a kid at home,' she says. 'I've locked up downstairs, but I can't be out much longer. I'm so sorry, Anse.'

He wants to stop and tell Rachel it's not her fault, it could be a number of things—he could have broken down on the side of the road, or got caught talking with an old friend, or maybe he's downstairs right now, and they've just missed each other and all this worry is for nothing—but there's something that tells him this isn't just one of those near misses. This is the real thing, and as much as he wants to comfort Rachel, he needs to get down to the police station, so he squeezes her shoulder, tells her to go home and then grabs the keys to his car.

At the police station, a young officer looks up from her computer and says, 'Missing persons usually have to be gone twenty-four hours before we consider them missing.'

'This isn't like him,' Anse insists.

'What was he wearing the last time you saw him?'

Fuck, what was he wearing? 'Um, it was a black leather jacket because he was riding the Vespa.'

A glance to her computer, and then, back at Anse. 'Details on the vehicle?'

'It's red. I don't know its plate number. It's just a red Vespa, not a common sight around here.'

Her mouth purses into a long thin line and she rises from her desk. 'Come with me, sir.'

His stomach churns as he walks into behind the office and into a small, sterile room. The police officer instructs him to sit, and then he's alone for five minutes—just him, and his thoughts, and a heavy weight in his gut—before a woman enters and says, 'Mr Meyer, I'm Constable Diaz. My colleague mentioned you made a report about a red Vespa?'

'I'm looking for my boyfriend,' Anse clarifies. 'He drives a red Vespa. Luciano Jilani.'

She slides into the chair across from Anse. He can already tell it's not good news.

'Mr Jilani has been involved in a car crash, and he's been taken to hospital with serious but non-life-threatening injuries. We've tried to contact his next-of-kin, his mother, Loretta.' She pauses to let the information sink in and all Anse can hear is how he sucks in air, breathing deep, his heart a flurry of worry. 'How long have you known Mr Jilani?'

He pulls his phone out of his pocket, finds the photo of them
—the *only* photo of them—in the Blue Mountains three weeks
ago and slides it across the table. 'He's my boyfriend. We've
been together for six months.'

Constable Diaz glances at the photo before sliding Anse's
phone back.

'His mother is dead.' It comes out harsher than he means.

'I'm sorry.'

'Can I see him, please?' Anse says. 'I can give you the details
to contact his sister, Corina.'

'I'll give you a ride to the hospital, Mr Meyer,' Constable
Diaz says. 'But I need to get a statement from you when we're
there.'

He texts Corina to meet them at the hospital and that Luciano
is hurt but he's going to be okay. In the car, he tells the constable
about his night, how he'd worked until seven-thirty when the
security kicked him out of the office, how he'd gone home and
ate dinner and showered, and that was when Rachel had knocked
on the door. The constable drives in silence. Anse can hear his
heartbeat thumping in his ears. An ambulance whirls past them
and he shuts his eyes tight.

When he arrives, Rohan's standing in the waiting room, his
phone pressed to his ear.

'Anse's here now with the police,' he says into the phone as
they pass. 'Yeah, I'll ask Corina to call you tomorrow. No, no,
the doctor said he's going to be fine. You don't have to come
until the weekend, Marzia—,'

The constable finds a nurse, who shows Anse through the
too-bright hallways and into a recovery room. Corina sits beside
the bed. A limp, bloodied hand rests in hers.

'Corina,' he squeezes her shoulder and looks down at

Luciano. Tubes criss-cross over his chest, which is stained yellow from the antiseptic and littered with adhesive bandages. His right shoulder has been splintered and his arm put into a cast. Already, the skin around his left eye is mottled purple and blue.

Corina's other hand covers his. 'He's fractured his right arm and collarbone, and he has a few broken ribs from the fall, but he'll be okay. They said he kept asking for you, but his phone was destroyed during the crash.'

'Who hit him?'

A sob escapes her throat. 'They just left him. They left him on the road, Anse. How could someone *do* that?'

Rohan slips back into the room and gives Anse a meaningful look before crouching down next to Corina and offering her a tissue. 'Let's go get a coffee, huh? Decaf. Luciano will be okay here with Anse.'

Corina nods. 'Yeah. Coffee would be good.'

Settling into the chair beside Luciano, he checks the time on his phone. It's close to eleven. He should tell Franz what's happened and take tomorrow off. His eye catches the approach of a nurse, who checks Luciano's vitals and goes over his charts, only offering Anse a tight smile. His name badge says 'Michael'.

'When will he wake up?' Anse asks.

'Usually it takes thirty minutes or so,' Michael replies. 'Give him a bit.'

Anse waits. He rubs at the blood underneath Luciano's fingernails, cleans around his cuticle, traces the veins of his wrist with feather-light touches. There are scrapes up his arm and bruises underneath his bandages. His right hand, which rests on his stomach, is encased in plaster and his fingers are slightly swollen. Anse brings his good hand up to his lips, kisses his knuckles, his fingertips, moves to rub them against his cheek.

A few minutes later, Anse's pulled out of his thoughts by a grunt. Luciano lurches and the hand Anse holds in his jerks, pulls back. Suddenly, Michael is back by their bedside, urging Luciano to lay back down.

'Take it easy, Luciano. You're in the hospital.'

Luciano groans and collapses back against the pillow. One of his eyes open but the other, Anse realises, is swollen shut.

Anse feels him squeeze his hand.

He clears the cotton from his throat at the hazy look in Luciano's eyes and feels his hand begin to tremble. 'Hey. Do you feel okay?'

His body shivers violently.

'Jitters are normal,' Michael assures. 'Luciano, do you know where you are?'

'Hospital.'

'And how are you feeling?'

It takes Luciano a moment to respond. 'Good. Can we go home now?'

'Soon,' Michael says. 'You were in a car crash. Do you remember that?'

Luciano hesitates. 'There was a bright light and then I was on the ground.' His eyes flit to Anse. 'You're crying.'

'I know.' Anse wipes his face on his sleeve. 'Sorry, I'll try to stop.'

'I'm okay,' Luciano tries to assure him.

'I know you are,' Anse replies but the tears won't stop. He can't *make* them stop. Michael hands him a tissue with a knowing smile.

'Comes with the job. I'll give you guys another twenty minutes but then I have to transfer you to a ward where he can get some rest. We can discuss recovery and rehabilitation options in the foyer.'

When Michael leaves, Anse slips in next to Luciano on the bedside, careful not to brush against him. He rubs his thumb over Luciano's cheek, catching an eyelash that's fallen. Luciano leans into his touch.

'Are you in pain?' Anse asks, barely a whisper.

'Not anymore. I think I'm on a lot of drugs.'

Anse laughs. 'I think you are, too.'

He covers his hand on top of Luciano's in a futile attempt to stop the jittering, as if he can warm him just from the one spot. His body looks so delicate, so damaged on the bed, it's hard to see him like this.

Corina rushes in. Her breath is heavy with the smell of coffee as she crowds in close. 'Fuck, Luciano, I was so worried.'

'I'm okay,' he assures. 'What about the Vespa?'

Corina bristles at the question. 'The *Vespa?* Luciano, you almost *died* and you ask me about the *Vespa?* Just wait until Marzia hears about this.'

Luciano laughs weakly. 'No, don't tell her.'

'Oh, I am telling her *everything*. Get prepared for a lecture of massive proportions.'

'Please, have mercy.'

After twenty minutes, Luciano is transferred to a ward to sleep and Corina and Rohan drive Anse back to the Kingston apartment. Not Luciano's apartment, which is where he now keeps most of his clothes, as well as his toothbrush, but he's too drained to protest. He steps into the apartment and inhales the scent of fake leather and synthetic carpet—a smell the apartment has never lost—before collapsing in his bed.

CHAPTER THIRTY-FIVE

L uciano hears Marzia before he sees her. The tell-tale *click click click* of her heels on the tiled hallway precede the brisk demand to the nurse, 'I'm looking for my idiot brother, Luciano Jilani.'

'Oh no,' Corina whispers. 'Incoming. Prepare yourself, Anse.'

Anse gives Luciano a look to ask, *is she joking?* But then Marzia steps into Luciano's cubicle and immediately cries, 'I told you that thing was a fucking death machine.'

Luciano calmly finishes his porridge and puts down his spoon. It's bland and gloopy but he's starving and Michael, his nurse, has promised that if Luciano eats his breakfast, he'll get him a *real* coffee from the cafeteria. 'Nice to see you too, Marzia.'

'Holy fuck,' Marzia says as she approaches his bedside. 'Your eye. Your *face*.'

'I promise it feels as bad as it looks,' Luciano says. 'Or at least, they say it will when the drugs wear off. Thanks for coming.'

'No one called me,' Marzia says. 'I had no idea. How did they not call me?'

'Government records still have Mum as our next-of-kin,' Corina explains. 'If Anse didn't call me, it could have been hours before the police tracked us down.'

Luciano turns to Anse and pushes a lock of long hair away from his eyes. He looks a wreck; hair untamed and falling about his face, dressed in a pair of jeans and a hoodie.

'You look like you could use a coffee,' Marzia says and Luciano realises she's talking to Anse. 'Come on, my shout.'

'Thanks Mar,' Luciano says before urging Anse to go.

He gives Luciano a look like he doesn't want to leave but wordlessly gets up and follows Marzia out of the cubicle.

'To be a fly on the wall in that café,' Corina jokes. 'How are you holding up? The doctor said you can probably go home tomorrow.'

'Fine,' Luciano says. 'Except I can't shower, or wipe my own arse, or feed myself and I can't work or play football and I'm really fucking sick of hospitals.' He sits back on the too-hard pillows. Deep down, he knows he shouldn't complain, but after everything their mother went through, hospitals are still a sore spot for them all. 'You know, Anse gave me the weirdest shower this morning. He literally had to help me put on underwear and not in a sexy way.'

'He loves you,' Corina says. 'It probably wasn't that weird for him.'

'I feel so stupid, Cor.'

'Hey. It wasn't your fault. You weren't in the wrong here.'

'That doesn't make me feel any better.'

The police come later and take Luciano's statement. A hit-and-run, no witnesses, no CCTV camera, and though neighbours heard the crash, it's not enough to go on. Even the driver who found Luciano on the side of the road—a seventeen-year-old coming home from a late-night ice-cream run—couldn't identify the car. Shit, he barely remembers being found, barely remembers anything about last night except for working his rounds and waking up in a hospital bed.

'There's a gap between when I saw you for dinner and when I woke up in hospital,' he admits to Anse later. 'I don't think there's much more than I can tell them.'

'You don't want to find the person who did this?' Anse asks.

He knows that he's supposed to want to find the driver; supposed to want closure and a resolution, supposed to want a sense of justice. But he also knows the street was dark and the night was cold and foggy. There's a tiredness in him he can't quite explain; something more than physical. He's exhausted.

'I just want to get on with my life.'

———

'Now, it's normal to be in pain for a few days after you leave hospital.' Michael sits by Luciano's bedside with a prescription notepad and a lollipop. 'Take the medication as you need. You'll have enough for a week. It's also completely normal to suffer broken sleep, insomnia, and vivid dreaming for up to a week after surgery. Talking to someone can help.'

'How do you—,'

'I have access to your medical records which I promise to use for good and not evil.' Luciano knows it's supposed to be a joke, because Michael's face lights up, as if expecting a laugh.

'Tough crowd. Anyway, talking to your therapist about it could help'

'Creepy. What else do you know about me?'

'I know that in a few weeks' time when I come to the restaurant, you're going to give me a free meal for taking such good care of you.'

Luciano scoffs. 'A free glass of wine. *House* wine.'

'I nursed you back to health! Surely I'm at least worth a discount off a meal.' Michael hands Luciano the prescriptions and the lollipop. 'Don't skip out on your doctor's appointments and keep wearing the sling. I hope I don't see you back here again, Luciano.'

Anse takes him home. He almost cries with relief as he sinks into his own bed again. Anse says something, but he's already drifting off to sleep, lulled by the strong prescription painkillers.

Rohan has made dinner by the time Luciano wakes up, groggy and tired. He still smells like the hospital, like sickly-sweet chemicals mixed with his own sweat. Anse helps him shower again, dresses him, and brushes leave-in conditioner through his hair.

'I love your curls,' he murmurs as he drags the comb through again. The attention feels nice. Luciano feels less like a burden and more like a figure of worship under Anse's ministrations.

Still, six months he worked to reopen the restaurant, and now, barely two months into service, he'll be out for weeks. What's worse is that he can't even watch Anse cook without feeling a pang of jealously. Of guilt. Of frustration. Because as hard as Anse tries, and as well as he takes direction and adds more pepper when Luciano tells him to, *he is still a bad cook.*

The pain only gets worse.

He spends the majority of his second day home in bed,

exhausted at the mere feat of getting up the stairs to his apartment.

'Shouldn't you be at work?' Luciano asks as Anse feeds him luke-warm soup for lunch.

'I can't leave you by yourself, Luciano.'

'But what about the promotion?' Another mouthful.

'Won't hinge on whether I take a day or two off to look after you,' he says. 'Do you like the soup?'

'Yeah.' he tries to sound enthusiastic but he knows that Anse doesn't buy it. He's fed another mouthful.

Luciano sleeps for most of the afternoon and by the time he wakes, it's four in the morning. The bed is cold and empty. Blearily, he gets up, manages to piss without causing a mess, and checks the loungeroom. Anse sleeps on the lounge, his body curled under a thin blanket. The light from his laptop screen gives his skin a dull white glow. Luciano can see there's eighteen unread messages in his inbox.

'Hey,' Luciano whispers. His fingers brush Anse's fringe from his eyes, trying to stir him gently.

He jolts awake. 'Fuck, Luc!'

'Why are you out here?'

Anse sits up and rubs his face. 'I didn't want to roll over and hurt you.'

'It's freezing. Come back to bed.'

Anse doesn't protest and oafishly stumbles into the bedroom. Luciano curls around the warmth of his body, using his freehand to trace the contours of Anse's face: his long, narrow aquiline nose, the roundness of his top lip, the deep ridges of his cheek-bones, the sharpness of his jaw. Anse, in return, tugs him across the mattress until their bodies are against each other. Carefully, very carefully, their mouths find each other.

CHAPTER THIRTY-SIX

Rohan knocks on the door just as Anse is heading out for work.

'Nice suit.' Rohan gives him the up-and-down. 'I forgot you were a lawyer or something.'

'Attaché. A late one,' he corrects. 'Luc's medications on the stand. Don't get up to anything too crazy.'

'No worries, mate, I brought the PlayStation.'

Anse looks down at the gaming system in Rohan's arms. 'You know he has one hand, right?'

'Ah, fuck.'

Anse laughs as he side-steps Rohan. 'He's still asleep. Have a nice day.'

Work is as busy as ever. He meets Franz to discuss the Ambassador's next trip to Brisbane; they'll both accompany her. At one, he eats lunch with Hannah in the courtyard. The sky is clear and the early August day is uncharacteristically warm.

They get *bahn mi* from a Vietnamese café in Kingston and eat on the street. It's a better alternative than the awful soup he'd made earlier in the week; how Luciano had managed to stomach it, he has no idea.

'So, Franz is leaving, huh. Finally.'

'Apparently he'll be leading the Canadian team.'

She regards him seriously. 'What are your plans, then? Will you go back to Austria?'

'If I don't get any other offers, I'll have to,' he says. 'My job transfers back.'

'But you'll try to come back, right? You won't be over there for too long?'

Honestly, he's not sure. To come back would mean quitting his job with the government. It would mean getting a visa and finding whatever work he could do here; putting a hold on his career. It's not that Luciano's not worth it. It's just a lot to consider.

Hannah's quiet for a moment and Anse thinks it's just because she's enjoying her *banh mi,* but then she blurts, 'I'm getting married in May, Anse, and I want you there. I want you standing next to me.'

His brain doesn't have time to process what Hannah's suggesting before he responds, 'What?'

Hannah reaches over the table and takes his hand. 'Anse Meyer,' she says dramatically. 'You're my best friend. Will you be my bridesman?'

'You're serious?'

'Of course!' she says. 'I wouldn't be holding your hand if I wasn't. It's very soft, by the way.'

'I moisturise.'

Hannah clears her throat, seemingly done with his playing. 'Anse Meyer, will you be my bridesman?'

The rational side of his brain tells him not to commit to something he's not sure he can see through. He feels the dread slip down his spine and settle in his gut as he says, 'Of course I will.'

At six, Hannah hassles him out of the door.

'New policy states you have to work from home after six in winter,' she says though he doesn't recall the new policy being communicated before. 'Too dark otherwise.'

It's a ridiculous policy, but Hannah won't leave without him and he really should check on Luciano. He hasn't heard from Luciano except a brief text of *me and Rohan are going out for lunch! See you later tonight xx*

When he arrives at Trattoria, the restaurant is full of people. He parks around the back and finds Ned throwing bottles into the recycling bin. The lights are off in the apartment. Surely they're not still out? On a hunch, heads back down the stairs and slips into the busy kitchen.

'Rachel, have you seen—,'

'He's in the office,' the chef responds sharply as she adds a generous splash of red wine to a hot pan.

Anse shakes his head as he trudges down the hallway. It's been three days since he was let out of the hospital, and he's already trying to go back to work? Frustration simmers in his stomach; he'd been lucky to escape the car crash with minimal injuries. Why he couldn't he just spend a few days on the couch?

The door to the study is shut, but a slither of light escapes from underneath.

'Luciano? Are you in there?' He grasps the doorknob. 'You know shouldn't be working.'

Anse's unprepared for what he sees as the door swings open. Luciano stands in front of a group of people. All at once, the crowd erupt into a cheer. There are balloons everywhere.

'Happy birthday!'

The office has been transformed into a dinner party. Daniel and Emmy are here, Hannah and Cameron too, as well as the other usual suspects.

Luciano strings his good arm around Anse's shoulders. 'Happy birthday, baby. Were you surprised?'

He kisses him. His brother whoops. It's entirely embarrassing, but he doesn't care because *no one* has made a big deal about his birthday in years.

'How'd you find out?' Anse says as he's led to the table. Hannah coughs and hides her smile behind her hand.

'We definitely didn't bend data privacy regulations,' she smiles.

'Hannah told me you were a Virgo so I checked your passport,' Luciano says. 'You know, Aquarius and Virgo are not very compatible together.'

'Spare me. Not you, too.'

'Obviously we're an exception to the rule.'

Daniel hands him a cold beer and claps him on the shoulder. 'Nice to spend your birthday together; I think the last time was your eighteenth.'

Dinner's called and they gather around the table. It's a hodge-podge menu of Anse's favourites: bruschetta and schnitzel with *sauerkraut* and the best damn *Käsespätzle* Daniel says he's has had in years. Once everyone's settled in, Luciano taps his spoon against his glass of wine.

'To Anse,' he says, leading the toast. 'Our world is so much brighter with you in it.'

Luciano wakes to Anse sitting on the edge of their bed, dressed in a fine navy suit with a black tie. Luciano thinks, wildly, one day he'll buy Anse one of those striking floral-patterned suits. He'd be a dream in hydrangea print.

'I need to leave now.' His hand pushes the curls away from Luciano's forehead to kiss just above his brow. 'See you in a week's time.'

Luciano stumbles out of bed to see Anse off and then showers, manages to dress himself and potters around in the kitchen for most of the morning, listening to podcasts and doing his best to cook with one hand. It's not easy. He douses pieces of tough steak with red wine and lets them cook on a low heat for most of the afternoon. The courtyard garden has suffered over the winter, but it's early September and the weather is warming again. He plants basil and parsley seedlings and takes the cheesecloth shade off the lemon myrtle tree.

The next morning, Rohan drives him to his therapist appointment, and he spends the better part of an hour talking about things he'd rather not: his sleeping patterns, his mother's death, what will happen if Anse can't stay? If he leaves him?

The first time he met with Therese, his therapist, he'd expected to lay back on a lounge and go into some kind of trance, and at the end of it, she'd prescribe him a bottle of pills.

Instead, he just talks and she listens and there's no judgement. Sometimes she'll stop him to ask a question, or probe into something else further, but most of the time, he just unloads on her and it feels nice.

'You seem to have a lot of anxiety about factors in your life you can't control,' she says. 'But you can control how you react to them. I want you to write down a list of what the worst-case and best-case scenarios look like and try to plan out what you'll do for each.'

He's not sure it'll help, but he does it anyway.

BEST CASE SCENARIO

- Anse gets a job and he can stay here for a few more years
- We move in together (officially)
- Anse applies for permanent residency
- We get married
- I would continue running the restaurant

WORST CASE SCENARIO

- Anse doesn't get offered an extension
- He goes back to live in Austria
- The restaurant burns down (it could happen!)

'There,' says Therese, after the exercise. 'We've identified our fears. Now, we can take steps to address them. What would you do if the worst-case scenario did happen?'

'Maybe you visit him?' Rohan asks over lunch as Luciano discusses his session over a pint and a schnitzel. 'Austria's like seriously beautiful, you know.'

He's sure it is. And he wants to travel. But if Anse moves back, it means that he's not in Luciano's bed every night; his cologne won't linger in the apartment, even hours after he's left for work; that when Luciano looks up from the football scrum, he won't see Anse watching from the sideline.

'I don't *want* to visit him,' Luciano mutters. 'I don't want him to go.'

The list offers no clarity. It just depresses him more because it's September, and the official termination date on Anse's contract is the fifteenth of December, and they still don't have a plan.

CHAPTER THIRTY-EIGHT

Brisbane is gloriously warm. It's midday, and the sun is high in the cloudless sky. Luciano would love it here, Anse thinks. It is so similar to their Wollongong trip that when he sees the long stretch of beach on the way to their hotel, he thinks of Luciano, and the beach and then—awkwardly—all the things he can do with that mouth.

Franz sits beside him in the cab, running through his emails. He disregards the memory quickly.

There's no time for the beach; after they check into the hotel, they take fifteen minutes to freshen up before catching another taxi to their first meeting with a client, and then a train across town for a lunch meeting, before going over papers in a café and dialling into a teleconference.

Franz retires to his hotel room as soon as they conclude business, which leaves Anse with a free evening.

He calls Luciano but can't get a hold of him so instead he

goes for a run. They communicate mostly through texts and memes but when Anse calls on Tuesday night, the same thing happens. Suspicious, he calls the line to the restaurant.

Luciano picks up with a chirpy, 'This is Trattoria!'

'It's me.'

'Fuck.'

'You need to be resting.'

'I feel fine! It's nice to be back on my feet,' comes the answer. 'And I'm only supervising, I promise. And maybe a bit of office work.'

'You should be doing *no work*.'

'But I'm bored,' Luciano whines. 'And I miss you. It's fucking freezing in bed.'

'I have the air conditioner on. It's almost thirty degrees here.'

'Don't be cruel,' Luciano says and hangs up.

On Wednesday, he works on the small dining table in Franz's room; they barely speak to each other. Franz looks pallid, and Anse notices he barely eats anything all day. It confirms Anse's suspicions when Franz suggest they clock off just after three. The day is still bright and warm, so Anse goes for a run on the beach and cools off in the hotel pool, the smell of chlorine burning his nostrils.

He sends a picture of the coastline, wide and white and blue, to Luciano.

Anse: The sea reminds me of you

Of our date

Luciano: Omg, the things I wanted to do to you on that beach…

Anse: Why didn't you?

Luciano: Sand is an unpleasant thing to get in places, I've heard

Anse laughs at the response as he falls on the bed. His hand drifts lower and stops just at the waistband of his swimmers.

Anse: Tell me more pleasant things

Luciano types a message but doesn't send it, because the icon disappears. Anse hesitates. Perhaps he was too forward. But then—

Luciano: Really?

Anse: Yes.

Luciano: Ok hold on ;)

I am, he thinks, a little impatient; very horny.

Luciano: I'm home. In our bedroom. On our bed.

Did you make the bed? Anse wants to ask, but he knows the answer. Luciano never makes his bed. Instead, he focuses back on the beach, on the memories, and the messages from the man he wishes was beside him.

Anse: What are you wearing?

It's not exactly the most original way to start off the conversation, but he's not in any mood to play games.

Luciano: Nothing, except my sling

Anse rolls his eyes. Of course, the stupid fucking sling. He can't tell if Luciano's making fun of him or not.

Luciano: That's the right answer?

Anse: It's fine. I'm naked as well.

Luciano: That was quick.

Anse: I miss you. Just… touch yourself and think of me.

Luciano: Bossy ;)

Anse: But are you doing it?

There's a long stretch of time where no message comes through, and Anse, frustrated, considers searching the web for some relief. But then his phone vibrates in his hand.

It's Luciano.

'Turns out I kind of need one hand to type and one hand to…
do what you want me to do,' he says. 'And I like it more like
this. I can hear you. I want to hear you.'

'Fuck, Luciano,' Anse sighs.

'Yes, like that.'

This, Anse thinks, is a much better idea.

———

On the last day they're together, Franz does the unthinkable.

'Drink?' he suggests as he closes his laptop.

'Yes, definitely,' Anse replies.

It's been six days of work. He is mentally and physically
exhausted and ready for home. Even if it means leaving the mild
summery afternoons, the golden shoreline of the beach, and the
gentle sea-breeze that drifts through the open windows of his
hotel room. Brisbane has been kind to him.

But his lover's arms will be kinder. The mildly cold bite of
Canberra spring. The feeling of warm flesh pressed against his,
of lips, teeth and tongue and a well-deserved four days off.

They head to the hotel bar. It's an underwhelming affair
décor-wise, but it has gorgeous views and a decent wine list, and
he's in no mood to venture outside of the hotel and wade through
the city foot traffic to find a bar. Franz lets out a long sigh as they
collapse into the armchairs.

'I'm exhausted,' he says. 'I caught a bug over the weekend.
I'm afraid I still haven't completely shaken it.'

'That's awful,' Anse replies. Franz so rarely offers up tidbits
of his personal life. Anse wonders if he should reciprocate. 'You
should have said something.'

Franz shrugs. 'By all accounts, you've had your own concerns. How is your boyfriend?'

'He's well. He wants to get back to work, despite doctor's orders.'

'I can understand that.'

Anse sips on his beer. Franz nurses a gin and tonic. There's a bowl of complimentary peanuts on the table between them, but neither touch it.

'How was Canada?' Anse asks just to break the silence.

Franz shrugs. 'It was pleasant enough. Everything is set up over there. The outbound Ambassador to Canada is moving to the United Kingdom, and he's taking most of his staff with him. There are more vacancies to fill than we first expected,' he says and then takes a sip of his gin and tonic. 'The Ambassador wants you on her staff.'

He almost chokes on his beer.

'In Canada?'

'Ottawa, yes,' Franz corrects. 'It's quite the commendation.'

He doesn't doubt it.

'You speak French, German and English, and for what it's worth, I enjoy working with you, Anse. You don't have to give me an answer now. I am aware of your *attachments* here,' he chooses the word carefully. 'But I see this as a great opportunity in what will be an extremely rewarding career for you.'

Ottawa. He needs time to think. The beer hits him. Everything is off-centre and out of focus.

'It is a great opportunity. If I decline?'

'I can't guarantee you a place at the Australian office with a new Ambassador, but I could write you a letter of commendation. Or you'd go back to Vienna.' Franz offers him a tight smile. 'Think it over.'

———

The flight back to Canberra is short; just over two hours. Anse finishes a book while Franz taps through his mobile phone. One day when man and machine are fused together, Franz will be the first to have his phone integrated through his being, Anse thinks.

As soon as he steps a foot into the apartment, Luciano leaps into his arms, pressing frenzied kisses against his lips, jaw and throat.

'I love you,' he gasps. 'I missed you. Take me to bed.'

'Your arm.'

'Carefully. Take me to bed *carefully*.' He squeals as Anse walks him down the hallway.

———

Later, when Luciano is tucked into his side and the night is quiet except for the shallow breathing of his lover and the distant sounds of traffic, Anse allows himself to think.

The job in Ottowa isn't an official offer. There's nothing on paper and words mean very little in his line of work.

But Franz wouldn't bluff about something like this.

He would have been happy with a few more years in Australia.

He would have been ecstatic.

It had been his goal; what they'd been working towards.

But now there is Ottawa.

For the first time in months, he thinks about Max and the long, silent drive from his old apartment to the airport, and how, as he'd lingered by the departures gate, he'd almost hoped to hear Max calling out his name, telling him to wait; telling him he didn't have to do this alone, that he'd changed his mind—

He runs his hand through Luciano's curls and revels in the sigh that brushes against his ribs.

CHAPTER THIRTY-NINE

The morning greets them unhurried and yet unwelcome. Luciano has no desire to rise from the warmth of the bed, despite hearing Anse's alarm ring at seven. It's turned off quickly and he feels his lover press his mouth into the crook of his shoulder. Luciano groans. Outside, he can hear the howl of the wind, the rattle of the old windows, and closer still, the hitch in Anse's breath as Luciano presses back against him, until finally, he slides in. Anse whispers sweet, lustful nothings against the shell of Luciano's ear as he rocks slowly.

It's an all-round pleasant way to start the morning.

They doze for another hour, only rousing when Anse's phone buzzes once more.

Luciano groans into his shoulder. 'If that's the office, I'm going to break your phone.'

'It's Daniel,' Anse replies before answering. '*Servus?*'

They converse in German for a few minutes as Luciano plants

kisses across Anse's chest and avoids the hand that bats him away. When he finally hangs up, Luciano twists his tongue around Anse's nipple and revels in the, 'Fuck, Luciano, do you have to?'

'What did he want?'

'He's got a job.'

Luciano sits up. 'What? That's great!'

'In Canberra. At the library.'

'For real?' he grins. 'They're moving here? What about Emmy?'

'She's been looking to move for a while.'

'Good for them.' He kisses his chest. 'I can't believe I'll have to share you with your family now, though.'

'I'm sure you'll manage.' Anse runs his hand through Luciano's hair, down his neck and settles between his shoulder blades. 'They also asked if we wanted to spend Christmas with them.'

Christmas. He doesn't even want to think about Christmas.

'Will you even be here for it?' Luciano asks. Anse's hand drifts down to his lower back.

'I'm not sure. I could book my flights after the New Year. My visa doesn't run out until the fifth.'

'You haven't heard anything from work?'

'No.'

And before he can stop himself, Luciano says, 'Marry me.'

Anse looks at him, astonished. '*What*?'

Luciano throws his leg over Anse and scrambles to the floor before getting down on one knee.

'I love you and all I keep thinking is how much more I want of you. I want to share a home with you, a life, a family. I know it might be stupid and that we've only known each other since the start of the year, but I'm not ready to let you go yet. Or ever. So, please, Anse Meyer, will you marry me?'

Luciano can barely see through the tears, and he can't wipe them away because he's using his only good hand to hold Anse's and he can't let go.

'Luciano.' Anse lets out a long breath and it hits Luciano like a punch in the gut.

Oh no.

It feels like he's falling. A horrible twist in his stomach grows tighter the longer Anse remains quiet, holding Luciano's hand in his. Luciano waits to be jolted awake; he waits for Anse to say something, to move, to do anything and break this sudden freeze-frame they've found themselves in.

'I don't want it like this.'

What does that mean? He has no idea. He can't bear to look at him, so he keeps his gazed fixed on their fingers, how they thread together, how Anse's thumb brushes over the contours of his knuckles.

He hears Anse take a deep, shaking breath.

'I don't want it to just be for a quick visa.'

'It's not *just*—,' his voice sounds wet, broken.

'It is,' Anse replies and then his fingers are on Luciano's jawline and Luciano looks up to see tears brimming in his ocean blue eyes. 'Come up here.'

Clambering onto Anse's lap, they hold each other silently until the silence becomes too much, too heavy, and Luciano needs to know. 'Where do we go from here?'

'We don't have to go anywhere,' Anse murmurs into his hair. His fingertips run up and down his spine. 'We can just stay here, like this.'

'Not forever though.'

'No,' Anse says against his shoulder. 'Not forever.'

———

There's something stifling about the apartment, so Luciano decides to take Anse out. It's a gorgeous, warm spring day. A rainbow forms in the mist of the giant fountain in the middle of the lake as they drive over Commonwealth bridge.

Luciano buys coffee from a van as Anse wanders around a vast bed of fuchsia tulips, and Luciano shamelessly takes a picture of his lover amongst the blooms. Floriade. The celebration of spring. It's been a long cold winter and he's got the scars to prove it, and yet, if he could stay in that winter, if he could replay it over and over again, he would. He's never hated spring more.

They walk, wordlessly, through the garden beds. In one, crimson slowly fades to bright orange, and then to pink. In another, black and white tulips grow in lattice patterns. There's a sea of endless yellow, and then a mottling of various colours. This is what Luciano likes the most: there's no sense to the way these flowers are planted, no way to know exactly what colour they'll come up. It's a perfect, vibrant mess.

He should have proposed here.

Anse would have hated that. He's not sure he was thrilled with the proposal this morning, but he knows this would have been worse.

Luciano feels sick for thinking it, but in public, maybe he would have said yes—just to avoid that embarrassment—and Luciano could have experienced that brief sense of elation.

He loves Anse so much it hurts.

And it's so entirely selfish.

He knows that.

But he wants that future together; the future that's easy even when it's hard.

And he doesn't want to make sacrifices.

Because hasn't he sacrificed enough this year?

He knows that's not how it works; there's not some cosmic force pulling them together or tearing them apart. There's no relationship karma that counts how much misfortune he's received as of late and decides he's suffered enough, though he desperately wants, just this once, to ask the universe to give him this; to give him Anse, to give him the life he can so clearly see carved out for them.

Because Anse is slipping away.

He can feel it.

And he knows Anse isn't a reward; isn't something he got from being good or going to Sunday service when he was a kid. He knows the hard had to come, that the hard is unavoidable.

'Luciano.' Anse tugs at his arm, pulling him out of his reverie. 'Take a photo with me.'

'Huh?'

'I said before we don't have enough photos together. Take one with me now.'

Luciano presses himself against Anse's shoulder as he raises the camera high. It's a beautiful photo. He smiles. Behind them, the flowers are a field of deep crimson.

He's right. They don't have enough photos together.

CHAPTER FORTY

He doesn't hear anything else about the Canadian job. Anse acts like nothing's happened; words are just that in this industry and Franz doesn't bring up the job again. Hannah throws a Halloween party and Luciano gets drunk on peach schnapps and gin and convinces everyone to go out clubbing, and Anse experiences the worst hangover of his life.

Luciano supervises Anse make dinner. After the horror soup incident, he's back to only being allowed to cook supervised. Luciano watches as he dices the onion and places it in a hot pan. He adds mushrooms, garlic, and a handful of cooked chicken.

'I'm sick of this sling.' Luciano puts a handful of homemade pasta into a small pot of boiling water. 'I'm sick of not being able to work, or cook, or shower properly.'

'Only a few more weeks.'

The silence between them is uncomfortable; the proposal hangs heavy between them. It's been a week since Luciano asked him to marry him, kneeling naked on his bedroom floor.

He knows he needs to tell Luciano about the job.

Even if it's not a real job yet.

They still need to discuss their options.

But if he does, Anse knows he'll lose this: a quiet Sunday night cooking with his boyfriend who sways to the soft music playing through their speaker system as he moves thickening sauce around a pan. Crossing the floor, Anse places a kiss on Luciano's cheek and revels in the way his lover leans into the touch. The ragù smells amazing.

'Get the plates, please, dear.'

Anse sets their small kitchenette table and helps Luciano dish up the rich spaghetti sauce.

'I made a list.'

Anse looks up from his meal. 'You made a list?'

'You know,' he elaborates. 'To be prepared for whatever happens.'

'Luc…' He's tired of this circular conversation. 'Please, let's just leave it for tonight.'

Luciano puts down his fork and Anse knows he's said the wrong thing.

'I just don't want to ruin the time we have by worrying about what will happen in the future.'

Luciano shoots him a fiery glare. 'I'm ruining it, then?'

'That's not what I meant.'

'It's my fault.'

He opens his mouth to protest, but there's no point digging himself a bigger hole. Luciano downs the rest of his wine and steps away from the table, his food half-eaten.

'Luciano!' Anse calls after him. 'Come back. Finish your meal.'

He hears the bathroom door close. Fuck.

The shower begins to run and Anse sighs, cleaning up dinner, before heading to the lounge to work through his emails. Luciano emerges fifteen minutes, his hair wet, and wordlessly sits down next to Anse, placing his hand on his thigh.

'I don't want to lose you. I'm sorry I made a scene.'

He doesn't look at him. 'I don't have an answer for you.'

'I know.'

Should he just end it? Now would be the best time. If there's such thing as a best time. But then Luciano settles in against his side and he smells like coconut shampoo and his lemongrass soap, and his body is a comforting warmth against him. Anse runs his hand though Luciano's damp curls.

He should just end it.

They only have a few weeks left together before he's supposed to go back to Vienna. Or Canada. The tickets will need to be booked soon, either way.

'You know I probably won't be able to stay,' Anse says. He knows he's baiting Luciano to start the argument again and the guilt of trapping him like this twists in his gut. It would be an easy escape.

Luciano sighs, his breath warm against where he's settled against Anse's ribs. 'I don't want to talk about it anymore.'

———

Franz gives him the job offer the following morning.

'You would be an asset to the team over there, Anse.'

Anse glances over the position description. There's a generous salary with benefits and an early January-start date.

'You'd be overseeing a team of six,' Franz continues. 'All the other benefits are included of course: you'll get an apartment, use of a company car, five weeks of annual leave.'

'What if I wanted to bring my partner with me?' Anse asks.

Franz hesitates. 'Visas would have to be worked out, but you could. So long as they paid their way there. Australians can get Canadian working visas easily if that's what you're asking. Being the Commonwealth and all.'

'When do I have to let you know?'

Franz raises his thin brow. 'I was hoping you'd give me an answer now.' When Anse doesn't reply, he nods. 'By the end of the week, Anse.'

———

That afternoon, he works through exactly what he's going to say on the treadmill, refines his arguments on the leg press, and finally decides on an approach during a five-kilometre stint on the rower. By the time he gets to Trattoria, it's close to seven and his argument is fully formed in his mind. Luciano is working the floor of the restaurant, talking to customers. It's only another week until he gets his sling off and he's desperate to get back to work.

'You're not supposed to be working,' Anse reminds him.

'I'm not. I'm *mingling*.' Luciano steers him towards a booth in the back. 'Sit. I'll get you dinner.'

He catches Luciano's hand as he turns to leave. 'Have dinner with me. I want to talk to you about something.'

A heaviness settles over Luciano's posture, like his body has suddenly taken on extra weight. Wordlessly, he nods.

It takes Luciano over half-an-hour to get back with dinner, and Anse spends the time stewing over his decision.

'Sorry. The kitchen needed a hand. Luckily, I have one.' It's a stupid joke, but Anse laughs anyway. Madison places their meals in front of them before resuming her rounds. 'So what did you want to talk about?'

'Eat first.' He chickens out. Luciano knows it too. 'How was your day?'

'Fine,' Luciano replies. 'Can we quit the small talk? Something's obviously bothering you. I can't enjoy my food until I know what.'

Anse puts down his fork. 'I was offered a position today.'

'What?' Luciano grins. 'That's fantastic. Oh my god, Anse, that's amazing.'

The obvious delight on Luciano's face wrenches something deep within him. 'The position is based in Ottawa.'

Luciano's delight dies immediately, like a candle snuffed out. 'As in Canada?'

'Yes.' Luciano is silent so Anse continues. 'I know it's a big move but I discussed visa requirements for partners, and Franz said you could probably get a working visa—,'

'A working visa?'

'If we applied now, you'd probably hear before Christmas. You have a passport, right?'

'You.' Luciano licks his lips. 'You want me to move to Canada with you?'

'It wouldn't be forever. A year or two. Maybe three.'

'I can't go to Canada.'

'You haven't even thought about it,' Anse replies. 'You could—,'

'Anse,' Luciano replies. 'I've thought about it. Fuck, it's the only thing I've thought about for these past few months. Everything I am, and everything I want to be, is here. Not there.'

'But I'd be there.'

Luciano hasn't eaten a bite of his dinner yet. 'So don't go.'

The meticulous arguments he's constructed fall apart. But this is his career. This job is everything he's worked for; it's the culmination of his late nights studying, his shitty internships, his low-paying barista job. All of it had been for this job, and then, for the next.

And in that moment, as Luciano squeezes his hand, Anse realises it's exactly the thing he's asking Luciano to give up for him.

'You've already decided, haven't you? I can see it on your face.'

Luciano tries to pull his hand away again and this time Anse lets go.

It doesn't end with an argument, or with heated words, or with tears. It ends quietly over a nice meal in Luciano's restaurant, their silent agreement heavy between them as they finish their dinner. Then, he goes upstairs to pack his things.

If he'd known that last night would have been the last time they'd be together, he wouldn't have started the argument again; he would have listened to his concerns, even if it was the hundredth time they'd had the same conversation about what could happen. He wouldn't have fallen asleep with his back to Luciano. He wouldn't have fallen asleep at all.

And Canada had never officially been on the table.

Until the job offer was literally placed on his table.

'I love you,' is the last thing Anse says to Luciano that night, standing next to his car.

'I know. I love you too.'

———

He drives back to his apartment.

Anse: I'll confirm formally via email tomorrow, but I will accept the role.

Franz: Wonderful! And the partner visa?

Anse: Won't be needed.

CHAPTER FORTY-ONE

'Fuck him,' Rohan says as he pours Luciano another glass of wine.

It's late. They're in Trattoria, drinking, because Luciano doesn't want to go back up to his apartment.

It's been four days since Anse left.

The apartment is empty.

The bed is cold.

They haven't spoken since.

'What a piece of shit,' Rohan continues. 'What an absolute asshole.'

'He's not an asshole, Rohan. I'm pretty sure he was the love of my life. Like, I even proposed to him.'

Rohan takes a swig of his drink. 'Sorry. I thought I was supposed to go best friend ballistic on your behalf.'

'I'll let you know when you can. For now, I just want to drink.'

Rohan wraps his arm around Luciano's shoulder. 'You

proposed to him, huh?'

'It was stupid. I don't even know what I was doing. I was naked and I got on one knee and-,'

'You were *naked*?'

'Don't tell anyone, please, it wasn't not my finest moment.'

'We both do stupid things for love, my friend. I tried to impress Corina by taking her to a fancy seafood restaurant down in Bateman's Bay—,'

'She's allergic to shellfish.'

'And I *knew* that,' Rohan replies. 'Like on a subconscious level, but you Italians really know how to romance a bloke and I wanted to impress her so badly. She barely stepped into the restaurant and she'd broken out in a rash. She ended up in the hospital overnight and made me promise not to tell you. So, now you promise me you won't tell her I told you.'

He swirls the wine around his glass. 'So you guys are serious, huh?'

A warm smile graces Rohan's face. Love looks good on him, Luciano considers.

'Yeah,' he hums. 'I think so.'

———

November melts—because it's the hottest November on record—into December. A bushfire burns along the coastline and the wind blows toxic smoke into Canberra. His social media feed is full of death and destruction and loss.

Anse has left but pieces of him remain. By the door, Luciano's gathered a box of his forgotten belongings: a few shirts left in the wash, a pair of pants, runners that were hidden under the bed, and a bottle of expensive cologne Luciano's thought about keeping but the smell still triggers memories of him. Of them together.

Fuck, he really needs to get rid of that box. With a groan, Luciano lifts it up, dashes down the stairs, and throws it in the back of his car.

The Vespa is gone. The first thing he did after getting the sling off was purchase a red Fiat.

Old habits die hard and all that.

Really, he should just throw the box out. If Anse really needed any of it, he'd come by and collect it. Besides, it's not like Anse can't just repurchase a couple of shirts and a bottle of cologne.

Anse's contract ends in two weeks' time and there's been radio silence since the breakup. No phone calls texts, no tweets, no new photos on Instagram or even a fucking Facebook status. He'd never thought Anse would be so *callous* as an ex, and the longer he doesn't hear from him, the more he resolves not to be the first one to reach out.

The fact is, he's writing to Anse three times to break the silence between them. Two out of those three times he was drunk. The current message in his drafts reads, *What, you're not even going to text me goodbye? We dated for ten fucking months and you don't even say goodbye? I proposed to you*

He knows the way to Anse's apartment too well. Parking across the road from the complex, he grabs the box from the back seat. It's three on a Wednesday afternoon, and Anse should be at work.

God, he hopes he's at work.

He punches in the access code to Anse's apartment and is let into the foyer. He must still live here, then. If he'd moved the access code would have been reset. As the elevator doors open,

Luciano hitches the box onto his hip and struts into the hallway. He's just going to leave it at Anse's door, and if anyone pinches it, that's not his issue.

And he's definitely not going to knock on the door just in case.

Because Anse should be at work.

Because it's a workday.

He knocks on the door twice just to prove himself right. The door opens before he can scramble away.

'Oh, Luciano.' Daniel looks surprised to see him. Immediately, he pulls Luciano in for a hug.

'Hey,' Luciano mutters into Daniel's shoulder. The hug is thankfully brief and Luciano bends down to pick up the box. 'This is just a bunch of stuff Anse left at my place that I thought he might want.'

Daniel takes the box. 'Oh sure. We're helping him move out. Do you want to talk to him?

Shit. 'No, no, definitely not,' Luciano backs off. 'Thanks Daniel, see you another time.'

Dashing down the hallway, he frantically smashes the elevator button just as he hears someone call out his name. He doesn't need to turn to know it's Anse.

He wills the elevator to come faster. 'Come on, come on, come on, *come on.*'

'Luciano!' Anse stumbles out into the hallway.

The elevator door opens and Luciano slips in, hitting the button to close the doors. Anse lunges forward to grab at the doors, and for a brief moment, Luciano makes eye-contact with him. He looks desperate. His hand reaches out to stop the door, but it's too late. They close and Anse withdraws his hand. Luciano lets out a breath.

As soon as the elevator doors open to the foyer, Luciano races back to his car. Just as he's left the apartment building, he hears the door to the stairwell open and Anse staggers out, red-faced and panting.

'Luciano, wait! Please! I just want to talk.'

'*Talk!*' he whirls around. 'You haven't *talked* to me in weeks!'

Anse stands before him, panting, dressed in a tight white t-shirt and a pair of shorts.

'I know. I'm sorry.' Luciano notices the haircut first: it's much shorter and Luciano hates it. He liked it when he could card his fingers through it to work out the hard gel used to sweep it back every day. He liked it when his fringe would fall around his eyes whenever it got wet. 'I wanted to come to the restaurant, but it's been so busy at work and now with the move—,'

Luciano resists the urge to smack his stupid, awful, handsome face. 'I'm sorry you've been *so* busy.'

'I don't want to fight with you.'

He doesn't want to fight either, of course he doesn't want to fight, he *loves* this infuriating man, but then Anse continues—

'Come with me, please. Change your mind.'

The fire sparks within him again. It rises from his stomach, up his throat until he can taste the bitterness like salt on his tongue. 'Why did you make me choose between my life and you? It's fucking with my head. If I can't have you, I just want to be *rid* of you. So just leave, Anse. And don't call me, or text me, or tell me your sorry, and don't come back.'

Luciano wipes his nose on the collar of his t-shirt, and then his eyes, and feels himself come together again. Taking a deep breath, he gives Anse one final look: he looks stricken, hollow, like something is eating at him from the inside, withering him, breaking him down to rot.

And he hates being angry at Anse.

Hates that he's angry because he desperately doesn't want to be.

'I should go. We're making scene.'

'Come inside.'

'And what? Get a drink, talk it out?' he raises his eyebrow. '*Fuck* one last time?'

Anse winces. 'Don't be crass.'

'I'm madly in love with you, Anse, but I hate you so fucking much.' He snorts. 'I don't know how it's possible. What do you *want*, Anse?'

'It's not a case of not knowing what I want,' Anse says finally. 'I can't have it all, Luciano.

That's the end of them.

The real end.

CHAPTER FORTY-TWO

'You're a fucking idiot,' Daniel says as Anse trudges back up the stairs. The boxes are packed in the hall. Everything he owns fits in eight boxes.

Daniel and Emmy's new home is a temporary rental with too-thin plaster walls. They haven't unpacked all of their belongings yet but a Christmas tree sits in the front alcove, glittering with tinsel and fairy lights.

The bed in the study is hard and uncomfortable.

He is hard and uncomfortable.

God, he misses Luciano.

The fight today had been awful. The image of Luciano, red-faced and crying, on the footpath, is fresh in his mind. Of the shitty ways he's ever broken up with someone, it's is a solid second. The first was when he'd slipped out of Lukas's bed, caught a plane back to Austria, and never spoke to him again.

God, he's an awful person.

He thought a clean break would have been easier. It's been

hard not to text Luciano, not to say 'this happened, and I thought of you. I thought of *us*'. It's hard not wake and search, subconsciously, for a body curled up against his. It's hard not to think of him every time he smells Emmy's coconut hand moisturiser.

It's hard, every day, without him.

'You're making a mistake,' says Daniel as he turns the steak on the BBQ.

———

He breaks up with Hannah.

She cries.

She asks if he'll be back in May.

He hugs her. 'I don't think so. I'm sorry.'

She pulls back. 'And Luciano?'

'It's not fair to ask him to leave,' Anse says even though he asked him to leave. 'It's better this way.'

———

Daniel is writing in his study when Anse brings home a six-pack of beer and chucks him a can.

'Take a break?' he asks.

Daniel rolls his eyes but cracks the beer. 'I'm still mad at you, you know. Five beers aren't going to make up for it.'

Anse looks down at the four remaining beers and hands the pack to Daniel.

'I know you're an adult,' Daniel continues. 'And I don't really have a right to tell you how to live your life, but what the fuck, Anse?'

'I asked Luciano to come but he wouldn't. He made the choice.'

'You made him choose between you and his job? That is fucked up.'

Anse scoffs. 'Whose side are you on?'

'Obviously, I'm on Luciano's.'

'But I'm your brother. And how is that any different to what Luciano wanted me to choose—it was him or the job.'

Daniel shakes his head. 'Sit down, you giant idiot.' Anse does, falling back onto the daybed. 'Why are you doing this? For real now.'

'I've worked my entire life for this job.'

'That's all?'

'What do you mean 'that's all'?' He's getting annoyed now. The conversation is just going around in circles. 'You know, it would be nice to get some support from my family in my career. Especially because I've always supported *yours*.'

Daniel stares down at the beer can in his hands.

'Forget it.' Anse to his feet again. 'I should have known we couldn't have a mature conversation about this.'

He gets to the study door only for Daniel to say, 'jobs come and go, Anse.'

'Spare me.'

But Daniel continues, undeterred. 'There are other ways you can get where you want to go and probably a hundred jobs out there you'd do well in, but I think you know there are not many like Luciano.'

Anse takes a sip of beer, his mouth suddenly dry.

Daniel rises to his feet and gives him a gentle pat on the shoulder. 'You still have time to make this right.'

Emmy gives him a pair of monogrammed cufflinks for Christmas. Daniel buys him a new pair of oxfords in brown with a pair of novelty cat socks. They're wonderful gifts.

'There's still one more present,' Emmy says as she reaches underneath the Christmas tree and retrieves a large flat box.

'You shouldn't have,' he says and means it because he'd only got them one gift each: an eyeshadow palette Emmy's had her eye on, and a voucher for the local bookshop for Daniel.

'We didn't,' Daniel says.

'Someone wanted you to have this.'

He knows immediately who the gift was from. 'He was here?'

'We went out for dinner last week,' explains Emmy. 'Apparently, he ordered this for you when, um, anyway, he said he still wanted you to have it.'

Anse tugs at the black silk ribbon and removes the lid. A jacket lies carefully folded on a pillow of black tissue paper. Clusters of lush rhododendron flowers, buds and leaves dot the navy jacket. Anse runs his fingers down the silk collar and notices there's a matching set of pants. It's completely ostentatious and he has absolutely no reason to wear such a flamboyant suit *every day*, but it's not meant to be worn every day, is it? Only for special occasions. Special occasions Luciano would have created for him just for an excuse to see him wear the suit.

'I should tell him thank you,' Anse says after a long while.

Daniel can't wipe the smile off his face.

CHAPTER FORTY-THREE

___

Luciano tries not to dwell on the fact that this will be the first Christmas without his mother, but then he hears *Hark the Herald Angels Sing* in the shopping plaza, and he thinks of her. It's not the first time Mariah Carey's made him cry, and it certainly won't be the last.

The staff decorate the restaurant until it, in Rohan's words, 'shits Christmas.'

The night before Christmas finds him snug as a bug, nestled between his sisters and cradling a mug of warm milo. Corina flicks through the cheesy Christmas movies before settling on one about a corporate lawyer giving up a lucrative career to get back together with a café owner. It's on the nose even for Luciano but he suffers through it. At least there's a happy ending.

Christmas day is a balmy forty-two degrees and Luciano spends most of the morning in Trattoria's kitchen while Marzia and Corina make frozen cocktails. When loud RnB music suddenly replaces his mellow Christmas jazz soundtrack, Luciano knows Rohan and Omala have arrived.

'The party is here!' Rohan cries as he steps into the kitchen with a case of beer. He kisses Corina before turning to Luciano. 'Anything we can do to help?

'Put my music back on and get out of my kitchen. Make yourselves useful and set the table or something.'

Omala hands him a bottle of wine wrapped in tinsel. The Ahujas don't celebrate Christmas, but they've always been invited to share Christmas lunch since Luciano can remember. It's been a few years since they were all together, but as everyone gathers around the table, it's like no time has passed at all.

The food is served a little later than expected, but Luciano doesn't think anyone really cares because they've all been drinking since ten and will probably continue into the small hours of the morning.

Corina and Marzia have decorated one of the long tables with candles and tinsel. It's tacky at best, but no one cares when the roast lamb leg is placed in the middle of the table. Over the next five minutes, he loads the table with potatoes cooked in fat, honeyed carrots, roasted pumpkins, brussels sprouts with bacon bits, cauliflower with white sauce and parmesan, and finally, a wonderfully sunken, cream-topped pavlova. When the table is brimming with food, Luciano takes a seat. 'Okay, let's eat!'

'Wait,' Marzia says and gestures for everyone to raise their glass. 'To a bloody hard year and a bloody remarkable woman.'

'Here, here,' says Rohan and they all drink.

But Marzia raises her glass again. 'And to my little brother, who against everything—and sometimes everyone—has achieved something really special.'

Luciano tries to shrug off the praise but it sticks to him, warm like the afternoon sun. 'Okay you guys, just shut up and eat.'

Rohan makes everyone crack the crackers and they all don the ridiculous paper crowns. Luciano's is red because of course it is.

'I have an announcement to make!' Corina stands suddenly, the ruffles of her pink dress swaying.

Marzia gives Luciano a look as if to say *is she drunk?*

Out of the corner of his eye, Luciano sees Rohan smile, a sparkle of amusement dancing in his eye.

Corina continues on, undeterred. 'Rohan and I are having a baby!'

'Well, fuck,' Marzia says immediately.

'Holy shit!' cries Omala.

He's drunk. He must be. That can't be right. He can't be becoming *an uncle*.

'Are you for real?' Marzia says again.

'Of course, I'm for real!'

'I can't believe it,' he says as Corina brings him in for a hug. Marzia loops her arms over the other side.

'Hold on, let me get in on the action,' Rohan complains as he nudges his way underneath Luciano's arm. 'I did *some* of the work.'

'Gross,' Marzia complains.

'Get used to it. We're family now.'

On Boxing Day, he wakes up to a splitting headache, the realisation that yesterday *really* happened, his sister is pregnant to his best friend, and that there are three messages from Anse on his phone.

Shit.

Anse: I got your gift. Thank you

It's not at all my style but I think that was what you're going for

Anyway it was a very thoughtful gift and I just wanted to let you know I appreciated it. And I'm sorry

Really sorry.

He's not sure what to write back. He needs coffee first.

Even after coffee, he's still not sure.

Sitting down at his kitchen table, he writes and deletes a message three times until he finally settles a semi-decent response.

Luciano: I'm glad you liked it. Did you have a nice Christmas?

Anse: It was fine. Quiet. How was yours?

Luciano: Not so.

Corina's pregnant.

Anse: Fuck me

It's out of line to say that was quick, but…

Luciano: They're really in love

I can't believe I'm going to be an uncle

Anse: I know what that feels like

The in love part

Not the uncle part

I'm happy for you, Luciano

Luciano: Thanks.

He doesn't want to bring up the move, though he desperately wants to know when he'll be leaving—when he can finally stop looking over his shoulder, stop thinking every knock at the door is him, stop thinking he's coming back.

Anse: I fly out just after New Year

You should come and visit me in Canada.

I still want to keep in touch.

I want to be friends

If we could

The barrage of messages is overwhelming. Luciano takes a deep breath; replies—

I don't want to be friends, Anse.

CHAPTER FORTY-FOUR

'I can't believe you're doing this,' says Daniel for what Anse thinks is the sixth time that morning.

'We all liked Luciano, Dan,' reminds Emmy from the front seat. 'Anse is a big boy now, he can make his own decisions.'

'Stupid decision,' mutters Daniel.

'Ignore him,' Emmy says. 'This is an adventure. A new start. Are you excited?'

Outside, the morning sky is a blur of navy, red and yellow as the sun slowly rises over Canberra. It's barely six in the morning but the temperature gauge in the car already reads twenty-eight. He's not going to miss the heat.

'Sure,' he says. 'I'm just not excited about the flight.'

'Pop a pill and it'll be over before you know it.'

He feels how he did before he left Vienna: filled with a dread he can't shake, a worry that keeps eating at him. *Is this the right decision?*

He'd had those worries back then and Canberra had turned out just fine. More than fine. It had been the best thing that's ever happened to him.

These worries are normal. If he had them in Vienna, it's normal to have them again now. Because Ottawa is the right decision. He knows it. The worries just mean he's moving forward. That he's challenging himself.

The airport is small. Daniel stops in the five minute-drop off zone.

Five minutes. That's all he has left.

Again.

'Don't make it so long between drinks, mate,' Daniel says as he hugs his brother. Anse fingers dig into the cotton of Daniel's shirt.

'Don't get any greyer.'

Daniel pushes him away with a laugh. 'Fuck off.'

Emmy fusses over him, smooths the short hair away from his face and places her hands against his cheeks. 'Take care of yourself, Anse.'

'You too, Emmy.'

'I hope you find what you're looking for over there.'

He almost says, 'me too,' but stops himself.

'We gotta go, Em,' Daniel says as he wheels Anse's luggage over. He gives his brother one last look over and Anse can't help but feel he's trying to soak him all in. 'See you.'

He boards the flight, finds his seat, watches as Canberra falls away from beneath him. He can see the lake, glistening and golden in the morning sun, and the memory of their wonderfully disastrous first date comes back to him. He can see Red Hill, thinks he spies the lookout where they'd kissed. His eyes skim over the summit and down, tracing the line to Trattoria like he's connecting the dots. He thinks he can see the roof of the restaurant, where everything else wonderful had followed and, just as quickly, ended.

And then he rises above the clouds and Canberra disappears.

CHAPTER FORTY-FIVE

O n the fourth day of January, Luciano opens the restaurant to the sound of a plane flying overhead. He looks up and can see its sleek white belly. To the passengers above, he is nothing, not even visible amongst a maze of streets and suburbs.

Anse hasn't been online for eight hours.

Luciano knows he's gone.

He says goodbye to the plane, silently, before continuing into the restaurant to start prep.

It's quiet in Canberra. The bushfires still burn to the east. He'd spent New Years Eve inside with Rohan and Corina and they'd tried not to talk about it.

'What will you do if the restaurant burns down?' she's said. 'What's your plan?'

It's a quiet Friday night when Ned pokes his head into the office and says, 'Chef, someone's asking for you.'

Luciano looks up from his accounts. It's six-thirty. 'What? Who?'

'Some tall bloke. Didn't give me his name.'

Not Anse.

Ned knows Anse.

He straightens his shirt and steps out onto the floor of the restaurant.

The nurse stands by the bar, dressed in a pair of black skinny jeans and a bright retro button-up shirt.

'Thought I'd finally make you pay up on that dinner you owed me.' As if reading the look on Luciano's face, the nurse laughs. 'It's Michael.'

Of course. Michael.

'Sorry. It's been a few months,' Luciano replies. 'Take a seat. But I'm quite sure I said it was just a free glass of house wine.'

Michael laughs; he has wonderful light melodic laugh, Luciano thinks, and his smile reaches his cornflower blue eyes.

———

Luciano brings him a menu, which he browses for only a brief second before handing it back to him. 'Surprise me.'

Luciano scoffs. 'Are you serious? I don't even know you. That's so risky.'

'I play a risky game,' Michael smiles. 'Surprise me.'

'Any allergies?'

'Nope.'

'Anything you don't like?'

'Not a huge fan of oysters.'

'Right,' Luciano mutters. 'It'll be around twenty minutes.'

'I bought a book.' He flashes the cover and settles in.

He returns half an hour later with the best cut of sirloin steak he could find. Michael's eyes light up as he places the dish in front of him.

'It's paired best with a merlot.' Luciano places the bottle on the table.

Michael gapes at him. 'Luciano, I couldn't possibly—,'

'It's on the house,' he says. 'You nursed me back to health, as you said.'

'Yeah, but I mean it was mostly my job.'

'And this is mine.' Luciano uncorks the bottle and pours Michael a glass. 'Enjoy.'

'Join me.'

Luciano pauses. He has a lot of bookwork to do, but then again it *is* a bloody good bottle of merlot and Michael is looking at him like he's just hung the moon.

'Sure.'

CHAPTER FORTY-SIX

When he arrives in Ottawa, it is dark and cold and snowing. Anse greets a man holding a sign that reads MEYER and is directed to a nondescript black car. The ride through the streets of Ottawa is silent, and in the dark, the streets look the same as all the other cities he's visited. He's dropped off at the apartment complex and he drags his suitcase up to yet another sterile, entirely unremarkable apartment. This one is smaller than his Kingston apartment but has sweeping views of the city.

He showers and climbs into the bed. The stiff sheets rub against his skin as he watches snow fall outside his bedroom window.

He turns on his phone, connects to WiFi, and the messages trickle in.

From his brother.

From Emmy.

From his old gym.

Three from Hannah.

None from Luciano.

And one from Max.

Anse stares at his phone, at Max's photo, at Max's message.

Max: Hey.

Hey, like it hasn't been a year.

Max: I'm thinking of taking a trip. You're still in Sydney, right? Is it worth the 24 hr trip?

Anse switches off his phone and presses his face into his pillow.

He forgets to set his alarm.

Anse wakes up at midday the next day, groggy and tired. Pulling on a jumper, he runs the snowy streets of his neighbourhood. Crowds of people swarm the streets. He struggles to navigate past them and avoid the ice that lines the edges of the footpath.

He finds a park and jogs around the large frozen lake before getting Chinese takeaway and going back to his apartment.

The routine is hauntingly familiar.

The new office is huge. Where Canberra was a home-turned-embassy, his new office is on the thirteenth floor of a tall skyscraper in the middle of the city. There's no Hannah on the front desk. There's no front desk at all. Now, Anse needs to be swiped in by a security foreman. Then, it's up the lift to a large foyer, where he waits for Franz to collect him. Through the glass doors, he can see bullpens of offices. People work at their computers diligently, getting up only to print out a document or take a call.

The door on the other side of the room opens and Franz emerges.

'You made it!' he shakes Anse's hand. He's smiling brilliantly. The 'old' Franz never smiled.

'This is a big change from the Australian office.'

Franz laughs at his observation. *Laughs*. This cannot be the same man he'd worked with for a year in Canberra; the same surly man who locked himself inside his office every day.

'You'll get used to it,' he says. 'Come on, I'll introduce you to the team.'

There are six people in his team, not including Franz. There's Winifred, who monitors the media and communication channels. Thomas, who seems entirely too young to have a job title with 'senior' before it, but who manages finances part-time. Then there's Gabriel, the speechwriter, and Celine and Ashlyn in policy. Finally, Phoebe, who is currently on leave in New York with her family but will be back in a week's time, looks after account and admin two days a week.

Anse is shown to his office. This time he has a corner window and the view looks straight into a floor of bullpens in the buildings next door. He can see dozens of other people sitting at their desks, typing wildly on their computers. There's no jacaranda tree, no filtered sunlight. The only greenery is the fake plant in the corner of his sterile office.

'Do you need anything?' Franz asks from the doorway. 'Security set up your emails last week but call the number on the post-it if you still can't access them.'

'First point me to the coffee.'

'Jet lag?'

'Yeah, it's bad.'

'Kitchen is down the hall to the left. They had one of those fancy capsule coffee machines, but there's been a real push for more sustainable methods, so they got rid of it. I'm afraid it's just instant.'

'It'll do.'

———

'I'm taking the team out for drinks tonight,' Franz says that afternoon. 'Just to the bar across the road. I'd like for you to come if you have the time.'

Franz never took the team out in Canberra.

They both know he has the time. Frankly, he'd rather accept his invite than decline and have Franz know that he's going home alone.

The bar Franz chooses is lively with a whimsical culture that reminds Anse of a university bar, but for tailored for the after 5pm crowd. Franz finds a table and, surprisingly, orders the first round.

'So, Anse, how are you settling in?' asks Winifred but he's distracted with the way Thomas and Franz are talking, their heads angled low towards each other like they're sharing a secret. How have they haven't become friends so quickly? It took him almost a year to even get Franz to have a beer with him.

'Anse?' says Winifred.

'Oh, um, it's cold,' he replies. 'But otherwise, fine.'

He's about to ask Winifred a question when Franz raises his beer.

'To a new team,' he toasts. 'A new adventure.'

Everyone cheers.

That night, he takes a photo of the floral suit hanging in his cupboard and sends a photo to Hannah.

Anse sent a photo

Anse: Christmas gift from Luciano

Hannah: Oh my god I love him

I mean I love the suit

You NEED to wear that

Anse: How's work?

Hannah: Boring without you. How's Canada?

Anse: Weird

Franz is popular here

Hannah: Wtf! Like in what way?

Anse: Just seems to vibe with the team

They're all friends

It took me months to even decide if he liked me as a colleague, let alone go out for a drink with him but they go out every week.

Hannah: Anse Meyer my robotic talking friend. Did you just use the word vibe?

Anse: I am a natural-sounding English speaker now.

I use lingo like vibe

And yeet

Hannah: STOP

Or I'll yeet this phone

———

It snows all week.

Disgusted with the instant coffee, Anse takes to making a coffee at the apartment and takes it into work with a small thermos. No one asks him to go get a coffee, anyway, and he can spend more time getting on top of his emails.

At lunch, he eats a salad at his desk and finishes a report.

His staff skate around him, and on more than one occasion, Anse's experienced the bizarre sensation of laughter leaving the room as soon as he enters.

Still, his team are competent, approachable and obviously collaborative. During their Wednesday team meeting, the efficiency of his staff is both impressive and troubling: he has no doubt the meeting would have been just as efficient if he wasn't in the room, and the thought haunts him for the rest of the day.

What is he *really* doing here?

Thursday is a string of meetings for media and policy and events coordination. He spends two hours running through Her Excellency's calendar organisation and invitations with Winifred.

On Friday, he rocks up to work wearing a suit only to realise the rest of his colleagues are wearing jeans and sneakers.

'Casual Fridays,' Franz says later that afternoon. 'Company culture is important, Anse.'

Anse resists the urge to put his head through his desk.

———

He calls Daniel. The video takes a moment to buffer, but then he can see Daniel, awash in the bright morning light. His hair is messy. Perhaps he's only just out of bed. Anse checks his watch. It's just after eight in the morning in Canberra, so it's a possibility.

'How's Canada?' Daniel asks.

'Cold. Snowing,' he says. 'How's the new job?'

'Wonderful,' Daniel sighs, and Anse tries not to roll his eyes. 'Good company, meaningful work. Discount at the bookshop and the café, and oh my god they have the best avocado—'

'Daniel,' Anse interrupts him. 'I've made a mistake.'

CHAPTER FORTY-SEVEN

He loves his sister. He really does. But as his knees threaten to buckle while lugging Rohan's PlayStation and all twenty-two games up the four-floor walk-up to Corina's apartment, he wonders exactly how far that love extends. Sure, Corina has always supported him through his endeavours, and there was that one time she completely renovated his restaurant, but hell, that was all *one floor*.

Both Corina and Rohan had agreed that they should move into Corina's small apartment in preparation for the baby, which makes zero sense to Luciano because there's no way Corina will be able to carry a pram and a baby up these steps so they'll *obviously* have to move again before the baby's born. So here he is, lugging shit up the four-floor walk-up, knowing full well in a few months' time, he'll be bringing it back down.

'This is a trial run,' Corina says. 'To see if we'll bite each other's head off *before* we sign a lease together. Just because I'm having his baby doesn't mean we're happy families immediately.'

'Right,' says Luciano because he's too exhausted to argue.

'Don't give me that look, Luc, you and Anse were practically living together and you weren't together that long. This is just a test run.'

'Take it my future niece or nephew wasn't exactly a planned event, then.'

Corina rolls her eyes. 'Yes, Luciano, we decided that six months into dating would be a perfect time for the condom to break. I went off the pill because, and I quote Rohan on this, it 'fucks me up'.' She shakes her head as Rohan comes back up the stairs with another big box of clothes that *somehow* will squeeze into Corina's overflowing wardrobe. 'Anyway, it happened, and even though it's wonderful, we just have to be realistic about this—,'

'You talking about the time to condom broke and the subsequent spill that we're going to be cleaning up for the rest of our lives?' Rohan asks as he throws his surround-sound speaker system on the lounge. Corina eyes it with disapproval. 'All done. Beer time.' Rohan chucks Luciano a cold beer and Luciano catches it on the full.

'You sure it's just one?' Luciano asks. 'Being a fraternal twin increases your chances of having twins.'

Rohan chokes on his beer.

'We're sure.' He looks to Corina for reassurance. 'Aren't we, babe?'

'Yes,' Corina grits out as she gives Luciano the dirtiest stare she can muster. 'Just one.'

———

He's covered in flour when he gets the email. It's a Wednesday morning and he's elbow deep (literally) in pasta dough. The gentle lo-fi music he plays during prep is suddenly interrupted as his phone chimes.

Luciano wipes the flour down his pristine navy apron and checks his messages.

'Holy shit.'

———

When the restaurant is empty and Michael is on his third glass of rosé, Luciano shows him the email.

'Fuck me,' Michael says as he gets to the bottom of the email. 'Are you going to do it?'

'I mean I have to, don't I?' Luciano says. 'Opportunities like this don't just fall into someone's lap.'

'Apparently they do for you.' Michael grabs the bottle and refills Luciano's glass. 'Cheers to you. Chef. Business owner and *New York Times* Best Selling Author to-be.'

'It won't get that far.' Luciano clinks their glasses together. 'Honestly, they'll read my writing and rethink the entire offer.'

'They don't want you to write. They want you to tell a story. Your mother's story, and yours.'

'This time last year, I was broke and my sister was telling me we'd have to sell the house and the restaurant. I was barely making ends meet delivering takeaway food.'

'Oh my god, you were one of those QIK-EATS guys?'

'I was. I had this little Vespa.'

'Surely not the same one you crashed.'

'The very same.'

'Luciano!'

Luciano laughs as Michael's face flushes red. It doesn't take much. A glass of wine. A good joke. It's easy to make Michael laugh.

Michael stretches and glances at the half-empty bottle of wine. 'I should head off. Unless I could tempt you in finishing this bottle upstairs?'

It's not an unwelcome come-on, and the way Michael says it makes it all sounds so easy. Luciano has no doubts that's how the rest of the night would go; wonderful in its simplicity, a night shared between two friends who could be more. Some part of him wants this. Maybe if had it been another night, in another few months, maybe he would have taken Michael upstairs.

But it's only been a handful of weeks.

And he still aches in ways he can't explain.

'I can't.'

'What? Finish off the wine?'

'Do this,' he gestures to the space between them.

'I thought as much,' Michael replies. 'Still.'

'Still,' Luciano echoes.

It's not fair to either of them to pretend like he's ready to move on.

Luciano hears the chair scrape against the floor and then Michael is leaning across the table and his mouth is on his. It's gentle, barely enough to taste.

'Whenever you're ready,' Michael says and then he grabs the bottle of wine and leaves.

———

To: hello@trattoria.com.au
 From: gdemetriou@wandering.com.au

Subject line: Query—Family cookbook

Good afternoon, Luciano.

I hope this email finds you well. My name is Grace Demetriou, commissioning editor at Wandering Press. We publish a range of cookbooks, as well as selected commercial fiction and non-fiction. The team and I are huge fans of your late mother (we ate at Ragazza twice over two days back in 2011—I know that technically she didn't own it back then, but we checked they were all her recipes!) and I would love to discuss the possibility of collaborating on a cookbook that could share her amazing stories and recipes with the world.

Look forward to hearing from you.

Kind regards,

Grace Demetriou

Commissioning Editor

Wandering Press

Please note I work Monday—Thursday 10—4 pm.

CHAPTER FORTY-EIGHT

He hands in his resignation on Monday morning.

Specifically, at 9:02am Monday morning.

He's had the weekend to think about it; to draw up the pros and cons; to let it settle in his stomach that this is the *right* decision.

And it does feel right. It's felt right ever since he'd confessed to Daniel he'd made a mistake and they'd spend the next two hours figuring out how he could get back to Australia.

The first step: he needs to resign.

Franz's eyebrows raise higher the further he gets down the letter.

'You're resigning?' he says. 'Anse, it's been two weeks.'

'I know this must be terribly disappointing.'

'Don't be ridiculous,' Franz closes the door to his office. 'Sit down.' He presses a button on his phone. 'Louis, can you bring in two coffees? The real kind, no not the instant in the kitchen. Yes *now*, please.'

With that taken care of, Franz gives him a hard look.

'Franz, I—,'

'I assume this is to do with the attachment back in Canberra.'

There's no point in lying. 'Yes.'

'You want to go back, then?'

'I do, yes.'

Franz reads over his letter once more. 'And you're sure about all of this?'

'I'm—,'

'Anse,' Franz interrupts. 'You're a bright young man. I just want to make sure you've thought about what you're giving up if you do this.'

'I have,' Anse says. 'My position remains firm.'

Franz sighs deeply and sinks into his chair. 'Right. I have a contact who might be able to help us out. Let me make a few calls and I'll get back to you this afternoon.'

'For what?'

'Your visa. The sooner you start the process, the sooner you can get back to Australia.' His fingers fly over the keyboard.

'You're emailing them now?'

Franz scoffs. 'No. I'm emailing the Ambassador to let her know you resigned. She'll be disappointed, of course, but she'll be pleased she won the bet.'

'You bet to see if I would take the position?'

Franz sniggers. 'Quite unethical, I know.' Franz takes a long sip and then leans back into his chair. Louis arrives with their coffees. 'Now, let's talk about your replacement.'

———

Two weeks later, Anse is back at the airport. There is a lightness in his step as he walks into the terminal carrying a large sign that says RIDLEY.

'You stupid, love-sick goof,' Hannah laughs as Anse pulls her into a hug. Her luggage is strewn about them, dropped in the excitement of reunion. 'You absolute fool. Thank you. *Thank you.*'

'You're perfect for the job,' Anse says as Hannah takes a step back and collects her luggage. 'I missed you.'

'I missed you too,' she says as he directs her to the waiting car. They catch up on the drive back to Anse's apartment—he tries to brief her on the job, what she'll expect come Monday morning and a little about Thomas, who is taking over Anse's job, and whom she'll be replacing—but Hannah only wants to talk about one thing. 'When do you leave?'

'As soon as my visa comes through. Maybe in a month or two. I have an interview with a representative from the Australian Embassy this week.'

'And Luciano?' she asks. 'Have you told him?'

'No.'

'Anse—,'

'I just need to figure out how to get back first. I'll go from there.'

———

'You have to send me Milo once a quarter,' Hannah instructs as they walk from the subway station to the office. 'And Tim-Tams.'

'When's Cameron coming over?' Anse asks

'About a month. He had to give the radio station notice.'

'And he's excited?

'Hell yeah.'

Anse smiles, 'I'm happy for you.'

'Thanks. I think he's keen for a couple of months travelling. I don't mind, even if I am chained to the nine-to-five. He used to write music before he started at the radio station, just these great acoustic songs. He got into radio because he knew he couldn't get a job in the music industry, but I don't know, I kind of want him to find himself again.'

A pang of jealously hits him as he realises how Hannah and Cameron's relationship has reshaped in the face of change. In their phone call two weeks ago, she'd been clear she wouldn't take the job without Cameron. He realises that not once had he ever put Luciano on the same step as his career. Not really. He'd asked Luciano to come with him, just as he'd asked Max to do the same.

Would he have stayed if he hadn't got the job? He isn't sure. The 'what-if's seem meaningless now.

'Ugh, I can't believe I'm working with Franz again,' Hannah scoffs as they reach the entrance to the office. 'Three years and I'm finally free of the goof, just to follow him halfway across the globe.'

'I think you'll find the new Franz a changed man,' Anse says as he swipes through the security gate. 'A man who always buys the first round.'

———

That afternoon, Anse is aware of three things: that it's excruciatingly hot in Franz's office, that the ball of his foot is itchy and there's no polite way to scratch it, and that he's possibly failing this interview. He's *never* failed an interview.

Chris, the representative from Australian Immigration Services, has a cold, hard stare and a long line of a mouth. Every so often, he scribbles a note in illegible handwriting on Anse's application paper.

'How long were you in Australia?'

'Eleven months and eighteen days,' Anse says. He counted.

'On a sponsored working visa, yes?' Chris directs this question at Franz.

'Correct,' Franz answers. 'The Embassy sponsored Mr Meyer to fill an attaché position. It was a rigorous selection process in which we considered Australian applicants and those international. After an impressive series of interviews, we decided to invest in Mr Meyer for the role in Canberra, and then later for the role he has just resigned from.'

'And you've been in Canada for—,'

'Four weeks and six days,' Anse answers.

Chris writes that down.

'And why do want to go back to Australia, Mr Meyer? Why not Vienna?'

He says what he thinks he's supposed to. 'I enjoyed my time in Australia and I have skills that align with the key job requirements—,'

'Mr Meyer, with all due respect, your profession is in foreign law and policy,' Chris interrupts. 'You have to admit that it's quite niche. If you were a medical professional or some sort of trade—,'

'He's going there for love,' Franz says suddenly.

Chris stops writing. 'Excuse me?'

Anse thinks he might punch Franz in the face.

'You're going there for *love*?' Chris clarifies.

'My partner,' Anse clears his throat. 'Ex-partner lives in

Canberra. I made a mistake. I know that's not what you want to hear and I know I can certainly contribute to the economy in other ways, but Franz is right. The main motivation is to work things out with my partner.'

Chris takes a deep breath and looks down at his notes.

'With all you've told me, Mr Meyer, I would suggest applying for a working holiday visa. You don't need a reason,' he pauses, 'even if it is love. You'll have twelve months in Australia to do what you wish. If you want to apply for a second working visa, you will need to complete twelve weeks of what the government call *specified work*. Usually, this is on a farm or orchard of some sort. Otherwise, you can apply online.'

He applies that afternoon.

———

Hannah finds him in his office later that week, frantically tapping away on his keyboard.

'Close your email. Let me take you out for lunch, sad boy.'

'I'm not sad,' he lies.

'You are. Come on. Dumplings will make you feel better.'

He takes his coat from behind the door and follows her to a small hole-in-the-wall dumpling restaurant. A waiter hands him a small note pad and pen to write his order on and Anse marvels at the efficiency.

'You should tell him you're coming back,' says Hannah. It's been three days since he applied for the visa. It could be a month before he knows if he can go back or not. 'I don't see the harm in messaging him. I'm ordering pan fried.'

'We'll get pan-fried *and* steamed,' Anse says. 'I'm not messaging him.'

'Why?'

'I know he'll tell me not to come back.' He hands the piece of paper back to the waiter. 'I need to see him face-to-face. It's the only way he'll realise that I'm serious about this.'

Hannah goes to speak, pauses, takes a sip of beer. 'Well then how will you do it?'

'Do what?'

'Win him back?'

Anse laughs, 'God, I don't know. I was just planning on falling at his feet. Telling him how wrong I was and begging. A lot of begging.'

'Hot,' replies Hannah and Anse raises a brow. 'But seriously, you gotta do a grand gesture.'

'Oh my god, Hannah, this is not a movie.'

'Anse, your boss just claimed, on record, that the reason for your visa is *love*,' she says. 'You need a grand gesture to convince Luciano to take you back after you broke his heart and fled the country.'

'I get the picture.'

'You could do an entire dance routine in the square.'

'I'm just going to tell him I made a mistake, isn't that enough?' Anse shrugs and rubs at his eyes. 'I don't even know if he will. I fucked this up so badly, Hannah.'

'Get it together, Anse,' she says. 'You've got a man to win back.'

———

The next week, Anse gets the email he's been waiting for.

Approved.

How? How is he approved? He only submitted it ten days

ago. He rushes into Franz's office with the approval printed and waves it in front of his face. Franz takes the piece of paper with a smile and Anse knows he's done something, and he simply cannot thank him enough.

'Here's your ticket home, as stipulated in your contract,' Franz says and the word *home* hits Anse harder than it should when he sees the destination is printed as CANBERRA. 'Get out of my office, Anse. Your flight leaves in six hours.'

'But-,'

Franz laughs. 'Why spend longer here than you need to? Go. Email me when you're there.'

There's no arguing with Franz at the best of times so he just hugs him. 'Thank you.'

He finds Hannah on the way out, says goodbye to his staff who he knows he won't miss in the slightest, and then jumps on the subway to his apartment. He repacks his things and catches a cab to the airport.

Passport.

Wallet.

Required documentation.

It's a dance he's done dozens of times before.

'Mr Meyer,' confirms the air hostess as he throws his passport at her. 'To Sydney, Australia.'

'And then onto Canberra,' he replies. Just in case. Just in case his luggage is lost or he's not checked into the domestic change and he misses it and it takes him any more time to get to Canberra than it needs to take. His heart cannot afford a delay.

It takes him thirty hours to arrive back in Canberra. The flight arrives at seven-thirty in the evening. The immigration officer checks his visa and his passport and then his visa *again* before stamping the document and letting him through.

The airport is empty as he waits for his luggage to come around the carousel. Finally, he sees it coming, hurls it off the conveyer belt and disappears into the bathroom.

Quickly he throws off his sweat-stained t-shirt and pants and slips on a fresh white shirt. He hangs the suit jacket on the back of the stall door and runs his fingers down the fine floral embroidery.

This is it.

He tells the cabbie to take him to the Pearce shops and tries to ignore the occasional glances he gets in the rear vision mirror. The streets are slick with rain. Thunder rumbles above them, and every so often the clouds flash.

'You had an event or—,'

'I have a date,' Anse replies.

'Fancy date,' comments the taxi driver. 'Spose it is Valentine's Day.'

He feels the heavyweight of dread settle in his stomach as the taxi pulls over. They're here.

The lights are on in Trattoria. It's almost nine o'clock at night and Luciano's speaking with the last of his customers while Ned clears their table.

His heart is suddenly heavy in his chest.

'Hey!' The cabbie snaps his fingers in Anse's face. 'You getting out? This is the place, right?'

CHAPTER FORTY-NINE

The rain does not stop the crowds. It's been a dry few months, both for weather and cash-flow, but Valentine's day has broken the drought. The hanging tendrils of crepe paper were cute at the start of the night, a not-so-subtle nod to the first *Sex and the City* movie, but are now tedious and trite as Luciano begins to tear them down.

'You want help with that, or—,' Ned trails off as he steps out of the dark kitchen. Luciano can hear the dishwasher running as it works through the last of the night's dishes.

'No, it's fine,' Luciano replies. 'You head on home. Thanks for tonight.'

Ned gives him a tight smile. 'You too. It'll all still be here in the morning, Luc.'

Tomorrow he has to order a few kegs for the bar, make two cakes, a new tub of pesto, and probably marinara sauce. 'Have a nice night.'

The front door closes and Luciano continues cleaning up.

Outside, it starts to rain heavily. It's a welcome respite from a horror summer—bushfires have ravaged the countryside and decimated the coastal towns. The last time he'd seen the beach was in Wollongong, and he misses it. Mourns it.

The sound of the front door opening makes Luciano turn. 'Did you forget something?'

Rain slaps against the pavement outside, the sound carrying through the open front door. A tall figure stands in the doorway, briefly distorted by the rolling beams of light from a departing car.

'Luciano.'

His skin prickles. That accent. No one says his name quite like that. No one but—

Anse.

He stands in the doorway dressed in a ridiculously floral suit. Wet hair clings to his face.

He crosses the floor wordlessly, his gaze never wavering from Anse's figure.

'I want to apply for a job,' Anse hands Luciano his resume.

Luciano looks down at the stack of papers. 'You want a job?'

'I'm on a working holiday visa,' Anse explains as Luciano flicks through the document. 'My career aspirations have recently changed, but I do have experience in table service and I'm willing to work late nights and weekends. I have qualifications and written references.'

Luciano flicks to the letters of reference. There's one from Daniel, from Hannah and even Her Excellency.

My brother's an idiot, but I think he was meant to be your idiot.

Please take him back, Luciano. He was insufferable without you.

Anse Meyer has the courage to admit when he made a mistake and do his best to make up for it—that's a wonderful quality not found in a lot of people.

'Anse—,' he starts.

'Turn the page.'

Apprehensively, Luciano turns the page and manages to suppress a sob. It's certificate to his culinary school, the one he'd given Anse as a joke when he'd cooked three hundred sausages and a very nice roast chicken.

'Wow, that's a prestigious school.' He can't help but laugh but his voice cracks, wavers under the strain of keeping down his heart.

'I learnt from the best.'

Luciano closes the resume and hands it back to Anse. 'Why did you choose to come to Australia?'

'I made a mistake,' Anse says. 'I left the man I loved.'

He swallows thickly. 'And why do you want to work here, specifically?'

'Luciano.' A plead.

'Answer my question, please.'

Anse takes a deep breath. 'This is where I'm supposed to be. By your side. I'm sorry it took me so long to figure that out.' There's silence. 'Say something, please.'

Luciano looks through Anse's resume once more before handing it back. 'I'm sorry, Anse, but I can't hire you.'

'Luciano, I—,'

He holds up his hand, silencing him. 'Please, let me finish, Anse.' Anse doesn't speak, so Luciano continues. 'I don't need you and even if I did, you'd be the most overqualified waiter on my team. How do I know that as soon as the right job appeared, you wouldn't just leave?'

'I don't care about the *job*, Luciano.' He reaches out to touch Luciano's shoulders, thumbs smoothing over the white cotton of his shirt, but he's not pulled closer and Luciano doesn't shrug him off. 'I am madly in love with you. I made a mistake, and I flew halfway across the world to try and make it right.'

'I'm not sure it's enough.'

'I know I hurt you, Luciano. God, fuck, I *know*.'

'I can't—,'

'No,' he says, 'Let me finish now, please. I know you don't need me; you've never needed me. But I do. I *do*.'

Anse says the words with such conviction that it feels like they strike him and he begins to sob.

'The city, the job, it only reminded me how much I was alone. Luciano, you are what it means to love and be loved. I need you.'

Is it enough? He's not sure. But Anse is standing in front of him, soaked to the bone, wearing an expensive floral suit, and begging for another chance.

He feels Anse's thumbs rise to rub at his cheeks. 'I'm sorry it took me so long to realise it. I'm sorry I hurt you. And I know it'll take time for you to trust me again but please, just let me try.'

Tears rim his Anse's eyes and Luciano feels like he's drowning, sobbing so violently he's unable to do anything but bring Anse into his arms and hold him. When his arms raise to pull him closer, Luciano melts against his damp clothes, inhales the familiar scent of his cologne and knows he's home.

'I'm so madly in love with you, Luciano.'

'You came back.' Luciano pulls back a little, just enough to see his face. 'I didn't think you would.'

And it maybe it won't be as easy as before, but that's okay.

Anse is back in his arms. He rises onto his tip-toes, a silent invitation, and Anse leans forward and kisses him fiercely.

'I'm sorry,' he says against his lips.

Luciano wipes the tears from Anse's cheeks. 'Come inside. You must be hungry.'

The end.

ACKNOWLEDGMENTS

I was unsure if I'd ever get to the point in my career that I'd get to write an acknowledgement passage in a book. If you're here too, then thank you for reading as far as you did. It means a lot.

Thank you to my family for supporting me and who believed in my work from the moment I said I wanted to be a writer. Thanks for reading first drafts, fifth drafts, and fifteenth drafts.

Thank you also to my editors, Tegan Lyon and Connie Dowell, and my friends Rebecca Cocks, Sasha Clarke, Caitlin Robinson, Kim Chown (and the Chown family), Tayla Steele, Nigel Chee, Adina Thavisin, Jayden Mascuilli, Tegan Lyon, Georgia Sheales, Tia Talge, Lee Allison, Dr Kate Highfield, Connie Dowell, Kimberly Skye, Will Middleton, Dr Amanda Walsh, Jennifer Sullivan, Clare McHugh, Scott Woodard and Clair McDonald. Your support, kind words, and willingness to help made this book possible.

Thanks to the team at the ACT Writers Centre and Romance

Writers of Australia. Become a member of your local writers centre. It will mean more than you know.

Everything included in this book is (at the time of writing these acknowledgements) a place you can visit in Canberra; including Tidbinbilla Nature Reserve, the Red Hill lookout, Lake Burley Griffin and Floriade. Cheers Canberra, you're a wonderfully weird city, and I love you.

ABOUT THE AUTHOR

Abra Pressler grew up in rural NSW and currently lives in Canberra, Australia. She's been writing since she was thirteen and holds a Bachelor of Arts (Creative Writing).

More is her first novel.

Want more?

Visit Abra's website for recipes and updates about new releases: www.abrapressler.com

Stream the Spotify playlist 'More'!

Twitter: @abra_pressler

Instagram: @abrapresslerauthor

Facebook: @abrapresslerauthor

Reviews help this book reach more readers. Please consider reviewing this book on your preferred platform.

BRUSCHETTA

Serves: 3-4

Preparation time: 15 minutes

Ingredients:

- 3-4 fresh tomatoes, roughly chopped
- 2 cloves of garlic, crushed
- A handful of fresh basil
- Good quality baguette or bread, sliced approximately 1cm thick
- A dash of good quality olive oil
- Salt and pepper to taste

Method:

1. Combine the tomatoes, garlic and olive oil in a small bowl

2. Toast the bread until desired crispness
3. Spoon tomatoes over the bread
4. Garnish with basil leaves if desired.

AVOCADO TOAST

Serves: 1
Preparation: 10 minutes
Cooking time: 2-5 minutes

Ingredients:

- 1/2 ripe avocado
- 1 teaspoon of lemon juice
- ½ garlic clove, crushed
- A bit of onion, diced
- Feta cheese (the most important bit, in my opinion)

Method:

1. Chop avocado into cubes, place in a bowl and smash
   with the bottom of a fork

2. Add the garlic, onion, lemon and a pinch of salt and pepper and combine
3. Spread over toast, with or without butter and sprinkle with feta cheese or other toppings (such as bacon, capsicum, spinach, mushrooms) as desired.

CHICKEN CACCIATORE

Serves: 3 – 4
Preparation: 10 minutes
Cooking time: 20 minutes

Ingredients:

- 500g of chicken breast, roughly sliced
- One onion, diced
- Three cloves of garlic, crushed
- 1 ½ cups of passata or tomato puree
- 1 cup of water½ cup of dry white wine
- ½ cup of olives
- ¼ cup of flour
- a generous handful of basil
- Salt and pepper to taste

Method:

1. Coat the chicken in flour and cook in a heatproof casserole dish or saucepan until brown. Remove from pan.
2. Add onion and garlic, cooking until fragrant and the onion is soft. Return chicken to the pan.
3. Add white wine and cook until reduced (approximately 1-2 minutes).
4. Add passata and water, and half of the basil. Bring the sauce to the boil, simmering for 2-3 minutes, or until sauce is thick.
5. Add cooked pasta to the dish, stirring it through the sauce.
6. Garnish with basil, parmesan and olives as desired.

COMPLETELY WHIPPED TIRAMISU

Serves: 6 – 8

Preparation time: 30 minutes

Cooking time: 20 minutes for the ladyfingers, and 2 hours refrigeration for the tiramisu.

Ingredients:

- 6 eggs
- 250g of mascarpone cheese
- 150mls of good quality coffee, brewed and cooled
- ½ cup of white sugar
- ½ cup of milk
- 50mls of Kahlua (can be switched out for Bailey's Irish Cream or Tia Maria if desired)—optional but recommended
- Cocoa powder, for dusting.

For the ladyfingers

(Makes approximately 25 ladyfingers)

- 3 large eggs at room temperature
- 2/3 cup of sugar
- 1 cup plain flour

Method:

For the ladyfingers:

1. Prepare a large tray with baking paper and preheat the oven to 180C.
2. Separate egg whites from the yolks, placing whites in a small bowl and putting to the side.
3. Combine egg yolks and sugar and whisk until pale yellow. The mixture should triple in size.
4. Fold in the egg whites and flour until smooth.
5. Spoon mixture into a piping bag with a ¾ inch tube and pipe ladyfingers approximately 3 inches in length.
6. Bake for 15 – 20 minutes, until just firm.

For the tiramisu:

1. Grease and line the base and sides of a large baking dish.
2. To make the custard, combine the yolks of the eggs and half the sugar in a bowl over boiling water, ensuring the water does not touch the bowl. Gradually add milk. Stir until the custard thickens (approximately 8 – 10 minutes).

3. Take the custard off the heat and transfer into a sink of cold (iced, if possible) water, stirring as the mixture cools to avoid a skin forming on the custard.
4. Fold the mascarpone into the custard mixture.
5. Mix the coffee and kahlua (if using) in a shallow dish.
6. Dunk the ladyfingers in the coffee mixture and arrange in the baking dish until the base is covered.
7. Cover with a layer of custard and repeat, alternating direction of ladyfingers each time.
8. Dust with cocoa powder and refrigerate for at least two hours.

LUCIANO'S CHOCOLATE PIE

Serves: 10 – 12 slices

Preparation: 30 minutes + 2 hours chilling

Cooking time:

30-40 minutes for the pie crust

5-10 minutes for the filling

Ingredients:

For the crust:

- 1 ½ cups of self-raising flour
- 100g of unsalted butter, room temperature
- 1 egg, room temperature
- 2 teaspoons of good quality cocoa powder
- ¼ teaspoon of vanilla bean paste

For the filling:

- 360 grams of high-quality, dark cooking chocolate
- 1 cup of thickened cream
- 25 grams of butter

Method:

1. Grease and flour an eight-inch tart or pie pan and set aside.
2. Combine flour, butter and cocoa powder until it forms breadcrumbs between your fingers.
3. With a wooden spoon, add an egg and around a teaspoon of cold water, and mix, ensuring the ingredients don't separate.
4. Coat your work surface generously with flour and knead the dough until it forms a malleable ball, then cover in plastic and rest in the fridge for thirty minutes.
5. Roll crust to approximately ½ centimetre thick, place in a pie pan, add pie weights (old beans or chick-peas will also work fine) and bake on 180 degrees for twenty minutes.
6. For the filling, warm the cream and the butter, but do not boil. Stir in the chocolate, pieces at a time, until it's thick and glossy.
7. Pour filling into the cooled tart crust, leave standing for fifteen minutes and then place in the fridge for at least two hours.
8. Using a warmed knife, slice the pie.

NON-TRADITIONAL SCHNITZEL

Serves: 2-4

Preparation: 10 minutes

Cooking time: 10 minutes

Ingredients:

- 2-4 cuts of thin veal or pork (approximately 100-150 grams each)
- ½ cup of Greek yoghurt (or natural yoghurt)
- 1 cup of panko crumb
- ½ cup of flour
- Vegetable oil for frying
- Salt and pepper to taste

Method:

1. Season the panko crumbs with salt and pepper.

2. Dip veal into the flour, coating both sides and shaking off the excess.
3. Liberally coat both sides the veal with yoghurt.
4. Dip veal into the panko crumb, pressing the crumbs onto the surface of the meat where needed until both sides are evenly coated.
5. Place the schnitzel into hot oil and fry until is crisp and golden.

SIMPLE SAUERKRAUT

Serves: 5-6 people

Preparation: 40 minutes plus 2-3 weeks for fermentation

Ingredients

- ¼ of fresh cabbage, sliced thinly
- 1 tablespoon of salt
- Peppercorns (for taste, if desired)

Method:

1. Sterilize all equipment, including a large airtight container, and wash hands thoroughly.
2. In a large bowl, sprinkle the salt over the cabbage and begin gently kneading the cabbage with your hands.
3. Continue kneading until cabbage juice fill the bowl and the cabbage becomes tender. There should be enough brine to cover the cabbage.

4. Add peppercorns if desired.
5. Fill the large airtight container ensuring the brine covers all the cabbage. If not, add a little more salt water to the mixture until all the cabbage is submerged.
6. Keep container in a cool dry place while fermenting (up to 3-4 weeks). The sauerkraut can be eaten as early as 4-5 days if preferred.

Note: cabbage bought out of season may not yield the same results, and the amount of brine created is highly dependent on the cabbage type and age. This recipe makes approximately 500-700g of sauerkraut using ¼ of a cabbage.

Leave 1-2cm between the brine and the lid of the container, as the brine may overflow. Check your sauerkraut regularly but wash hands thoroughly and sterilise any equipment as outside bacteria may impact on the fermentation process.

Sauerkraut will smell while fermenting. It is often described as a 'sour egg' smell.

CLASSIC PAVLOVA

Serves: 8-10

Preparation: 20 minutes

Cooking time: 1 hour

Ingredients

- 4 egg whites, at room temperature
- 1 cup caster sugar
- 2 teaspoons cornflour
- 1 teaspoon lemon juice
- 2 teaspoon vanilla essence
- 300ml thickened cream

Method:

1. Preheat oven to 150°C fan-forced.
2. On a baking paper, trace around a 20cm dinner plate and place on the tray.

3. Use an electric beater or mixer to whisk egg whites until soft peaks form. Add the sugar gradually until gone and continue to whisk until the meringue forms soft peaks.
4. Add cornflour, lemon juice and half the vanilla essence and beat until the meringue forms hard peaks and becomes glossy. This may take up to ten minutes.
5. Pile into the circle on the baking tray, making the centre slightly hollow (you'll fill it with cream and fruit later!), and bake for one hour, until the pavlova is dry to the touch.
6. Turn off the oven and let the pavlova cool completely before removing. The pavlova may crack or break in sections: this is normal, and still delicious.
7. Mix the cream, vanilla essence and a teaspoon of icing sugar (if on hand), and spoon onto the now-cool pavlova. Add seasonal fruit or toppings of choice.

LEMON MYRTLE CAKE

Serves: 8 - 10

Preparation: 20 minutes

Cooking time: 30-40 minutes

Ingredients:

- 2 teaspoons of lemon myrtle powder crushed
- 125g of unsalted butter
- ½ cup of honey
- 2 eggs
- 1 teaspoon of vanilla extract
- 1 ½ cups of self-raising flour
- ½ cup of milk

Method:

1. Preheat oven to 180°C (fan-forced).

2. Cream sugar and butter until it is combined and pale.
3. Add eggs, one by one, until combined.
4. Add vanilla extract and combine.
5. Fold lemon myrtle powder and sifted flour into the batter, before adding milk and folding until smooth. Spoon into a pre-greased, lined pan and bake for thirty minutes, or until knife comes out clean. Can be served with a simple glaze, icing sugar, or by itself.

Note: Harvest mature leaves of a lemon myrtle tree, wash, dry and bake around 110 degrees Celsius with the door open for approximately 30-40 minutes or until the leaves are crispy. Wait until cool and then ground into a fine powder using a mortar and pestle.

Alternatively, lemon myrtle powder can be purchased from some culinary retailers.

CHICKEN NOODLE SOUP

Serves: 3-4

Preparation: 5 minutes

Cooking time: 15 minutes

Ingredients:

- 1-litre good quality chicken stock
- 1 fresh chicken breast, diced
- 4 large spring onions, chopped
- 2cm knob of ginger (fresh is best), grated
- 1 tablespoon of minced garlic
- 1 can of corn kernels
- 1 can of creamed corn
- 100g thin egg noodles, such as vermicelli
- 2 eggs, whisked
- Salt and pepper to taste

Method:

1. Bring the chicken stock to the boil and add chicken,
    spring onions, garlic and ginger, and allow to simmer
    for five minutes.
2. Stir in creamed corn and half of the corn kernels,
    ensuring the mixture is well combined before adding
    pasta.
3. Add noodles and allow soup to simmer for as much
    time as needed for the noodles to cook.
4. Bring soup to the boil and stir through eggs.
5. Adjust soup to taste, adding more ginger and garlic as
    needed.

www.ingramcontent.com/pod-product-compliance
Lightning Source LLC
Chambersburg PA
CBHW030232120726
47903CB00005B/1454